D0193296

ROMEO & JULIET

TWENTIETH CENTURY FOX PRESENTS A BAZMARK PRODUCTION LEONARDO DiCAPRIO CLAIRE DANES

"WILLIAM SHAKESPEARE'S ROMEO & JULIET" BRIAN DENNEHY JOHN LEGUIZAMO

PETE POSTLETHWAITE PAUL SORVINO DIANE VENORA MUSIC BY NELLEE HOOPER

COSTUME DESIGNER KYM BARRETT CO-PRODUCER MARTIN BROWN FILM EDITOR JILL BILCOCK PRODUCTION DESIGNER CATHERINE MARTIN

DIRECTOR OF PHOTOGRAPHY DONALD M. McALPINE, A.S.C. PRODUCED BY GABRIELLA MARTINELLI AND BAZ LUHRMANN

SCREENPLAY BY CRAIG PEARCE & BAZ LUHRMANN DIRECTED BY BAZ LUHRMANN

DOLBY IN SELECTED THEATRES ORIGINAL SOUNDTRACK ALBUM AVAILABLE ON Capitol COMPACT DISCS AND CASSETTES © 1996 TWENTIETH CENTURY FOX

William Shakespeare's
ROMEO & JULIET

The Contemporary Film, The Classic Play

*The screenplay by Craig Pearce & Baz Luhrmann
and the text of Shakespeare's original play
together in one volume*

*Notes to William Shakespeare's play by
John Bettenbender*

LAUREL-LEAF BOOKS

Published by
Bantam Doubleday Dell Books for Young Readers
a division of
Bantam Doubleday Dell Publishing Group, Inc.
1540 Broadway
New York, New York 10036

If you purchased this book without a cover you should be aware
that this book is stolen property. It was reported as "unsold and
destroyed" to the publisher and neither the author nor the publisher
has received any payment for this "stripped book."

"The Contemporary Film"
Copyright © 1996 by Twentieth Century Fox Film Corporation. All
Rights Reserved.

"The Classic Play"
Copyright © 1965 by Dell Publishing Co., Inc.
Text of ROMEO AND JULIET reprinted by arrangement with
Harper and Row, New York, N.Y.

Photographs courtesy of Merrick Morton

All rights reserved. No part of this book may be reproduced or
transmitted in any form or by any means, electronic or mechanical,
including photocopying, recording, or by any information storage
and retrieval system, without the written permission of the
Publisher, except where permitted by law.

The trademark Laurel-Leaf Library® is registered in the U.S. Patent
and Trademark Office.
The trademark Dell® is registered in the U.S. Patent and Trademark
Office.

ISBN: 0-440-22712-7

RL: 5.9

Printed in the United States of America

November 1996

10   9   8   7

Director, Co-Writer, and Producer of
William Shakespeare's Romeo & Juliet

I've always wanted to do *Romeo and Juliet*. Shakespeare's plays touched everyone, from the street sweeper to the Queen of England. He was a rambunctious, sexy, violent, entertaining storyteller. We're trying to make this movie rambunctious, sexy, violent, and entertaining the way Shakespeare might have if he had been a filmmaker. We have not shied away from clashing low comedy with high tragedy, which is the style of the play, for it's the low comedy that allows you to embrace the very high emotions of the tragedy.

I thought that Leonardo DiCaprio was an extraordinary young actor and would make a great Romeo. It's important to reveal these eternal characters anew for every generation, and Leonardo is particularly suited for this. He does seem to symbolize his generation.

When he arrived the first time, I really didn't know how he'd handle the language. After the initial read-through, we went through the text very thoroughly and when we went back to it, the words just came out of his mouth as if it was the most natural language possible. To me, the language in Leonardo's mouth is a wonderful thing to hear because the words have resonance. He speaks them as if they really are his words, and that's something you don't always get in a Shakespearean performance.

When I met Claire Danes, I was really struck by her. Juliet is written as a very smart, active character.

She decides to get married, *she* resolves to take the sleeping potion, *she* really drives the piece. The extraordinary, unmissable characteristic about Claire is that here is a sixteen-year-old girl with the poise and maturity of a thirty-year-old.

Everything that's in the movie is drawn from Shakespeare's play. Violence, murder, lust, love, poison, drugs that mimic death, it's all there.

· · · · · · · · · · · · · · · Cast · · · · · · · · · · · · · · ·

ROMEO	Leonardo DiCaprio
JULIET	Claire Danes
BENVOLIO	Dash Mihok
MERCUTIO	Harold Perrineau
TYBALT	John Leguizamo
BALTHASAR	Jesse Bradford
GREGORY	Zak Orth
SAMPSON	Jamie Kennedy
ABRA	Vincent Laresca
FATHER LAURENCE	Pete Postlethwaite
NURSE	Miriam Margolyes
GLORIA CAPULET	Diane Venora
FULGENCIO CAPULET	Paul Sorvino
CAPTAIN PRINCE	Vondie Curtis-Hall
TED MONTAGUE	Brian Dennehy
CAROLINE MONTAGUE	Christina Pickles
DAVE PARIS	Paul Rudd
UNDERTAKER	Farnesio de Bernal
PHARMACIST	M. Emmet Walsh
ANCHORWOMAN	Edwina Moore
EXPRESS CLERK	Catalina Botello
RICH RANCHIDIS	Michael Corbett
SUSAN SANTANDIAGO	Harriet Harris
PETER	Pedro Altamirano
LITTLE BOY'S MOTHER	Margarita Wynne
LITTLE BOY WITH TOY GUN	Rodrigo Escandon
ATTRACTIVE GIRL	Lupita Ochoa
NUN	Gloria Silva
GAS STATION ATTENDANT	German Fabregat
EXPRESS DELIVERY MAN	Jorge Abraham
MONTAGUE LIMO DRIVER	Harry Porter
ALTAR BOY	Ricardo Barona
ALTAR BOY	Fausto Barona
SACRISTAN	John Sterlini
HUGE BOUNCER	Mario Cimarro
MIDDLE-AGED OCCUPANT	Carolyn Valero
MIDDLE-AGED OCCUPANT	Paco Morayta

ABBREVIATIONS

In the script, directions for the camera are written in capital letters. Some terms are abbreviated; below is a guide to the abbreviations:

E.C.U. = extreme close-up
EXT. = exterior
INT. = interior
O.S. = off screen
P.O.V. = point of view
V.O. = voice-over

EXT. HIGHWAY. AFTERNOON.

A ribbon of freeway stretching into a blue and pink late afternoon sky. A huge dark sedan, windows tinted gold, powers directly for us.

CUT TO: A heavy, low-slung pickup truck traveling toward the sedan.

WIDE SHOT: Sky, freeway, the cars closing.

TIGHT ON: The sedan.

TIGHT ON: The pickup.

Like thunderous, jousting opponents, the cars pass in a deafening cacophony of noise.

INT. TRUCK. AFTERNOON.

TIGHT ON: The fat face of GREGORY, yelling at the disappearing sedan.

> GREGORY
> A dog of the house of Capulet moves me!

He and the pimply-faced front-seat passenger, SAMPSON, explode with laughter.

The red-haired driver, BENVOLIO, keeps his eyes on the road.

INT. TV STUDIO. DAY.

An ANCHORWOMAN; behind her the faces of two middle-aged men. The caption reads, "Montague; Capulet. The feud continues."

She speaks to camera.

ANCHORWOMAN
Two households, both alike in dignity.
(In fair Verona, where we lay our scene)
From ancient grudge break to new mutiny,
Where civil blood makes civil hands unclean.

EXT. GAS STATION. AFTERNOON.

The truck is in the busy driveway of a large gas
    station, being filled with gas. The surrounding
    walls are painted with murals of blue sky and
    palm trees.

INT. TRUCK. AFTERNOON.

Inside the truck, Gregory and Sampson are boasting
    outrageously. The driver's seat is empty.

GREGORY
I will take the wall of any man or maid of
    Capulets.

EXT. GAS STATION. AFTERNOON.
SAMPSON
I will show myself a tyrant: when I have fought
    with the men I will be civil with the maids, I
    will cut off their heads.

Gregory; mock outrage.

> GREGORY
> The heads of the maids?

Sampson leers lecherously at a minibus full of Catholic schoolgirls next to them.

> SAMPSON
> Ay, the heads of the maids, or their maidenheads,
> Take it in what sense thou wilt.
> GREGORY
> They must take it in sense that feel it.

Gregory and Sampson pump up the song on the sound system while gyrating crudely at the girls.

> GREGORY/SAMPSON
> (singing)
> I am a pretty piece of flesh!
> I am a pretty piece of flesh!
> Me, they shall feel while I am able to stand;
> I am a pretty piece of flesh!

**EXT. GAS STATION—MINIMART.
AFTERNOON.**
The teacher nun from the minibus returns to the vehicle.
GREGORY'S P.O.V.: The girls' minibus pulls away, revealing . . . a tough-looking Latino boy, ABRA, leaning against the huge dark sedan.

INT. TRUCK. AFTERNOON.
Gregory suddenly stops gyrating.
CLOSE ON:

>   SAMPSON
> Here comes of the House of Capulet.

EXT. GAS STATION. AFTERNOON.
Abra stares coldly toward the boys. His goateed side-
kick PETRUCHIO takes notice.

INT. TRUCK. AFTERNOON.
CLOSE ON: Gregory; eyes locked to the Capulets.
   With fake bravado he pulls back his shirt to reveal
   a handgun. He nudges Sampson.

>   GREGORY
> Quarrel!
> I will back thee.

CUT TO: Abra. He unfolds his arms to reveal an
   even more ferocious holstered gun.
CLOSE ON: Sampson. Trying to quell his rising
   panic. He nervously unbuttons his shirt to clear
   his sidearm.

>   SAMPSON
> Let us take the law of our sides. Let them begin.

SUDDENLY: BANG! Gregory and Sampson jump.

WHIP PAN: It was the gas station attendant slamming the hood.
Gregory and Sampson are mortally embarrassed.

EXT. GAS STATION. AFTERNOON.
Abra; with a snort of contempt, he turns toward the car:

INT. TRUCK. AFTERNOON.
Sampson, furious, tries to save face.

> SAMPSON
> I will bite my thumb at them, which is a disgrace to them if they bear it.

Sampson quickly bites his thumb toward Abra's back as he gets into the sedan.

INT. SEDAN. AFTERNOON.
Abra's eyes flick to the rearview mirror.
E.C.U.: The rearview mirror; Sampson biting his thumb.

EXT. GAS STATION. AFTERNOON.
Suddenly, a bloodcurdling screech of tires. The sedan, rubber burning, reverses full speed toward Sampson and Gregory.

The Capulet car shudders to a halt inches from the truck, blocking its path.

INT. SEDAN. AFTERNOON.
CLOSE ON: A scurry of limbs scrabbling across seats and reaching for door handles.

EXT. GAS STATION. AFTERNOON.
Abra hauls Sampson from the truck. Gregory leaps out, Petruchio covers him. Abra slams Sampson against the side of the vehicle, then, goading him to go for his gun, screams:

> ABRA
> Do you bite your thumb at us, sir?

Sampson's shaking hand hovers, ready to draw.

> SAMPSON
> I do my bite my thumb, sir.

CUT TO: Attendants and customers run for cover.

INT. MINIMART. AFTERNOON.
A packet of bullets hits the counter. A hand with a cat ring picks them up.
TILT DOWN: To shiny, black boots decorated with cat-shaped spurs. A LITTLE BOY with a toy gun runs past. He stares through the glass doors

toward the confrontation outside. The LITTLE
BOY'S MOTHER has not heard the disturbance
through the thick glass of the minimart windows.

EXT. GAS STATION. AFTERNOON.
CLOSE ON: Abra, a hysterical rage; he shrieks:

>ABRA
Do you bite your thumb at *us*, sir?
>SAMPSON
>(sweating, murmurs to Gregory)
Is the law on our side if I say "Ay"?
>GREGORY
No.

CLOSE ON: Sampson, still sweating.

>SAMPSON
No, sir, I do not bite my thumb at you, sir, but I
bite my thumb, sir!

CUT TO: Gregory; a ridiculous inquiry.

>GREGORY
Do you quarrel, sir?

CUT TO: Abra; a dangerous smile.

>ABRA
Quarrel, sir, no sir.

CLOSE ON: Sampson; unconvincing bravado . . .

> SAMPSON
> But if you do, sir, I am for you. I serve as good a
> man as you.

CLOSE ON: Abra; a lethal question.

> ABRA
> No better?

CLOSE ON: Sampson, trapped.

> SAMPSON
> Well, sir . . .

WE HEAR: The sound of a toilet flushing.
CUT TO: Benvolio leaving the gas station wash-
room.

EXT. GAS STATION. AFTERNOON.
CUT TO: Gregory. He whispers maniacally.

> GREGORY
> Here comes our kinsman. Say "better"!

E.C.U.: Sampson; he screams:

> SAMPSON
> YES SIR, BETTER!

DISTORTED OUT-OF-CONTROL CLOSE-UP:
Abra shrieks:

ABRA
You lie. DRAW IF YOU BE MEN!

CUT TO: Benvolio. Terror-stricken, he sees the
boys.
LIGHTNING CUT: Four hands reaching for guns.
SLAM ZOOM: To Benvolio; weapon outstretched,
he screams:

BENVOLIO
Part, fools! You know not what you do!

MUSIC STING; A SUPER MACRO SLAM
ZOOM along the barrel of Benvolio's gun; the
engraved gun type reads:
"Sword 9mm series S"
CUT TO: Benvolio. He screams in desperation:

BENVOLIO
Put up your swords!

CUT TO: Gregory,
CUT TO: Sampson,
CUT TO: Abra,
CUT TO: Petruchio.
Frozen, still, weapons undrawn.
CUT TO: Benvolio. A moment, then, from behind,
the unmistakable sound of a match striking.
CLOSE UP: The match. It falls to the boot.

E.C.U.: The black cat-spurred boots.
CRANE UP: To find the dark cold eyes and feline
    smile of the wearer of the boots. His name is
    TYBALT; he lights the cigarette clenched between
    his teeth while holding his gun outstretched in
    the other hand.

          TYBALT
What, art thou drawn among these heartless
    hinds?
Turn thee Benvolio and look upon thy death.
          BENVOLIO
          (desperate)
I do but keep the peace: Put up thy sword,
Or manage it to part these men with me.

Tybalt; a mocking smile.

          TYBALT
What, drawn and talk of peace? I hate the word,
As I hate hell, all Montagues, and . . .

E.C.U.: Tybalt's finger squeezing the trigger . . .
Suddenly we hear firing from Tybalt's blind side.
Tybalt redirects his weapon, cracking off a single
    shot at the surprise attacker.

EXT./INT. MINIMART. AFTERNOON.
It is the five-year-old at the minimart door. The bullet shatters the glass of the minimart.

CUT TO: THE HYSTERICAL MOTHER, screaming as she throws herself on the child.

EXT. GAS STATION. AFTERNOON.
Tybalt; a lightning turn, his second gun out.
CUT TO: Benvolio. He brings his gun around on Tybalt.
Tybalt fires, blowing Benvolio's gun out of his hand.
CUT TO: Gregory firing at Tybalt. Tybalt combat-rolls.
CUT TO: Sampson firing toward Abra while simultaneously kicking over the truck.
CUT TO: The truck squealing away from the gas pump.
The gas hose bursts, spewing gas everywhere.
CUT TO: Gregory firing at Tybalt from the moving truck.
CUT TO: The windows blowing out of the car Tybalt is using for cover. He springs to his feet from the combat roll, simultaneously mounting his long-distance sight.
CUT TO: Abra and Petruchio's sedan screeching off after the truck.
CUT TO: Tybalt. Ignoring the gunfire, he slowly draws the high-powered sight to eye level, launching a shot that rips through Gregory's arm.
CUT TO: Gregory. He falls in his seat, screaming with pain. The truck races away, Capulet's sedan pursuing.
CUT TO: Benvolio picking up his gun; he runs onto the roadway.

Cars squeal to a stop. Benvolio fires back at Tybalt over a halted car.

Taking evasive action, Tybalt hits the ground. Benvolio turns and runs up the road.

CLOSE ON: Tybalt. He throws his spent cigarette to the ground and runs off in pursuit of Benvolio.

TIGHT ON: The discarded cigarette igniting a lick of gasoline.

CUT TO: Benvolio, running full tilt through the cars.

CUT TO: The flame traveling fast.

CUT TO: Tybalt, running full tilt against cars.

CUT TO: The flame whooshing toward the gasoline-soaked gas station as people and staff run in all directions.

AN ALMIGHTY ORCHESTRAL CHORD. The gas station ignites into flame. We push toward the painted walls of blue sky and palm trees as they are consumed in flame.

CRANE UP: Over the burning walls through the smoke to discover . . .

EXT. VERONA BEACH - MATTE SHOT. AFTERNOON.

STATIC SUPER WIDE SHOT: As the flame and smoke clear, we see in the distance towering over the smoggy city an enormous statue of Christ flanked by two glass towers. One is neon-crowned MONTAGUE, the other, CAPULET. On the horizon a squadron of choppers flies toward us.

EXT. AERIAL SHOTS. AFTERNOON.
CUT: From inside an armed chopper to another flying past Capulet Mansion (Chapultepec).

> VOICE-OVER
> From forth the fatal loins of these two foes
> A pair of star-crossed lovers take their life.

EXT. HIGH ANGLE WIDE. NEAR JESUS STATUE. AFTERNOON.
SECOND OPTICAL: From behind the towers. The words "Montague" and "Capulet" in reverse crown the frame. Jesus looks away from us. In the distance, we see fires burning all over town and, on the horizon, the faint outline of a beach.

> VOICE-OVER (cont.)
> Whose misadventured piteous overthrows doth
> with their death bury their parents' strife.

The choppers thunder through frame.

EXT. RIOT AREA. EVENING.
TIGHT ON: Tybalt, screaming demonically, gun outstretched.
TIGHT ON: Benvolio, screaming demonically, gun outstretched. A standoff over the hood of a car. The MIDDLE-AGED OCCUPANT screams maniacally.
CUT TO: Thundering close above them, a heavily

armed gunship. A command booms from the
chopper's public address system.

>   CAPTAIN PRINCE
>   (over PA)
> Rebellious subjects, enemies to peace,
> Throw your mistempered weapons to the ground.

CUT BACK: To the standoff.
WHIP PAN: VERONA BEACH POLICE patrol
  cars swerve to a halt. Cops leap out, rifles aimed.
WHIP PAN: To another patrol car sliding in.

INT. CHOPPER. EVENING.
CLOSE ON: The steely gray eyes of CAPTAIN
  PRINCE, chief of the Verona Beach Police De-
  partment. He repeats the command.

>   CAPTAIN PRINCE
> Throw your mistempered weapons to the ground!

CUT TO: Benvolio. He quickly looks to the guns
  pointed behind and above; Tybalt does the same.
TIGHT ON: Tybalt, considering.
TIGHT ON: Benvolio, his rage subsiding.
Like a surreal ballet, the boys mirror each other precisely; they slowly back away and, with perfect
  synchronicity, turn to the chopper and raise their
  guns into the air. As they do, we pull up into the
  chopper's P.O.V. The wider we get, the more

devastation we see. Riot police subduing looters,
cars burning, shop windows smashed.
TIGHT ON: Tybalt's gun.
TIGHT ON: Benvolio's gun.
CUT TO: the guns falling serenely through space.
ONE touches down, then the other, then . . .

**INT. CAPTAIN PRINCE'S PRECINCT OFFICE.
NIGHT.**
CLOSE ON: A golden badge. It reads: VERONA
   BEACH POLICE. IN GOD WE TRUST.
SLAM OUT TO: Captain Prince's grim features.

          CAPTAIN PRINCE
Three civil brawls, bred of an airy word
By thee, old Capulet, and Montague,
Have thrice disturbed the quiet of our streets.
If ever you disturb our streets again, your lives
   shall pay the forfeit of the peace.

TIGHT ON: The ruddy bulldog face of TED
   MONTAGUE.
TIGHT ON: The dark, dangerous eyes of
   FULGENCIO CAPULET.
PULL BACK: To reveal Tybalt and Benvolio hand-
   cuffed to POLICE OFFICERS. Montague's and
   Capulet's LAWYERS stand at the back of the
   room.

EXT. VERONA STREET. DAWN.

A majestic sunrise. Ted Montague's limousine skulks
   through deserted streets, one bodyguard's car
   drives ahead and another follows behind.

INT. MONTAGUE'S LIMOUSINE. DAWN.

Ted Montague, his wife, CAROLINE, and nephew
   Benvolio ride in uncomfortable silence.
Caroline finally speaks her anger.

> CAROLINE
> O where is Romeo, saw you him today?
>   (pointedly to Montague)
> Right glad I am he was not at this fray.

Montague snorts derisively and stares out the window. Embarrassed, Benvolio tries to be of assis-
   tance.

> BENVOLIO
> Madam, underneath the Grove of Sycamore
> So early walking did I see your son.

Ted Montague speaks with contempt.

> MONTAGUE
> Many a morning hath he there been seen
> With tears augmenting the fresh morning's dew.

Caroline struggles to contain her emotion.

CAROLINE
Away from light steals home my heavy son
And private in his chamber pens himself,
Shuts up his windows, locks fair daylight out
And makes himself an artificial night.

Montague barks into the car intercom.

MONTAGUE
Westward from this city side.

EXT. STREET. DAWN.
The limousine and bodyguards' cars U-turn, heading
west.

EXT. BEACH. DAWN.
To the melancholic strains of Mozart's "Serenade for
Winds," we discover the ornate arch of what is
left of a once splendid cinema. At the top of the
arch the words "Sycamore Grove" are clearly visi-
ble. The cinema has been demolished but for its
proscenium, through which we can see the grubby
shore of Verona Beach, housing a collection of sex
clubs and strip joints, populated with prostitutes,
drag queens, clients, and street people.
PAN DOWN: To discover a blond nineteen-year-old
boy sitting alone in the corner of the proscenium.
CLOSE ON: The boy, ROMEO. Looking out over
the ocean, he sucks on the last of a cigarette.

INT. MONTAGUE'S LIMOUSINE. DAWN.

The limo and bodyguards' cars are parked on a cross
street at a distance from the golden arch.

Ted, Caroline, and Benvolio sit watching the silhouette of Romeo.

> MONTAGUE
> Black and portentous must this humor prove
> Unless good counsel may the cause remove.

EXT. BEACH. DAWN.

P.O.V.: From the limousine: Romeo, noticing he is
being watched, rises and makes his way from the
demolished cinema, through the wire fence into
the parking lot of the adjacent pool hall.

CUT TO: Montague's limo as it begins to follow at
a discreet distance, turning the corner and heading directly for Romeo.

Seeing this, Romeo turns in the opposite direction
and heads off down the beach.

INT. MONTAGUE'S LIMOUSINE. DAWN.

> BENVOLIO
> So please you step aside.
> I'll know his grievance or be much denied.

Benvolio clambers out of the limo.

CLOSE ON: Montague; an encouraging smile.

MONTAGUE
Come, Madam. Let's away.

EXT. BEACHFRONT/BEACH. DAWN.
The limousine and bodyguards' cars pull away, and
Benvolio heads toward Romeo down on the
beach.

BENVOLIO
Good morrow, cousin.

Romeo turns. Sore, red, unfriendly eyes squint back
at Benvolio.

ROMEO
Is the day so young?
BENVOLIO
But new struck, coz.

Romeo rises and walks through the beach shacks.
Benvolio follows.

ROMEO
Ay me! Sad hours seem long.

Romeo stops as if taking in Benvolio for the first
time.

ROMEO (cont.)
Was that my father that went hence so fast?

BENVOLIO
(guilty)
It was. What sadness lengthens Romeo's hours?
ROMEO
Not having that which having makes them short.
BENVOLIO
In love?
ROMEO
Out.
BENVOLIO
Of love?
ROMEO
Out of her favor where I am in love.
BENVOLIO
Alas that love, so gentle in his view,
Should be so tyrannical and rough in proof!
ROMEO
Alas that love, whose view is muffled, still
Should without eyes, see pathways to his will.
Where shall we dine? O me, what fray was here?

Romeo is halted by the sight of last night's disturbance displayed on a small TV screen in an outdoor bar. Benvolio starts to reply.

ROMEO (cont.)
Yet tell me not, for I have heard it all. Here's
much to do with hate, but more with love.

Romeo begins to stride away from Benvolio, raging.

ROMEO (cont.)
Why then, O brawling love, O loving hate,
O anything, of nothing first create!
O heavy lightness, serious vanity,
Misshapen chaos of well-seeming forms,
Feather of lead, bright smoke, cold fire, sick
    health,
Still-waking sleep, that is not what it is!

Romeo screams at a huge bouncer who lounges in
    the doorway of one of the on-beach sex bars.

ROMEO (cont.)
This love feel I, that feel no love in this!

The bouncer's hand moves to his gun. Benvolio
    pulls Romeo back quickly, holding his own hands
    in the air, away from his own gun. Romeo laughs
    at the bouncer.

ROMEO (cont.)
Dost thou not laugh?
BENVOLIO
(calming Romeo)
No, coz, I rather weep.
ROMEO
Good heart, at what?
BENVOLIO
At thy good heart's oppression.
ROMEO
Farewell, my coz.

BENVOLIO
Soft! I will go along.
An if you leave me so, you do me wrong.
        ROMEO
Tut, I have left myself. I am not here.
This is not Romeo, he's some other where.
        BENVOLIO
Tell me in sadness, who is it that you love.
        ROMEO
In sadness, cousin, I do love a woman.
        BENVOLIO
I aimed so near when I supposed you loved.
        ROMEO
A right good marksman. And she's fair I love.
        BENVOLIO
A right fair mark, fair coz, is soonest hit.
        ROMEO
Well, in that hit you miss.

Romeo takes up a stick and writes the word
    "Rosaline," and a heart with an arrow piercing it,
    in the sand. Benvolio reacts with amazement.

        ROMEO
She'll not be hit
With Cupid's arrow. From love's weak childish
    bow she lives uncharmed.
She will not stay the siege of loving terms,
Nor bide th' encounter of assailing eyes,
Nor ope her lap to saint-seducing gold.
        BENVOLIO
Then she hath sworn that she will still live chaste?

ROMEO
She hath; and in that sparing makes huge waste.

BENVOLIO
Be ruled by me; forget to think of her.

ROMEO
O, teach me how I should forget to think!

BENVOLIO
(indicating nearby working girls)
By giving liberty unto thine eyes.
Examine other beauties.

ROMEO
Farewell. Thou canst not teach me to forget.

Romeo; a dismissive laugh as he enters the pool hall.

BENVOLIO
I'll pay that doctrine, or else die in debt.

Benvolio follows Romeo up into the club.
We pan to a newsstand and move in on the cover of
    TIMELY magazine. As it fills the screen, we see a
    picture of a square-jawed young man and a cap-
    tion that reads: 'Dave Paris, BACHELOR OF
    THE YEAR. Excellent breeding, sums of love and
    wealth, absolute power and a good name."

INT. ELEVATOR. CAPULET TOWER. DAY.
Fulgencio Capulet rides up in the stainless steel ele-
    vator side by side with the same DAVE PARIS,
    dressed in an exquisite Parisian suit.

CAPULET
But Montague is bound as well as I,
In penalty alike;
And 'tis not hard, I think
For men so old as we to keep the peace.

Dave smiles obligingly.

DAVE
Of honorable reckoning are you both,
And pity 'tis you lived at odds so long.

An awkward pause.

DAVE (cont.)
But now, my lord, what say you to my suit?

Capulet glances sideways at Paris.

CAPULET
But saying o'er what I have said before;
My child is yet a stranger in the world;
Let two more summers wither in their pride,
Ere we may think her ripe to be a bride.

Dave is politely insistent.

DAVE
Younger than she are happy mothers made.
CAPULET
(checking him hard)
And too soon marred are those so early made.

Earth hath swallowed all my hopes but she;
She is the hopeful lady of my earth.
But woo her, gentle Paris, get her heart.
My will to her consent is but a part,
And she agreed, within her scope of choice
Lies my consent and fair according voice.

The elevator arrives. Capulet places a fatherly hand
on Dave's shoulder, ushering him out the door.

EXT. CAPULET TOWER ROOFTOP. DAY.

Capulet and Dave emerge from a fire door into the
bright day. As the door closes behind them, we
see it forms part of a huge Capulet crest painted
on the wall. Capulet begins to raise his voice
above the noise of an approaching helicopter.
They walk.

> CAPULET
> This night I hold an old accustomed feast
> At my poor house, look to behold this night,
> Fresh female buds that make dark heaven light.
> Hear all; all see,
> And like her most whose merit most shall be.

Capulet smiles knowingly. Dave seems encouraged.

> CAPULET (cont.)
> (a hearty slap)
> Come go with me!

Capulet excitedly ushers Dave toward us, as, massive in foreground, Capulet's chopper drops into frame, landing on what we now see is a heliport on top of Capulet Tower.

As Capulet and Dave climb aboard, we take in the staggering vista.

INT. POOL HALL. DAY.
Dim, smoke filled. Benvolio and Romeo play pool.

> BENVOLIO
> (chalking his cue)
> Take thou some new infection to thy eye,

He lines up the six ball top pocket.

> BENVOLIO (cont.)
> And the rank poison of the old will die.

A hopeless shot that slams the eight ball toward the side pocket. Romeo stops it with his hand and hurls it against the other balls.

> BENVOLIO
> Why, Romeo, art thou mad?

Romeo sinks the other balls with his hands.

> ROMEO
> Not mad, but bound more than a madman is;
> shut up in prison, kept without my food,

Romeo stalks away from the table.

>   ROMEO (cont.)
> Whipped and tormented.

He stops at the gun check, rummaging in his
   pocket.

>   ROMEO
> Good day, good fellow.

A crusty old man looks up from the small television.
   Sixty-something, he has a face scarred with age
   and abuse. He is nursing a mangy cat.
The old man points to the sign that reads: "No
   ticket no gun." Romeo finally produces a ticket.
   Crusty goes out back. Romeo's attention is caught
   by the television.

INT. TV STUDIO SET. DAY.
An ostentatious woman and her overgroomed part-
   ner, RICH, host what looks to be a kind of *En-*
   tertainment Tonight show. The graphic behind
   them reads "Bacchanalian Nights with Susan Santandiago and Rich Ranchidis."
SUSAN SANTANDIAGO speaks conspiratorially to
   camera.

>   SUSAN
> Now I'll tell you without asking. The great
>   Rich Capulet, holds an old accustomed feast;

RICH RANCHIDIS chimes in:

>   RICH
> A fair Assembly.
>   SUSAN
> I pray you, sir, can you read?

A picture postcard shot of Capulet Mansion is inserted into the background behind Rich, as a list of names begins to scroll across the screen. Rich reads them off.

>   RICH
> Signor Placentio and his wife and daughters,
> Signor Martino, the Lady Widow
> Of Vitruvio and her lovely nieces, Rosaline and
>   Livia . . .

INT. POOL HALL. DAY.
Benvolio leans in to Romeo.

>   BENVOLIO
> At this same ancient feast of Capulet's
> Sups the fair Rosaline; whom thou so loves,
> With all the admired beauties of Verona.

INT. TV STUDIO SET. DAY.
>   SUSAN
> If you be not of the house of Montagues,
> Come and crush a cup of wine!

RICH
Rest you merry!

INT. POOL HALL. DAY.
Crusty returns. He hands the boys their guns, and
they move off.

EXT. POOL HALL STAIRS. DAY.
We follow Romeo and Benvolio down the stairs.

BENVOLIO
Go thither, and with unattainted eye
Compare her face with some that I shall show,
And I will make thee think thy swan a crow.

Romeo laughs dismissively.

ROMEO
One fairer than my love! The all-seeing sun
Ne'er saw her match since first the world begun.

We follow the boys as they cross the parking lot to
Romeo's magnificent silver car.
CLOSE ON: A fourteen-year-old boy asleep on the
hood of the car, BALTHASAR.
Three or four kids doze on the sidewalk. As Romeo
approaches, they jump up and begin vigorously
polishing the already gleaming car.
Balthasar wakes. He springs off the hood, chases the

kids away, then, producing a huge bunch of keys,
opens the car door for Romeo.

BENVOLIO
Tut, you saw her fair, none else being by.

Romeo throws the kids a few coins and slides into
the driver's seat. He nods to Balthasar. Balthasar
jumps in back.

ROMEO
I'll go along, no such sight to be shown,
But to rejoice in splendor of mine own.

Benvolio leaps into the passenger seat.
As the car drives off, we CRASH CRANE UP and
WIPE over the pool hall roof.

EXT. AERIAL OVER CITY. DAY.
COMPRESSED INFORMATION SHOT: As we
sweep through the city to Capulet Mansion, an
Italianate wonder of Florentine architecture.

EXT. CAPULET ESTATE. DAY.
We hurtle to a stop on a mouth screaming from a
top-story window.

GLORIA
J U L I E T !

The call echoes three times, and with each echo
  we see:
A wide flat shot of the mansion.
A side shot of the mansion with a giant Capulet
  crest cake being carried in the front door.
The other side shot of the mansion with red dec-
  orative cloth being unfurled.
CUT TO: GLORIA CAPULET in a dressing
  gown, closing the doors on the upper balcony.

INT. THE GRAND HALL. DAY.
The grand hall is crowded with workers and servants
  rushing to finish preparing for tonight's party.
  The Capulet cake is being carried through to the
  ballroom. Through the arches, in the ballroom,
  we see the cleaned chandeliers being raised back
  into position.
Gloria strides down the stairs just as the NURSE
  explodes out of the elevator on the ground floor.

> GLORIA
Nurse, where's my daughter? Call her forth to me.
> NURSE
I bade her come. God forbid! Juliet!

Gloria heads off as we follow the Nurse up the magnificent staircase and across the landing.

INT. JULIET'S BEDROOM. DAY.
The Nurse enters. She finds the room empty but

notices a pile of clothes on the floor by the bed.
She crosses to one of the pairs of French doors
and throws them open.

INT. CAPULET MANSION/JULIET'S
BALCONY. DAY.
> NURSE
> (yelling)
JULIET!

She looks down.
CUT TO: The Nurse's P.O.V. of the swimming
pool area.

INT. JULIET'S BATHROOM. DAY.
The still, serene, submerged features of a beautiful
young girl. Dark floating hair gently frames the
face. Heavy liquid eyes stare up through the water.
We hear, though faintly, the calling:

EXT. CAPULET MANSION/JULIET'S
BALCONY. DAY.
CUT TO: Reverse on the Nurse bellowing . . .

> NURSE (V.O.)
J U L I E T !

. . . out of Juliet's bedroom window. As it echoes

twice, we go wide on the set and then extra wide on location at Chapultepec.

INT. JULIET'S BATHROOM. DAY.
> NURSE (V.O.)
> J U L I E T !

With a rush, JULIET surfaces. As she gulps air, we realize that she is, in fact, in a bath. She turns to look at the Nurse standing in the bathroom door-way.

INT. ENTRANCE HALL CAPULET MANSION. DAY.
Gloria Capulet is chatting with the INTERIOR DECORATOR.
She calls maniacally.

> GLORIA
> J U L I E T !

CUT TO: Juliet, as if from nowhere, has appeared. She wears a bathrobe, and her hair is wet. Behind her stands the Nurse.

> JULIET
> (coolly)
> Madam, I am here. What is your will?

Gloria, startled, sweeps up the stairs and shuffles her
   daughter toward a doorway.

GLORIA
Nurse, give leave awhile, we must talk in secret.

INT. GLORIA'S DRESSING ROOM. DAY.
Gloria shepherds Juliet into her opulent dressing
   room and closes the door. She circles with ner-
   vous vexation, searching for words, stops, then
   suddenly opens the door and yells out to the
   Nurse.

GLORIA
Nurse, come back again.
I have remembered me. Thou's hear our counsel.

The Nurse enters. Gloria, still refusing eye contact,
   checks her appearance once more in the mirror.
   She takes a hairbrush and, feigning pleasantness,
   intensely brushes her hair.

GLORIA (cont.)
Nurse, thou knowest my daughter's of a pretty
   age.
NURSE
(to Juliet)
Thou wast the prettiest babe that e'er I nursed.

The hairbrush clatters onto the dresser. A moment
   of tense silence. Gloria grips herself and pours a

sherry. Back still turned, she speaks to her daughter.

GLORIA
By my count,
I was your mother much upon these years
That you are now a maid.

A Nembutal twists like a pin in the corner of Gloria's mouth. She slugs it down with the sherry and turns abruptly to face Juliet.

GLORIA (cont.)
Thus then in brief:
The valiant Paris seeks you for his love.

CUT TO: Juliet; an uncomprehending stare.
The Nurse, caught off guard, tries to buoy the situation.

NURSE
A man, young lady! Lady, such a man
As all the world—why, he's a man of wax.

The medication takes immediate effect upon Gloria. She joins Juliet on the couch and coos in Paris's favor.

GLORIA
Verona's summer hath not such a flower.
NURSE
Nay, he's a flower; in faith, a very flower.

GLORIA
This night you shall behold him at our feast;
Read o'er the volume of young Paris' face
And find delight writ there with beauty's pen.
This precious book of love, this unbound lover,
To beautify him only lacks a cover.
So shall you share all that he doth possess,
By having him, making yourself no less.
NURSE
No less, nay bigger. Women grow by men.

Gloria, ignoring the Nurse, probes Juliet's thoughts.

GLORIA
Speak briefly, can you like of Paris' love?

Juliet, adept at negotiating her mother's strange
moods, chooses her words precisely.

JULIET
I'll look to like, if looking liking move,
But no more deep will I endart mine eye,
Than your consent gives strength to make it fly.

PETER the chauffeur enters.

PETER
Madam. The guests are come.
GLORIA
(checks the mirror)
We follow thee.

Gloria exits.
Suddenly skyrockets outside light up her window.
CUT TO: The Nurse as she whispers in Juliet's ear.

> NURSE
> Go girl, seek happy nights to happy days.

EXT. NIGHT SKY. NIGHT.
A skyrocket cutting through the velvety blackness.

EXT. CAPULET MANSION. NIGHT.
A gigantic fireworks explosion; a zillion dots of
    shimmering light.

EXT. DEMOLISHED CINEMA. NIGHT.
Romeo looks up sharply; his eyes sparkle in the
    blinding white flash of light.

EXT. JULIET'S BALCONY. NIGHT.
Juliet, in party costume (not the wings). She stands
    on the balcony above the pool. Her face shares
    the same light.

EXT. DEMOLISHED CINEMA. NIGHT.
With the scene lit by fireworks, we discover Romeo
    dressed as the boy King Arthur, slumped in the
    side-box of the Sycamore Grove cinema. Through

the arch we see a bevy of freaks who are lit by
fireworks that whoosh up into the air from the
beach. Balthasar perches precariously on the balcony edge packing a bong. Below, on what's left
of the cinema's forestage, a bandaged Gregory,
dressed as a Viking, swigs beer while playing
head-butt with fellow Viking warrior Sampson.
Benvolio sits in his car in a monk's habit, punch-
ing the radio looking for good music.

TIGHT ON: The system light as the pumping intro
to "Young Hearts" kicks in.

Miraculously with the musical introduction, the
darkness is slashed by headlights. A reckless sports
car speeds toward the boys and skids to a halt.

CLOSE ON: A silver-stilettoed foot emerges from
the car and plants itself firmly in the dirt.

CUT TO: The boys, eyes wide with amazement.

PAN: Slowly up a shapely pair of black-stockinged
legs, past a hint of garter belt to a black sequined
miniskirt and sequined holster and up over a
muscular dark-skinned stomach and tiny sequined
bra top, to discover: the twenty-one-year-old male,
African American face of MERCUTIO. He begins
a raunchy, if poorly executed, drag act while magically producing invitations from somewhere
within his miniskirt.

CUT TO: The boys. They laugh and catcall raucously. Aggressively bumping and grinding, Mercutio distributes the invitations, singing the song
"Young Hearts" as he does so.

MERCUTIO
Nay, gentle Romeo, we must have you dance.

Mercutio dances Romeo onto the stage, continuing
to sing. Romeo pushes Mercutio away. The music
disappears into its naturalistic background state.

ROMEO
Not I, believe me. You have dancing shoes
With nimble soles. I have a soul of lead.
MERCUTIO
You are a lover, borrow Cupid's wings
And soar with them above a common bound.
ROMEO
Under love's heavy burden do I sink!

Mercutio in mock sympathy.

MERCUTIO
Too great oppression for a tender thing.
ROMEO
Is love a tender thing? It is too rough,
Too rude, too boisterous, and it pricks like thorn.
MERCUTIO
If love be rough with you, be rough with love.

Mercutio jumps on Romeo.

MERCUTIO (cont.)
Prick love for pricking, and you beat love down.

CUT TO: Benvolio, impatiently honking the horn.

BENVOLIO
Every man betake him to his legs!

Mercutio drags Romeo toward the car.

MERCUTIO
Come, we burn daylight, ho!

Romeo pulls away.

ROMEO
But 'tis no wit to go.

Mercutio turns, exasperated.

MERCUTIO
Why, may one ask?
ROMEO
I dreamt a dream tonight.
MERCUTIO
And so did I.
ROMEO
Well, what was yours?
MERCUTIO
That dreamers often lie.
ROMEO
In bed asleep, while they do dream things true.

Mercutio magically produces a tiny gold pill case.

MERCUTIO
O, then I see Queen Mab hath been with you.

She is the fairies' midwife, and she comes
In shape no bigger than an agate stone
On the forefinger of an alderman,
Drawn with a team of little atomies
Over men's noses as they lie asleep.

Tantalizingly, he passes the case beneath Romeo's
nose.

MERCUTIO (cont.)
Her chariot is an empty hazelnut,
Her wagoner a small gray-coated gnat.

With a conjurer's dexterity Mercutio extracts a small,
gray pill.

MERCUTIO (cont.)
And in this state she gallops night by night
Through lovers' brains, and then they dream of
love;

He palms the pill. It reappears from behind Romeo's
ear.

MERCUTIO (cont.)
O'er lawyers' fingers who straight dream on fees;
O'er ladies' lips, who straight on kisses dream,
Which oft the angry Mab with blisters plagues.
Because their breaths with sweetmeats tainted are.

The pillbox glints in the moonlight.

>MERCUTIO (cont.)
Sometime she driveth o'er a soldier's neck;
And then dreams he of cutting foreign throats.
And being thus frighted, swears a prayer or two
And sleeps again.

Mercutio now intensely angry:

>MERCUTIO (cont.)
This is that very Mab
That plaits the manes of horses in the night
And bakes the elf-locks in foul sluttish hairs.

He screams into the night.

>MERCUTIO (cont.)
This is the hag, when maids lie on their backs,
That presses them and learns them first to bear,
Making them women of good carriage.
This is she, this is she . . .

CLOSE ON: Mercutio. He breaks off. There is a
strange stillness among the group. Romeo goes to
his friend.

>ROMEO
Peace, peace, Mercutio, peace.
Thou talkest of nothing.

Mercutio meets Romeo's gaze. A sea wind blows the
fires on the beaches.

MERCUTIO
True, I talk of dreams;
Which are the children of an idle brain,
Begot of nothing but vain fantasy.
Which is as thin of substance as the air
And more inconstant than the wind, who woos
Even now the frozen bosom of the north.

CUT TO: On the shoreline the bevy of freaks surround a bonfire that is buffeted by strong winds. Benvolio is in the car.

BENVOLIO
This wind you talk of blows us from ourselves:
Supper is done and we shall come too late.

Romeo looks through the proscenium toward the sea.

ROMEO
I fear, too early, for my mind misgives
Some consequence yet hanging in the stars
Shall bitterly begin his fearful date
With this night's revels, and expire the term
Of a despised life closed in my breast,
By some vile forfeit of untimely death.

PAUSE: A green firework explodes above them. Romeo smiles.

>ROMEO (cont.)
>But he that hath the steerage of my course
>Direct my sail!

He takes the pill and drops it into his mouth.

>ROMEO (cont.)
>On, lusty gentleman!

CUT TO: The boys and Balthasar in Romeo's car.

CUT TO: Another green firework exploding in the sky.

We hear a trippy-disco reprise of the "Young Hearts" chorus.

CLOSE ON: Romeo's face bathed in the green light.

PULL OUT: From Romeo's serene face. His car is in a wash of fireworks doing a surreal 360-degree spin on the spot.

Mercutio, standing at the center of the whorl, sings a slow lyrical version of the "Young Hearts" chorus. The characters from Sycamore Grove walk by.

The car begins to spin faster as the trippy "Young Hearts" version transforms into a pounding Latin treatment.

INT. GRAND HALL. CAPULET MANSION. NIGHT.

We are close up inside Mercutio's dream, as, like some disco diva on Ecstasy, he mimes the big

Latin version of "Young Hearts" on top of the
vaulting staircase of the magnificently decorated
grand hall.
The world has transformed into a depraved musical
routine as we track with Mercutio, Gregory, and
Sampson, as they cavort and gambol their way
down the staircase, taking every opportunity to
ogle and grope bewildered guests.
Mercutio, still singing "Young Hearts," points at an
unamused Romeo.
Mercutio drags Romeo away from the column
toward the passing conga line.

> MERCUTIO
> Every man betake him to his legs!

Mercutio forces Romeo to join the tail end of the
conga line as it disappears into the ballroom. We
begin to hear "Young Hearts" in a cheesy club
version sung in Spanish.

INT. BALLROOM. NIGHT.
CUT TO: ROMEO'S P.O.V.; On stage fronting a
Latin big band, Capulet sings the cheesier version
of "Young Hearts" in Spanish.
CLOSE ON: Romeo jostled and squeezed through
the dancing crowd; his face betrays his discomfort.
TRACK WITH: Romeo as he breaks from the
conga line, and follow him through the crowd
into the grand hall.

INT. GRAND HALL. NIGHT.

Suddenly a large arm coils around Romeo's neck.
DISTORTED E.C.U.: A seriously intoxicated
   Fulgencio Capulet; his puffy red face squeezes
   against Romeo's mask as he screams above the
   music.

                CAPULET
Ah, I have seen the day that I could tell
A whispering tale in a fair lady's ear. Such as
   would please—

Capulet ogles some passing young ladies.

                CAPULET (cont.)
Welcome!

As Romeo breaks away from Capulet, he slams into
   an elephantine mask, which leers obscenely at
   him.
ROMEO'S P.O.V.: The grotesque images of avari-
   cious decadence build to a nightmarish peak, the
   chorus of "Young Hearts" in Spanish contorts to
   a horrifying nightmarish cacophony.

INT. BATHROOM. NIGHT.

Silent, underwater shot. Romeo's tranquil features
   submerged in a basin of water.
BEAT.
With a gasp, Romeo rises. A moment. His breathing

calms. Then, smoothing water into his hair, he
gazes into the bathroom mirror. He turns:
The entire wall opposite the mirror is a magnificent
saltwater fish tank.
Romeo, drawn by its submarine beauty, leans against
the fish tank. Applause echoes faintly through the
bathroom speakers.

INT. BALLROOM. NIGHT.
As the applause dies, a dark-haired diva takes the
spotlight. The band eases into the opening bars of
a love ballad.

INT. BATHROOM. NIGHT.
As the music swells, Romeo watches a mustached
catfish glide past a medieval castle.
Suddenly, Romeo pulls away. In the powder room
beyond, he sees a beautiful girl in an angel costume perched on an ornate chair reading a slim
leather-bound book.
The diva's first pure, achingly beautiful notes soar.
Confused, Romeo looks again. There is no mistake—it is a girl. Through a shimmering curtain
of ribbon weed, two dark wide eyes, a childish
nose, and sumptuous full lips.
Romeo pushes his face closer to the glass.

INT. POWDER ROOM. NIGHT.
CLOSE ON: Juliet, dressed as an angel, on the

other side of the tank. She senses someone watching her. We now realize that the girls' powder
room and the boys' bathroom are divided by this
watery wonderworld.

Juliet warily moves closer to the glass.

INT. BATHROOM. NIGHT.

Romeo leans his face against the glass. The love ballad builds.

SLOW TRACK: From Romeo's profile, in through
the water, and . . .

INT. POWDER ROOM. NIGHT.

. . . out the other side, to find Juliet in profile,
peering into the tank.

INT. BATHROOM. NIGHT.

Romeo presses his nose lightly against the glass.

INT. POWDER ROOM. NIGHT.

Juliet; a tiny smile.

Suddenly, CRASH! The door slams open. Juliet
turns, startled. It is the Nurse.

> NURSE
Juliet, your mother calls.

The Nurse bustles Juliet out the door. Juliet looks
   over her shoulder at the mystery boy.

INT. GRAND HALL. NIGHT.
Romeo, now without his mask, slams out of the
   bathroom. Juliet and the Nurse have disappeared
   into the crowd.
CUT TO: Juliet being dragged along by the Nurse.
   She glances back toward the mystery boy, but he
   is gone.

INT. BALLROOM. NIGHT.
Juliet and the Nurse rejoin Dave Paris, who is
   dressed as an astronaut, and Gloria, at the side of
   the dance floor.
Dave, with an irresistible smile, extends his hand to
   Juliet.

>   DAVE
> Will you now deny to dance?

Juliet looks to Dave, desperately searching for a reason to decline. Gloria, brushing aside her silly
   daughter's protests, slugs the last of her cham-
   pagne and herds them onto the dance floor.

>   GLORIA
>   (whispering to Juliet)
> A man, young lady, such a man.

As Juliet is dragged onto the floor her eyes furtively
   search for the boy.

INT. GRAND HALL. NIGHT.
Romeo crosses the grand hall. Desperate to find the
   girl, he roughly shunts aside a reveler dressed as
   Lucifer, Prince of Darkness.
HOLD ON: Lucifer. He removes his mask: it is
   Tybalt. He turns to Abra, who's dressed as a de-
   mon.

>   TYBALT
> What, dares the slave come hither to
> fleer and scorn at our solemnity?
> Now by the stock and honor of my kin
> To strike him dead I hold it not a sin.

Tybalt moves off aggressively but is halted as Capulet
   slams a hand into his chest.

>   CAPULET
> Why, how now, kinsman, wherefore storm you
>   so?
>   TYBALT
> Uncle, this is that villain Romeo.
> A Montague, our foe.

Capulet peers across the ballroom.

>   CAPULET
> Young Romeo is it?

TYBALT
'Tis he.
CAPULET
Content thee, gentle coz, let him alone.
I would not for the wealth of all this town
Here in my house do him disparagement.
Therefore be patient; take no note of him.

Tybalt can't believe it.

TYBALT
I'll not endure him.

CLOSE ON: Capulet, exploding with rage.

CAPULET
He shall be endured!
(slapping Tybalt viciously)
What, goodman boy! I say he shall! Go to.

Capulet violently shoves Tybalt to the ground.

CAPULET (cont.)
You'll make a mutiny among my guests!

A middle-aged couple looks on, shocked. Capulet
waves to them festively:

CAPULET (cont.)
What? Cheerly, my hearts!

Capulet snorts at Tybalt in disgust.

CAPULET (cont.)
You'll not endure him? Am I the master here or
you? Go to.

Smoothing his hair into place, Capulet makes his
way down the stairs.
CLOSE ON: Tybalt choking back tears of rage.

INT. BALLROOM. NIGHT.
Romeo is spying on the angel from around the
arches on the hall side of the dance floor.
CLOSE ON: Romeo whispers.

ROMEO
Did my heart love till now? Forswear it, sight.
For I ne'er saw true beauty till this night.

Romeo begins to circumnavigate the dance floor in
an attempt to get closer to Juliet.
CUT TO: Dave slow-dancing with Juliet. Romeo
tracks with them from behind the arches.
Juliet's eyes search the room for the boy.
CLOSE ON: Romeo.
CLOSE ON: Juliet.
Their eyes connect.
Juliet looks quickly back to Dave, who, oblivious,
returns his most devastating smile.
CUT TO: The songstress; her voice soars.
CUT TO: Juliet. Unable to look away from the boy,
she stares over Dave's shoulder.

CUT TO: Romeo, positioning himself behind an arch ever so near her.

With the diva's spiraling final notes, the ballad concludes. The crowd cheers and screams its applause. An avalanche of balloons, tinsel, and confetti rains down from the roof. The light dims. Juliet has her back against the arch, her eyes search the darkness, but the boy is gone.

CLOSE ON: Juliet. Suddenly: A gasp; Juliet's eyes widen, shocked.

In the dark, a hand has shot out from the folds of cloth in the curtained archway and clasped hers. Juliet barely dares breathe.

She glances furtively to Dave Paris. He watches the stage.

Slowly Juliet turns toward the hand; there through a break in the curtain she can see eye, cheek, and lips of the mystery boy. As the diva continues her curtain call, Romeo, ignoring the dangerous proximity of Dave Paris, maneuvers his lips to almost touch Juliet's ear. He whispers as he brings her hands to his lips.

> ROMEO
> If I profane with my unworthiest hand
> This holy shrine, the gentle sin is this.
> My lips, two blushing pilgrims, ready stand
> To smooth that rough touch with a tender kiss.

Juliet, pulling her hand away, slips around the column out of sight of Gloria and Dave.

INT. GRAND HALL. NIGHT.

> JULIET
> Good pilgrim, you do wrong your hand too
> much,
> Which mannerly devotion shows in this.
> For saints have hands that pilgrims' hands do
> touch,

She offers her hand in a chaste handshake.

> JULIET (cont.)
> And palm to palm is holy palmers' kiss.

Romeo, ignoring the polite, edges his way closer,
attempting a kiss.

> ROMEO
> Have not saints lips, and holy palmers too?

Juliet glides her lips out of range of his and moves
off.

> JULIET
> Ay, pilgrim, lips that they must use in prayer.

Juliet, turning in front of the elevator in the grand
hall, brings her hands together to mime a praying
angel.

> ROMEO
> O, then, dear saint, let lips do what hands do,

Gently parting her praying hands—

>   ROMEO (cont.)
>   They pray: grant thou,

His lips closer and closer—

>   ROMEO (cont.)
>   Lest faith turn to despair.

They are so close they can feel each other's breath.

>   JULIET
>   (attempting reason through short breaths)
>   Saints do not move, though grant for prayer's
>   sake.
>   ROMEO
>   Then move not while my prayer's effect I take.

CLOSE ON: Romeo's lips deliciously close to Juliet's. She does not deny him as ever so gently they . . .
SUDDENLY: Juliet's eyes awaken with horror.
CUT TO: JULIET'S P.O.V. Gloria and Dave are hunting toward them through the crowd.
SUDDENLY: BING. The elevator doors open. Juliet, seizing the moment, pulls Romeo inside.

INT. ELEVATOR. NIGHT.
The doors close, shrouding them from Gloria and Dave. Romeo and Juliet kiss, swept up in the mo-

mentum of the rising elevator. A gentle reticence; Juliet shies away.
Their hearts race; close, warm, breathless.

>   ROMEO (cont.)
> Thus from my lips, by thine, my sin is purged.
>   JULIET
> Then have my lips the sin that they have took.
>   ROMEO
> Sin from my lips? O trespass sweetly urged!
> Give me my sin again.

They fall toward each other to kiss again when . . .
BING, the doors of the elevator open.

INT. GRAND HALL LANDING. NIGHT.
JULIET'S P.O.V.: Gloria and Dave, having reached the top of the stairs, are petrifyingly close.
Juliet dares not move; her eyes fix on the approaching couple through the feathers of a passing peacock costume.

INT. ELEVATOR. NIGHT.
CLOSE ON: Juliet's hand working the "close" button.

INT. GRAND HALL LANDING. NIGHT.
The peacock has moved and Dave and Gloria stand, backs turned, directly in front of the elevator.

TIGHT ON: Gloria turning toward Romeo and Juliet as the doors close in the nick of time.

INT. ELEVATOR. NIGHT.

Romeo and Juliet kiss deep, long, entwined. All sense of time is lost in the dizzying vertiginous spin of the falling elevator. Suddenly, it stops with a thud. Juliet breaks away, catching her breath.

> JULIET
> You kiss by the book.

Light bursts through the crack of the opening elevator doors behind them. Our focus moves from the lovers' longing look to the shocked features of the Nurse, now standing in the open elevator doorway.

INT. GRAND HALL. NIGHT.

> NURSE
> Madam, your mother craves a word with you.

She eyes Romeo severely.

> NURSE (cont.)
> Come. Let's away.

She takes firm control of her charge.
Juliet furtively motions for the startled Romeo not to follow as he trails them across the grand hall.

CUT TO: ROMEO'S P.O.V.: The Nurse and Juliet reach the door, but instead of leaving, they turn and ascend the staircase that arcs around to the mezzanine level. They join a vexed Gloria Capulet, who clings to a patient Dave Paris.

Inaudible words are exchanged. Juliet flicks her eyes nervously to Romeo.

CUT TO: Romeo. He halts at the foot of the stairs, unsure.

CUT TO: Gloria. Catching Juliet's interest in the boy, she indicates to her daughter to "come along."

CUT TO: Romeo; a dawning realization.

> ROMEO
> (under his breath)
> Is she a Capulet?

CUT TO: Juliet. She stops halfway up the steps and turns back.

CUT TO: Romeo, comprehending the reality of who she is.

CUT TO: Juliet. The Nurse whispers in her ear.

> NURSE
> His name is Romeo, and a Montague,
> The only son of your great enemy.

HOLD ON: Juliet. Like a cloud passing across the sun, a dark coldness descends upon her.

CUT TO: Mercutio. He throws himself upon the shell-shocked Romeo.

> MERCUTIO
> Away, begone, the sport is at its best.

Mercutio shuttles Romeo toward the door.

> ROMEO
> Ay so I fear,

A covert glance over his shoulder.

> ROMEO (cont.)
> The more is my unrest.

EXT. CAPULET MANSION. NIGHT.
Mercutio bundles Romeo through the front door
and down the stairs, through the guard of honor.

INT. CAPULET MANSION/STAIRS. NIGHT.
Juliet, maneuvered up the stairs by the Nurse, breaks
away.

EXT. CAPULET MANSION. NIGHT.
Romeo, being dragged through the guard of honor,
looks up at Juliet's silhouette in the window.

EXT. CAPULET MANSION. NIGHT.
Gregory and Sampson are strapping on their guns
and holsters at the gun check at the outside gate.

CUT TO: Romeo staring up at the windows. Mercutio joins him, handing him his gun. Romeo takes no notice. He sees Juliet come out onto a small side balcony. Mercutio holsters Romeo's gun in his dress and pushes the dreamy one into the backseat of the car.

EXT. CAPULET MANSION/WINDOW. NIGHT.
CLOSE ON: Juliet on the balcony, staring at Romeo.

EXT. CAPULET MANSION/GATE. NIGHT.
A huge display combusts into blinding fireworks.
As the convertible passes beneath the fireworks, Romeo turns. Through a deluge of falling sparks, he glimpses the mystery girl high up on the balcony.

EXT. CAPULET MANSION/WINDOW. NIGHT.
CLOSE ON: Juliet leaning over the balcony. Brilliant sparkles light in her eyes.
PUSH IN: We hear her secret whisper.

> JULIET
> My only love, sprung from my only hate.
> Too early seen unknown, and known too late.
> Prodigious birth of love it is to me,

EXT. CAPULET MANSION/GATE. NIGHT.
JULIET'S P.O.V.: In slow motion, Romeo, through
the falling curtain of fiery embers.

> JULIET (cont. V.O.)
> That I must love a loathed enemy.

Warm wind blows the smoke from the expended
fireworks.

EXT. CAPULET MANSION FRONT DOOR. NIGHT.
PAN from Juliet on the balcony to the gun check to
discover someone else who cannot take his eyes
off the departing Romeo. It is Tybalt. The music
darkens as we push through the smoky wind.

> TYBALT
> I will withdraw. But this intrusion shall,
> Now seeming sweet, convert to
> bitterest gall.

INT. ROMEO'S CAR. NIGHT.
The car slows behind the jam of departing vehicles.
The boys sing along raucously with the radio.

> BOYS
> (singing)
> "I am a pretty piece of flesh,
> I am a pretty piece of flesh . . ."

PUSH IN: On Romeo; he leaps from the car.
   Benvolio yells after him.

        BENVOLIO
   Romeo! Cousin Romeo! Romeo!

Romeo runs back toward the estate.

EXT. BACK OF CAPULET MANSION. NIGHT.
PAN DOWN: From a tall satellite dish above which
   Capulet Mansion towers.
Romeo arrives at the base of the satellite structure.
   He stops and hears Mercutio call.

EXT. BACK OF CAPULET MANSION. NIGHT.
        MERCUTIO (V.O.)
   Romeo! Humors! Madman! Passion! Lover!
        ROMEO
   He jests at scars that never felt a wound.

EXT. BACK OF CAPULET MANSION. NIGHT.
CLOSE ON: A pair of stone cherubs on top of the
   retaining wall of a terraced garden. Romeo's face
   appears between them.
Romeo hauls himself up onto the wall. Below is an
   Italianate-style pool area. To the right, the dark-
   ened rear wing of Capulet Mansion. Suddenly
   light slashes from a window in the house. Romeo
   takes cover.

ROMEO
But soft, what light through yonder window
breaks?

Romeo's question is answered as the silhouette of an
angel forms in the window.

ROMEO (cont.)
It is the East, and Juliet is the sun!

The silhouette of Juliet as she removes her wings.

ROMEO (cont.)
Arise, fair sun, and kill the envious moon,
Who is already sick and pale with grief
That thou her maid art far more fair than she.

The silhouette now moves to a second window and
very slowly begins to remove her gown.

ROMEO (cont.)
Be not her maid, since she is envious.
Her vestal livery is but sick and green,
And none but fools do wear it.

The silhouette has partially removed her dress.

ROMEO (cont.)
Cast it off!

The silhouette removes her dress and walks away
from the window. Romeo turns toward camera.

Behind him we see her silhouette appear in a
third window momentarily. He turns, but she is
gone again. Suddenly, with a BING, elevator
doors open poolside, revealing the vision of Juliet
clad only in her robe.

> ROMEO (cont.)
> It is my lady. O, it is my love!
> O that she knew she were!

Juliet sighs.

> JULIET
> Ay me!
> ROMEO
> (whispers)
> She speaks.
> O, speak again, bright angel!

Juliet looks longingly toward the stars.

> JULIET
> O Romeo, Romeo!—Wherefore art thou Romeo?
> Deny thy father and refuse thy name.
> Or, if thou wilt not, be but sworn my love,
> And I'll no longer be a Capulet.

CLOSE ON: Romeo. Incredulous.

> ROMEO
> Shall I hear more, or shall I speak at this?

>   JULIET
> 'Tis but thy name that is my enemy.
> Thou art thyself, though not a Montague.
> What's Montague? It is nor hand nor foot
> Nor arm nor face nor any other part
> Belonging to a man. O, be some other name!
> What's in a name? That which we call a rose
> By any other word would smell as sweet.
> So Romeo would, were he not Romeo called,
> Retain that dear perfection which he owes
> Without that title. Romeo, doff thy name,
> And for thy name, which is no part of thee,
> Take all myself.

Romeo wildly calls:

>   ROMEO
> I take thee at thy word!
> Call me but love, and I'll be new baptized.
> Henceforth I never will be Romeo.

Romeo jumps down from the wall. Juliet screams and turns, toppling backward. Romeo grabs her hand, but her momentum overbalances him and they both plunge headlong into the pool.

EXT. CAPULET MANSION/POOL. UNDERWATER. NIGHT.

UNDERWATER SHOT: A slow-motion phosphorescent tangle of arms, legs, and bodies.

EXT. CAPULET MANSION/POOL GARDEN. NIGHT.

Above water, real time: Romeo and Juliet surface,
    spluttering. Juliet thrashes the water in an attempt
    to get distance from her attacker.

>   JULIET
> What man art thou that, thus bescreened in
>   night,
> So stumblest on my counsel?

Romeo: A calming gesture as he tries to tread water.

>   ROMEO
> By a name I know not how to tell thee who I
>   am:
> My name, dear saint, is hateful to myself
> Because it is an enemy to thee.

The ferocious barking of a guard dog arrests the
    teenagers' attention. A moment, then they slide
    beneath the water.

CUT TO: The security guard and dog appearing
    above the pool area.

GUARD'S P.O.V.: The rippling surface of the wa-
    ter.

CUT TO UNDERWATER SHOT: Romeo and Ju-
    liet submerged, hair streaming, stare at each other
    like two beautiful fish.

CUT TO: The guard. Frowning, he returns the way
    he came.

CUT TO: Romeo and Juliet. Gasping for air, they

cautiously surface. A moment—then Juliet gives a small smile.

>   JULIET
> Art thou not Romeo, and a Montague?
>   ROMEO
> Neither, fair maid, if either thee dislike.

Juliet looks nervously toward the house. She drags Romeo toward a small grotto at the end of the pool.

>   JULIET
> How cam'st thou hither, tell me, and wherefore?
> The garden walls are high and hard to climb,
> And the place death, considering who thou art.
>   ROMEO
>   (with splashy bravado)
> With love's light wings did I o'er perch these
>   walls.
> For stony limits cannot hold love out,
> And what love can do, that dares love attempt.
> Therefore thy kinsmen are no stop to me.

Juliet drags Romeo firmly into the grotto.

>   JULIET
>   (with real fear)
> If they do see thee, they will murder thee.

Romeo slowly pulls Juliet toward him.

ROMEO
I have night's cloak to hide me from their eyes.
And but thou love me, let them find me here.
My life were better ended by their hate
Than death prorogued, wanting of thy love.

The lovers kiss long and deep. Then Juliet, suddenly
fearful, pushes Romeo away.

JULIET
Thou knowest the mask of night is on my face,
Else would a maiden blush bepaint my cheek,
For that which thou hast heard me speak tonight.
Fain would I dwell on form—fain, fain deny
What I have spoke. But farewell compliment!
Dost thou love me?

Romeo tries to speak; Juliet silences him.

JULIET (cont.)
I know thou wilt say "Ay,"
And I will take thy word. Yet, if thou swearest,
Thou mayst prove false. O gentle Romeo,
If thou dost love, pronounce it faithfully.
Or if thou think'st I am too quickly won,
I'll frown, and be perverse, and say thee nay,
So thou wilt woo. But else, not for the world.
In truth, fair Montague, I am too fond,
And therefore thou mayst think my 'havior light.
But trust me, gentleman, I'll prove more true
Than those that have more cunning to be strange.

ROMEO
Lady, by yonder blessed moon I vow,
That tips with silver all these fruit-tree tops.
    JULIET
O, swear not by the moon, th' inconstant moon,
That monthly changes in her circled orb,
Lest that thy love prove likewise variable.
    ROMEO
What shall I swear by?
    JULIET
Do not swear at all.
Or if thou wilt, swear by thy gracious self,
Which is the god of my idolatry,
And I'll believe thee.

She touches his cheek. Romeo moves his lips close.

ROMEO
If my heart's dear love—

Confused, Juliet breaks away.

JULIET
Well, do not swear. Although I joy in thee,
I have no joy of this contract tonight.
It is too rash, too unadvised, too sudden;
Too like the lightning, which doth cease to be
Ere one can say "It lightens." Sweet, good night.
This bud of love, by summer's ripening breath,
May prove a beauteous flower when next we
    meet.

Good night, good night. As sweet repose and rest
Come to thy heart as that within my breast.

She rushes up the stairs.

> ROMEO
> O, wilt thou leave me so unsatisfied?

Juliet; a shocked look.

> JULIET
> What satisfaction canst thou have tonight?

CLOSE ON: Romeo.

> ROMEO
> The exchange of thy love's faithful vow for mine.

CLOSE ON: Juliet. She runs joyously to Romeo.
They fall once more into the pool.

> JULIET
> I gave thee mine before thou didst request it!

Kissing him passionately.

> JULIET (cont.)
> And yet I would it were to give again.
> ROMEO
> Wouldst thou withdraw it? For what purpose,
> love?

JULIET
But to be frank and give it thee again.

They kiss again. The Nurse calls from inside.

NURSE (O.S.)
Juliet!

Juliet looks to the house.

JULIET
(breathlessly)
Three words, dear Romeo, and good night indeed.
If that thy bent of love be honorable,
Thy purpose marriage, send me word tomorrow,
By one that I'll procure to come to thee,
Where and what time thou wilt perform the rite,
And all my fortunes at thy foot I'll lay
And follow thee, my lord, throughout the world.
NURSE (O.S.)
Madam!
JULIET
(to Nurse)
I come, anon,
(to Romeo)
But if thou meanest not well,
I do beseech thee . . .
NURSE (O.S.)
Madam!

JULIET
        (to Nurse)
By and by I come!
        (to Romeo)
To cease thy strife and leave me to my grief.
Tomorrow will I send.

Romeo holds Juliet's gaze.

ROMEO
So thrive my soul.
        NURSE (O.S.)
Madam!

Juliet breaks away.

JULIET
A thousand times good night!

With a final kiss, Juliet runs inside.

ROMEO
A thousand times the worse, to want thy light.
Love goes toward love as schoolboys from their
    books;
But love from love, toward school with heavy
    looks.

Juliet reappears at the upper balcony.

> JULIET
> Romeo! What o'clock tomorrow
> Shall I send to thee?
> ROMEO
> By the hour of nine.

Juliet unclasps a delicate silver necklace from around her neck.

> JULIET
> I will not fail. 'Tis twenty year till then.
> Good night, good night! Parting is such
> sweet sorrow.
> That I shall say good night till it be morrow.

She lets the necklace fall from her hand. Romeo catches it, and she is gone.

> ROMEO
> Sleep dwell upon thine eyes, peace in thy breast,
> Would I were sleep and peace, so sweet to rest.

EXT. CHURCH. DAY.
In the beautiful morning we find a monumental church crowned with a towering Madonna. On the roof, we notice a small oasis. As we move closer, we see it is a ramshackle greenhouse.

INT. GREENHOUSE. DAWN.
CRANE DOWN: Through a broken pane in the
   roof of the greenhouse.
Morning sunlight filters through the lush foliage of a
tropical rain forest as we hear:

> FATHER LAURENCE (O.S.)
> O mickle is the powerful grace that lies
> In plants, herbs, stones, and their true qualities.

We discover the intensely concentrating features of
   FATHER LAURENCE; in his fifties, wiry, and
   wearing a priest's collar, Laurence delicately makes
   an incision in the bulb of a small purple-flowered
   plant. A pair of fresh-faced ten-year-old ALTAR
   BOYS look on in wonderment as a vivid blue sap
   oozes from the incision.
CUT TO: Laurence's P.O.V. through the broken
   roof pane, of the Madonna backlit in the morning
   sun.

> FATHER LAURENCE (cont.)
> Within the infant rind of this weak flower
> Poison hath residence, and medicine power.

PULL BACK: The priest carefully gathers the sap
into a beaker.

> FATHER LAURENCE (cont.)
> For this, being smelt, with that part cheers each
>   part;
> Being tasted, stays all senses with the heart.

The boys follow the Father as he moves out of the greenhouse and into an adjoining work area. The walls are lined with bottles of herbs and dried plants.

>   FATHER LAURENCE (cont.)
> For naught so vile on the earth doth live,
> But to the earth some special good doth give;

With the precision of a chemist, Father Laurence funnels the sap into a small bottle and places it in the refrigerator.

>   FATHER LAURENCE (cont.)
> Nor aught so good but, strained from that fair
>   use,
> Revolts from true birth, stumbling on abuse.
> Two such opposed kings encamp them still in
>   man as well as herbs: grace and rude will;
> And where the worser is predominant,
> Full soon the canker death eats up that plant.

A feverish knocking breaks the priest's reverie.

INT. GREENHOUSE. DAWN.
>   ROMEO (O.S.)
> Good morrow, father!

Father Laurence opens the greenhouse door to discover the costumed Romeo. Romeo enters.

FATHER LAURENCE
Benedicite!
What early tongue so sweet saluteth me?
    ALTAR BOYS
Good morrow, Romeo.

The altar boys leave.

FATHER LAURENCE
Young son, it argues a distempered head
So soon to bid good morrow to thy bed.
Or if not so, then here I hit it right—
Our Romeo hath not been in bed tonight.

The priest ushers Romeo out.

EXT. ROOFTOP. DAWN.
The priest continues across the rooftop toward the
    spiral stair leading down from the roof.
Romeo, on fire to tell of his experience, follows the
    priest down the stairs.

ROMEO
The last is true. The sweeter rest was mine.
    FATHER LAURENCE
    (He stops.)
God pardon sin! Wast thou with Rosaline?
    ROMEO
With Rosaline, my ghostly father? No.
I have forgot that name and that name's woe.

They enter the stairwell at the back of the presbytery.

> FATHER LAURENCE
> That's my good son! But where hast thou been then?
>
> ROMEO
> I have been feasting with mine enemy,
> Where on a sudden one hath wounded me
> That's by me wounded. Both our remedies
> Within thy help and holy physic lies.
>
> FATHER LAURENCE
> Be plain, good son, and homely in thy drift.
> Riddling confession finds but riddling shrift.

They have reached the sacristy door. Father Laurence ushers Romeo in.

INT. SACRISTY. DAY.

> ROMEO
> Then plainly know my heart's dear love is set,
> On the fair daughter of rich Capulet.
> We met, we wooed, and made exchange of vow,
> I'll tell thee as we pass. But this I pray,
> That thou consent to marry us today.

CUT TO: The priest, thunderstruck. Two kids return, dressed in red altar boy robes; they enter.

The apoplectic priest waves the boys away. They get
the message and bolt.

          FATHER LAURENCE
     Holy Saint Francis! What a change is here!
     Is Rosaline, that thou didst love so dear,
     So soon forsaken? Young men's love then lies
     Not truly in their hearts, but in their eyes.
          ROMEO
     Thou chid'st me oft for loving Rosaline.
          FATHER LAURENCE
          (very angry)
     For doting, not for loving, pupil mine.

Unconsciously, Romeo helps the priest prepare. It is
clear he knows the routine by heart.

          ROMEO
     I pray thee chide me not. Her I love now
     Doth grace for grace and love for love allow.
     The other did not so.
          FATHER LAURENCE
                    O, she knew well
     Thy love did read by rote, that could not spell.

The Father considers. He looks through the sacristy
     door to where a small children's choir has assem-
     bled. Their angelic voices soar into the purest of
     hymns.
We recognize the hymn as "When Doves Cry" by
     Prince.

PUSH IN: On the priest; moved, he looks to Romeo.

> FATHER LAURENCE
> But come, young waverer, come, go with me.
> In one respect I'll thy assistant be.
> For this alliance may so happy prove
> To turn your households' rancor to pure love.

Romeo hurriedly assists the priest with his vestments.

> ROMEO
> O, let us hence! I stand on sudden haste.

Father Laurence holds Romeo in his powerful gaze.

> FATHER LAURENCE
> Wisely and slow. They stumble that run fast.

INT. CHURCH. DAWN.
The procession is joined by the two little altar boys and the Mass begins.

EXT. VERONA BEACH. DAY.
As the angelic voices of the choir soar, we see a pay phone near the cinema ruins.
A single leaning palm tree frames the image.
Benvolio speaks on the pay phone. Mercutio,

torso naked but for his holstered Sports Rapier
9mm, drums his fingers on the side of the
booth.

        MERCUTIO
Where the devil should this Romeo be?
Came he not home tonight?
        BENVOLIO
        (slamming down the phone)
Not to his father's. I spoke with his man.

Mercutio storms off down the beach.

        MERCUTIO
Why, that same pale hard-hearted wench, that
    Rosaline,
Torments him so that he will sure run mad.
        BENVOLIO
        (running to keep up)
Tybalt hath sent a letter to his father's house.
        MERCUTIO
        (halts abruptly)
A challenge, on my life.

CLOSE ON: Benvolio, unsure.

        BENVOLIO
Romeo will answer it?
        MERCUTIO
Any man that can write may answer a letter.

BENVOLIO
Nay, he will answer the letter's master,
    how he dares, being dared.

Mercutio clamps Benvolio into a headlock.

MERCUTIO
Alas, poor Romeo, he is already dead!
Stabbed with a white wench's black eye,

He whispers into Benvolio's ear:

MERCUTIO (cont.)
Run through the ear with a love song,
    the very pin of his heart cleft with
    the blind bow-boy's butt-shaft.
        (in disgust)
And is he a man to encounter Tybalt?
        BENVOLIO
        (struggling to break free)
Why, what is Tybalt?
        MERCUTIO
        (releasing him)
More than Prince of Cats, O, he's the courageous
    captain of compliments: he fights as you sing
    prick-song, keeps time, distance, and propor-
    tion. He rests his minim rests, one, two, and
    the third in your bosom: the very butcher of a
    silk button.

Lightning fast, Mercutio draws his gun. He twirls it
    in an impressive display of gunmanship that ends

with the barrel between the startled Benvolio's
eyes.

MERCUTIO (cont.)
A duelist, a duelist, a gentleman of the very first
    house, of the first and second cause. Ah, the
    immortal *passado*, the *punto reverso*, the
    hay!
        BENVOLIO
The what?
        MERCUTIO
The pox of such antic lisping affecting
    phantasimes, these new tuners of accent. By
    Jesu, a very good blade, a very tall man, a very
    good whore! Why, is not this a lamentable
    thing, grandsire, that we should be thus af-
    flicted with these strange flies, these fishmon-
    gers, these "pardon-me's," who stand so much
    on the new form that they cannot sit at ease
    on the old bench?

Romeo's car pulls into the beachside parking lot.
    Benvolio heads toward it.

        BENVOLIO
Here comes Romeo, here comes Romeo!
        MERCUTIO
Without his roe . . .
        BENVOLIO
Me, O.

MERCUTIO

. . . like dried herring. O flesh, flesh, how are thou fishified.

EXT. BEACH/PARKING LOT. DAY.

Romeo alights from his car and throws his keys to Balthasar, who lounges outside the beachside hang. Mercutio saunters up the beach.

MERCUTIO

Signor Romeo, *Bonjour.* There's a French salutation to your French slop. You gave us the counterfeit fairly last night.

ROMEO

Good morrow to you both. What counterfeit did I give you?

MERCUTIO

The slip, sir, the slip. Can you not conceive?

Romeo smiles smugly.

ROMEO

Pardon, good Mercutio. My business was great, and in such a case as mine a man may strain courtesy.

MERCUTIO

That's as much as to say, such a case as yours constrains a man to bow in the hams.

ROMEO

Meaning to curtsy.

MERCUTIO
Thou has most kindly hit it.
ROMEO
A most courteous exposition.
MERCUTIO
Nay, I am the very pink of courtesy.
ROMEO
(campily)
Pink for flower?

The boys laugh. Mercutio feigns anger.

MERCUTIO
Right.
ROMEO
Why, then is my pump well flowered.
MERCUTIO
Sure wit, follow me this jest now, till thou hast
    worn out thy pump, that when the single sole
    of it is worn, the jest may remain after the
    wearing solely singular.
ROMEO
O single-soled jest, solely singular for the single-
    ness.
MERCUTIO
Come between us, good Benvolio! My wits faint.

Mercutio flicks sand at Romeo, then sprints off
    down the beach. Romeo, laughing, gives chase.

ROMEO

Switch and spurs, switch and spurs, or I'll cry a
    match.

MERCUTIO

Nay, if our wits run the wild-goose chase I am
    done. For thou hast more of the wild-goose in
    one of thy wits than I am sure I have in my
    whole five. Was I with you there for the goose?

ROMEO

Thou was never there with me for anything, when
    thou wast not there for the goose.

MERCUTIO

I will bite thee on the ear for that jest!

Mercutio, goading Romeo to follow, backs off down
    the beach.

ROMEO

Nay, good goose, bite not.

MERCUTIO

Thy wit is a very bitter sweeting, it is a most
    sharp sauce.

ROMEO

And is it not then well served in to a sweet goose?

MERCUTIO

O here's a wit of cheveril, that stretches from an
    inch narrow to an ell broad.

ROMEO

I stretch it out for that word "broad,"
which, added to the goose, proves thee far and
    wide a broad goose.

MERCUTIO
Why, is not this better now than groaning for
love?
Now art thou sociable.
Now art thou Romeo. Now art thou . . .

Romeo tackles Mercutio on the sand. Mercutio falls,
suddenly serious.

MERCUTIO (cont.)
(quietly)
What thou art, by art as well as by nature. For
this driveling love is like a great natural that
runs lolling up and down to hide his bauble in
a hole.

A moment between the boys.

BENVOLIO
Stop there, stop there.
MERCUTIO
Thou desirest me to stop in my tale against the
hair.
BENVOLIO
Thou wouldst else have made thy tale large.
MERCUTIO
O, thou art deceived; I would have made it short;
for I was come to the whole depth of my tale
and meant indeed to occupy the argument no
longer.

A shadow falls across them. Romeo looks up.

ROMEO
Here's goodly gear.

Standing above the boys is the Nurse. She wears a
ridiculous, all-red, "Jackie O"–style disguise of
sunglasses, scarf, and parasol.

MERCUTIO
(bemused)
God ye good e'en, fair gentlewoman.

The Nurse, ignoring Mercutio, speaks dramatically
to Romeo.

NURSE
I desire some confidence with you.

She turns and walks back to the parking lot.
Benvolio and the other boys look on curiously.

MERCUTIO
A bawd, a bawd, a bawd! So ho!

But Romeo rises and to the amazement of Mercutio
actually follows this woman. Mercutio looks ques-
tioningly to Benvolio, who shrugs.

BENVOLIO
She will indite him to some supper?

Even more strangely, Romeo joins her.

MERCUTIO
(taken by surprise)
Romeo, will you come to your father's?
We'll to dinner thither.

Mercutio and Benvolio have made it to their cars.

ROMEO
I will follow you.
MERCUTIO
Farewell, ancient lady. Farewell.

Mercutio and Benvolio drive off.
Romeo and the Nurse walk.

NURSE
(deadly earnest)
If ye should lead her in a fool's paradise, as they
    say, it were a very gross kind of behavior, as
    they say. For the gentlewoman is young; and
    therefore . . .

Stopping by a large Town Car, where PETER, her
    enormous bodyguard, waits, the Nurse presses
    Romeo up against the car.

NURSE (cont.)
If you should deal double with her, truly it were
    an ill thing and very weak dealing.

BEAT: Romeo chooses his words carefully.

> ROMEO
> Bid her to come to confession this afternoon,
> And there she shall at Friar Laurence's cell
>   be shrived and
> (PUSH IN ON Romeo)
>   married.

INT. JULIET'S BEDROOM. DAY.
CLOSE ON: Juliet's face peering out her round
  bedroom window.

> JULIET
> O God, she comes!

EXT. CAPULET MANSION. JULIET'S P.O.V.
DAY.
Nurse's car arriving.

INT. NURSE'S QUARTERS. DAY.
The Nurse's domain is decorated with a mixture of
  religious iconography and travel posters.
Juliet bursts breathlessly into the room.

> JULIET
> O honey nurse, what news?

The Nurse, buried up to her ample hips inside the
  refrigerator, does not turn around.
Juliet cries out impatiently.

JULIET

Nurse!

The Nurse emerges from the icebox, laden with
food. Moving to the counter, she starts to make a
sandwich.

NURSE

I am aweary, give me leave awhile.
Fie, how my bones ache. What a jaunce have I.

Juliet under her breath:

JULIET

I would thou hadst my bones and I thy news.

Juliet goes to the Nurse.

JULIET

Nay, come, I pray thee, speak: good, good Nurse,
speak.

Sandwich made, the Nurse shuffles over to a corner
couch.

NURSE

Jesu, what haste. Can you not stay awhile?
Can you not see that I am out of breath?

Juliet cannot stand the suspense any longer.

JULIET
How art thou out of breath when thou hast
- breath
To say to me that thou art out of breath!
Is the news good or bad? Answer to that.

The Nurse takes a big bite from her sandwich and
answers through thoughtful chews.

NURSE
Well, you have made a simple choice. You know
not how to choose a man. Romeo? No, not he.
Though his face be better than any man's, yet
his leg excels all men's and for a hand and a
foot and a body, though they be not to be
talked on, yet they are past compare. Go thy
ways, wench, serve God. What, have you dined
at home?

Juliet is flabbergasted.

JULIET
No, no. But all this I did know before.
What says he of our marriage? What of that?
NURSE
Lord, how my head aches! What a head have I:
My back . . .

Juliet moves behind the Nurse and begins massaging
her back.

NURSE (cont.)
O' t'other side, ah, my back!

With sublime self-control, Juliet coos sweetly.

JULIET
I'faith I am sorry that thou art not well.
Sweet, sweet, sweet Nurse, tell me, what says my
    love?
NURSE
Your love says like an honest gentleman,
And a courteous, and a kind, and a handsome,
And I warrant a virtuous—Where is your mother?

Juliet cracks.

JULIET
Where is my mother? How oddly thou repliest!
"Your love says, like an honest gentleman, 'Where
    is your mother'!"

The Nurse sulks.

NURSE
O God's lady dear, are you so hot?
Henceforth do your messages yourself.

Juliet's frustration explodes.

JULIET
Here's such a coil! COME, WHAT SAYS RO-
    MEO?

PAUSE: The Nurse considers Juliet.

>NURSE
>Have you got leave to go to confession today?
>JULIET
>I have.
>NURSE
>Then hie you hence to Father Laurence's cell.
>There stays a husband to make you a wife!

Juliet, with a scream of joy, hugs the Nurse to her.
HOLD ON: Juliet's ecstatic features.

INT. CHURCH. DAY.
TIGHT ON: Father Laurence.

>FATHER LAURENCE
>These violent delights have violent ends!

PULL BACK: Father Laurence is preaching energeti-
cally from the pulpit. Romeo waits at the side of
the altar.

>FATHER LAURENCE (cont.)
>The sweetest honey
>Is loathsome in its own deliciousness,
>Therefore love moderately.

The Father glances toward Romeo.

FATHER LAURENCE (cont.)
Long love doth so.
Too swift arrives as tardy as too slow.

CUT TO: The choir sings a choral version of
Rozella's "Everybody's Free."
We TILT DOWN from the choir to find Juliet hur-
rying into the church.
Father Laurence moves to Romeo as Juliet breath-
lessly arrives.

JULIET
Good afternoon to my ghostly confessor.

But before the priest can reply, the two lovers embrace, kissing passionately.

FATHER LAURENCE
(dryly)
Romeo shall thank thee, daughter, for us both.

The choir completes the hymn, and the priest, realizing it is his cue, rushes back to the altar. He
quickly delivers a prayer to the congregation while
eyeing the increasingly amorous smooching of the
young couple.
The choir launches into a joyous chorus of "Everybody's Free," and the priest returns to Romeo and
Juliet. He delicately parts the couple.

FATHER LAURENCE (cont.)
Come, come, and we will make short work.

For, by your leaves, you shall not stay alone
Till Holy Church incorporate two in one.

A soulfully voiced young man steps forward. He
    launches into a wailing solo.
MACRO CLOSE-UP: A simple silver ring. Engraved
    on the inside of the band are the words "I love
    thee."
Romeo slips the ring onto Juliet's finger as the priest
    executes the formal sacrament of marriage.
Romeo and Juliet kiss as the music swells.

EXT. VERONA BEACH. DAY.
We see that Mercutio—wading in knee-deep water
    close to the beach—is using his gun to hunt fish.
Benvolio shelters in the shade of an unmanned life-
    guard tower.
A shimmering heat haze blankets the deserted beach,
    and the horizon is stacked with purple storm
    clouds.

                    BENVOLIO
    I pray thee, good Mercutio, let's retire.
    The day is hot,

Mercutio, ignoring him, plugs away at another fish.
    Benvolio nervously looks to see if there is any
    reaction to the sound of the shot.

BENVOLIO (cont.)
The Capels are abroad. And if we meet, we shall
    not 'scape a brawl.

Mercutio strides out of the water.

MERCUTIO
Thou art like one of these fellows that, when he
    enters the confines of a tavern, claps me his
    sword upon the table and says "God send me
    no need of thee!"
        (he hands Benvolio his gun)
and by the operation of the second cup draws
    him on the drawer, when indeed there is no
    need.

Another incredible sleight-of-hand routine and Mercutio has managed to draw Benvolio's pistol, re-
trieve his own gun, and trap Benvolio with a
barrel at each temple.
The joke has worn thin for Benvolio; he pushes past
Mercutio toward where Balthasar, Sampson, and
Gregory lounge in the shade of the beachside
hang.
Suddenly he stops dead—a monstrous dark blue sedan prowls into the beachside parking lot.

BENVOLIO
By my head, here comes the Capulets.
MERCUTIO
By my heel, I care not.

EXT. BEACH. PARKING LOT. DAY.

The sedan slides to a halt only yards from Benvolio
    and Mercutio.

Tybalt, Abra, and Petruchio alight from the sedan
    and walk menacingly toward Mercutio and
    Benvolio.

> TYBALT
> Gentlemen, good day. A word with one of you.

The boys from the hang draw near the Capulet car,
    converge; eyes dart nervously, hands stray toward
    guns. Mercutio smiles mockingly.

> MERCUTIO
> And but one word with one of us? Couple it with
> something. Make it a word and a . . .

Leaning close to Tybalt, he camps the implication.

> MERCUTIO (cont.)
> . . . blow.

Mercutio scores. The boys laugh.

> TYBALT
> (furious)
> You shall find me apt enough to that, sir,
> (clutching at his sidearm)
> And you will give me occasion.

CLOSE ON: Mercutio. He stops, eyeing the hand
on the gun. No one moves.

> MERCUTIO
> (a breathy, coquettish voice)
> Could you not take some occasion without giv-
> ing?

The boys fall about again. Tybalt cracks.

> TYBALT
> Mercutio, thou consortest with Romeo.

The accusation stings—Mercutio's anger flares.

> MERCUTIO
> Consort? What, dost thou make us minstrels? An
> thou make minstrels of us look to hear nothing
> but discords. Here's my fiddlestick.

Indicating his holstered gun.

> MERCUTIO (cont.)
> Here's that shall make you dance.
> (barking at Tybalt)
> Zounds,
> (goading him to go for his gun)
> consort!

CLOSE ON: Tybalt.
CLOSE ON: Mercutio. He will not back down.
Benvolio tries to diffuse things.

BENVOLIO
Either withdraw unto some private place, or rea-
son coldly of your grievances.
Or else depart. Here all eyes gaze on us.
    MERCUTIO
Men's eyes were made to look, and let them gaze.
I will not budge for no man's pleasure, I.

At that moment, Romeo's car drives onto the beach.
Tybalt smiles.

    TYBALT
Well sir, here comes my man.

Tybalt moves toward Romeo, who bounds from his
car full of happy news.

    TYBALT
Romeo, the love I bear thee can afford
No better term than this:

CLOSE ON: Tybalt. He clears his jacket from his
sidearm and issues the challenge.

    TYBALT (cont.)
Thou art a villain!

CLOSE ON: Mercutio.
CLOSE ON: Benvolio.
All eyes are on Romeo.
Romeo calmly approaches his now cousin.

ROMEO
Tybalt, the reason that I have to love thee
Doth much excuse the appertaining rage
To such a greeting: villain am I none,
Therefore farewell. I see thou knowest me not.

Romeo turns and, to the amazement of all, walks
back to his car. Tybalt, unable to shoot him in
the back, is confused. He runs the short distance
to Romeo's car.
Tybalt hauls Romeo out, slamming him against the
fuselage.

TYBALT
Boy, this shall not excuse the injuries
That thou hast done me!

He smashes Romeo across the face; Romeo crashes
to the roadway.

TYBALT
(yelling)
Turn and draw.

A cut has opened in the side of Romeo's mouth. He
unsteadily lifts himself up and, meeting Tybalt's
gaze, speaks through bloodied teeth.

ROMEO
I never injured thee,
And so, good Capulet, which name I tender
As dearly as mine own . . .

Romeo cautiously extracts his gun . . .

>   ROMEO (cont.)
>   . . . be satisfied.

. . . and throws it at Tybalt's feet.

Storm clouds obscure the sun as Romeo turns and walks from the parking lot.

Mercutio, Benvolio, and the others cannot believe their eyes.

>   MERCUTIO
>   O calm, dishonorable, vile submission!

EXT. BEACH. VACANT LOT. DAY.

Tybalt's anger must be answered. He ceremoniously disarms, gives his weapon to Abra, and sprints after Romeo, who is now passing the lot that houses the largely demolished cinema. A bone-cracking kick sends Romeo crumbling into the vacant lot. The boys swarm toward the fray.

Romeo, still refusing the fight, scrambles up the rubble of the demolished cinema. Tybalt trips him, and Romeo careens into a pile of derelict cinema chairs.

Tybalt kicks savagely at the helpless Romeo.

Suddenly, Mercutio appears running full tilt down the stage. He plucks up a broken chair leg and yells . . .

MERCUTIO (cont.)
Tybalt, you ratcatcher,

. . . as he bludgeons him across the face. Tybalt
goes down.

MERCUTIO (cont.)
Will you walk?

Tybalt leaps to his feet, grabbing a lump of wood.

TYBALT
What wouldst thou have with me?

He swipes at Mercutio.

MERCUTIO
(avoiding)
Good King of Cats, nothing but one of your nine
   lives.

Mercutio jabs, Tybalt sidesteps.

TYBALT
I am for you.

Tybalt aims a double-handed blow to Mercutio's
   head. Mercutio blocks, hooking Tybalt's stick
   away.
Unarmed, Tybalt throws his full body weight upon
   Mercutio, slamming him against a section of ornate plasterwork that explodes in a white cloud.

Lightning fast, Mercutio jackknifes to his feet. He raises his weapon to deliver a skull-crushing final blow to the trapped Tybalt. Romeo rushes between them.

ROMEO
Forbear this outrage, good Mercutio!

Seizing the opportunity, Tybalt lunges at Romeo with a lethal shard of glass. He misses, gouging instead a slash of flesh from Mercutio's stomach.
A scream of excruciating pain as Mercutio grabs at his bloodied side. Everyone is still. In the abrupt silence, sirens are heard in the distance. Abra tugs at Tybalt.

ABRA
Away Tybalt!

As they head for their vehicle, Tybalt hastily straps his holsters back on. Abra hands him back his guns.
Benvolio goes to Mercutio.

BENVOLIO
Art thou hurt?

But Mercutio, covering his wound with his hand, laughs.

MERCUTIO
Ay, ay, a scratch.

He turns to his assembled fans at the bottom of the
   pile of rubble that leads down to the beach. With
   outrageous bravado he plays at being Caesar the
   conqueror.

>   MERCUTIO (cont.)
> A scratch!

The boys cheer their conquering hero. Romeo helps
   Mercutio down the slope.

>   ROMEO
> Courage, man. The hurt cannot be much.

Mercutio, holding his bleeding side, jokes through
   the pain.

>   MERCUTIO
> 'Twill serve. Ask for me tomorrow and you shall
>   find me a grave man.

He turns the next thought to the assembled audi-
   ence.

>   MERCUTIO (cont.)
>   (through crazy laughter)
> A plague o' both your houses!

Mercutio turns from the cheering boys to Romeo,
   who is struggling to support his weight.
Mercutio, through weak and desperate breathing:

MERCUTIO (cont.)
Why the devil came you between us? I was hurt
under your arm.

Romeo starts to register the panic in Mercutio's eyes.

ROMEO
I thought all for the best.

Like an animal trying to break free from a mortal
trap, Mercutio pushes Romeo away. He screams
in horror, as if falling in the dark.

MERCUTIO
A plague o' both your houses!
They have made worms' meat of me.

Mercutio staggers down the rubble and collapses in
the sand. Romeo is there instantly, cradling his
friend's head out of the sand. The dying boy
stares back at Romeo, smiling through the chilling
cold.

MERCUTIO (cont.)
(a silent whisper)
Your houses!

Everything stands still, everything is quiet. The
storm finally breaks.

EXT. BEACH. RAIN. DUSK.
OPTICAL INSERT; the storm breaks.

EXT. BEACH. RAIN. DUSK.
Tiny drops of water bespeckle Mercutio's lifeless
    body. The droplets grow to a heavy rain. Romeo
    can hear the faint sound a thousand miles away of
    Benvolio whispering.

> BENVOLIO
> Mercutio is dead!

Tears streak Romeo's face. He cries out.

> ROMEO
> Oh sweet Juliet,
> Thy beauty hath made me effeminate
> And in my temper softened valor's steel!

EXT. BEACH/PARKING LOT. DUSK.
Tybalt's car fires to life. Romeo's sorrow turns to
    uncontrollable rage. Romeo struggles to get to his
    vehicle as Benvolio tries to restrain him.
Tybalt's car foreground, cuts through frame in a
    spraying U-turn of sand.

INT. ROMEO'S CAR. DUSK.
TIGHT ON: The ignition as Romeo kicks it. We
    note Juliet's locket on the key ring.

EXT. ROMEO'S CAR. DUSK.

Romeo's car 360's in a hardlock as we furiously
   countertrack counterclockwise.

INT. ROMEO'S CAR. DUSK. (WINDOW CAM.)

The 360-degree blur.

CUT TO: Romeo, the dizzying blur in the background.

INT. JULIET'S BEDROOM. DUSK.

An acoustic guitar version of Joy Division's "Love
   Will Tear Us Apart." Juliet traces the path of a
   raindrop on the windowpane as she speaks her
   thoughts to the storm.

>   JULIET
> Come gentle night, coming loving black browed
>   night,
> Give me my Romeo. And when I shall die,
> Take him and cut him out in little stars,
> And he will make the face of heaven so fine
> That all the world will be in love with night,
> And pay no worship to the garish sun.
> O, I have bought the mansion of a love
> But not possessed it, and though I am sold,
> Not yet enjoyed. So tedious is this day
> As is the night before some festival
> To an impatient child that hath new robes
> And may not wear them.

EXT. STREET. NIGHT.
PUSH IN: An aggressive jump cut catapults us into
    a music-driven window-cam P.O.V. of cars spray-
    ing left and right as Romeo rockets the wrong
    way down a one-way street.

EXT. ROMEO'S CAR. NIGHT.
TIGHT ON: Romeo as the monumental Jesus is
    reflected on the windscreen rushing toward him.

EXT. STREET. NIGHT.
PICK UP: Tybalt's car hammering into frame.
WHIP PAN: to Romeo's car approaching from the
    opposite direction.

INT. TYBALT'S CAR. NIGHT.
SLOW MOTION: Tybalt looks to the right.
CUT TO: His P.O.V. through windscreen as Ro-
    meo's car rushes at him.

INT. ROMEO'S CAR. NIGHT.
CLOSE UP: Romeo defiant.

INT. TYBALT'S CAR. NIGHT.
Tybalt wrenches on the wheel to avoid the collision.
THE ALMIGHTY NOISE OF TWO CARS COL-
LIDING.

SLOW MOTION: WASHING MACHINE TUM-
BLE SHOT to catastrophic music as Tybalt and
Abra are violently hurled around as the car rolls.
In the maelstrom we see Tybalt's guns falling
through space.

EXT. STREET. NIGHT.

Cars screeching.

Tybalt's car, upside down, grinds to a violent dead
stop.

CUT TO: Abra's head smacking into the windscreen, shattering it.

CUT TO: Romeo's car squealing to a halt, blocking
traffic.

Romeo leaps from his car.

CUT TO: Tybalt. He desperately grabs at a weapon
and scrambles from his car.

CUT TO: Romeo. He relentlessly marches through
waves of oncoming traffic toward Tybalt's outstretched gun.

Romeo screams through tears.

> ROMEO
> Mercutio's soul
> Is but a little way above our heads,

Romeo grabs the barrel of Tybalt's gun; forcing it
between his own eyes, he growls insanely at
Tybalt.

ROMEO (cont.)
Staying for thine to keep him company.

Tybalt tries to back off.

TYBALT
Thou, wretched boy, shalt with him hence.

Romeo, refusing to let go of the gun, forces Tybalt
    backward.

ROMEO
(with frightening intensity)
Either thou or I, or both, must go with him.

Cars swerve; Romeo is relentless. He grips Tybalt's
    hand, trying to force him to shoot.

ROMEO (cont.)
Either thou or I, or both, must go with him.

Panicked, Tybalt wrenches free and lurches onto the
    roadway. Blinded by the headlights of an oncom-
    ing car, he thuds onto its hood as it skids to a
    halt. The impact catapults his gun into the air.
The gun slides along the ground, stopping at Ro-
    meo's feet. Police sirens in the distance.
CUT TO: Tybalt. He has landed at the base of the
    stairs to the monument.
CUT TO: Romeo staring at the gun at his feet.
CUT TO: Tybalt. Panic on his face. Unarmed, he
    turns, scrambling up the stairs to the monument.

TIGHT ON: Romeo. The rain beats down. A harrowing symphonic tone and the echo of Mercutio's voice can be heard.

> MERCUTIO (V.O.)
> Why the devil came you between us?

Romeo looks slowly up to the escaping Tybalt.
Looking down from the monument, we see Tybalt almost reaching the pond of water at the top of the stairs. Romeo stares up.
CUT TO: Tybalt. He turns to see Romeo, gun outstretched.
CUT TO: Romeo. He fires three relentless shots at Tybalt.
CUT TO: Tybalt's body convulsing backward, collapsing into the pond, bloodying the water.
Finally, the storm breaks.
Romeo, dropping Tybalt's gun, screams through the rain up at the statue.

> ROMEO
> O, I am fortune's fool!

OPTICAL: From the top of Jesus' head looking down at Romeo. A violent wind hits.
Through the mayhem, a rusty sedan driven by Balthasar slides to a halt.
Balthasar screams out at Romeo:

> BALTHASAR
> Romeo, away, be gone! Stand not amazed!

INT. BALTHASAR'S CAR. NIGHT.

Romeo collapses into the backseat.

WINDOW CAM: Balthasar does a speeding circuit of the traffic circle.

We see the base of the statue in the background.

EXT. STATUE BASE. NIGHT.

Balthasar's car screams through frame, exiting the traffic circle in the gale-force wind.

WHIP PAN: Discover the calamity; the dead boy; his upturned vehicle; a frenzy of panic.

TOPOGRAPHICAL SHOT: In the foreground Tybalt's body is lowered from the stairs. We see ambulances, cop cars, lots of umbrellas and crowd control. Captain Prince's car slides into frame.

CUT TO: BANG, the door of Captain Prince's patrol car slams open.

HANDHELD: Run with him and his officers, forcing their way through the crowd, crossing the police line toward a cluster of officers at the end of an ambulance.

They part, revealing Montague and Capulet, bodyguards and assistants, canopied beneath black umbrellas.

Capulet restrains Gloria; her sumptuous red ballgown drags in the mud. She clutches at Tybalt's corpse as it is loaded onto the stretcher.

Tight on a distraught Gloria Capulet.

GLORIA
I beg for justice, which thou, Prince, must give;
Romeo slew Tybalt. Romeo must not live!

PULL BACK: Gloria is surrounded by Montague,
Capulet, and Captain Prince. A handcuffed
Benvolio looks on.

PRINCE
Romeo slew him, he slew Mercutio;
Who now the price of his dear blood doth owe?

Montague moves forward, attempting to draw in
Captain Prince.

MONTAGUE
(intimately)
Not Romeo, Prince, he was Mercutio's friend;
His fault concludes but what the law should end,
The life of Tybalt.

Captain Prince, dismissing Montague, moves toward
his assembled offices.

PRINCE
And for that offense
Immediately we do exile him.

Capulet attempts to draw him in again.

MONTAGUE
Noble Prince . . . !

Captain Prince silences him.

> PRINCE
> I will be deaf to pleading and excuses;
> Nor tears nor prayers shall purchase out abuses.
> Therefore use none.

The Captain turns and addresses his assembled officers.

> PRINCE (cont.)
> Let Romeo hence in haste,
> Else, when he is found that hour is his last.

CLOSE ON: Captain Prince.

EXT. STREET. NIGHT.
Balthasar's car flashes by.

INT. BALTHASAR'S CAR. NIGHT.
Balthasar hands Romeo back his gun.

EXT. JULIET'S BEDROOM. NIGHT.
Looking in through a rain-spattered window, we see
    the Nurse solemnly enter the room.
Juliet eagerly turns to greet her.
As the Nurse speaks, Juliet's joy turns to sorrow.
The music surges as we . . .
PUSH IN: Through the window.

INT. PRESBYTERY KITCHEN. NIGHT.

Romeo stands at the kitchen bench, crying. His
    wounds have been bandaged, and Balthasar
    crouches frightened in the corner.
The priest leads the Nurse into the room.
Romeo looks up.

>   ROMEO
> Nurse!

She goes to him.

>   NURSE
> Ah sir! Ah sir! Death's the end of all.
>   ROMEO
> Speakest thou of Juliet?
> Where is she? And how doth she? And what says
> My concealed lady to our canceled love?
>   NURSE
> O, she says nothing, sir, but weeps and weeps,
> And then on Romeo cries, and then falls down
>   again.

Romeo is wailing inconsolably.

>   ROMEO
> As if that name,
> Shot from the deadly level of a gun,
> Did murder her, as that name's cursed hand mur-
>   dered her kinsman!

Father Laurence shakes the hysterical boy.

FATHER LAURENCE
I thought thy disposition better tempered!
Thy Juliet is alive. There art thou happy.
The law that threatened death becomes thy friend
And turns it to exile. There art thou happy.
A pack of blessings light upon thy back.

Romeo calms. The Nurse gives him the ring.

NURSE
Here, sir, a ring my lady bid me give you.

Romeo enfolds the ring in his hand.

ROMEO
How well my comfort is revived by this.

The priest goes to a washing basket on the kitchen
table, removes a clean shirt, and helps Romeo put
it on.

FATHER LAURENCE
Go, get thee to thy love, as was decreed.
Ascend her chamber. Hence and comfort her.

Father Laurence ushers Romeo from the room.

INT. HALLWAY. NIGHT.
They hurry down the hallway.

FATHER LAURENCE (cont.)
But look thou stay not till the watch be set,
For then thou canst not pass to Mantua
Where thou shalt live till we can find a time
To blaze your marriage, reconcile your friends,
Beg pardon of the Prince and call thee back,
With twenty hundred thousand times more joy
Than thou wentst forth in lamentation.

The priest opens the front door. It is raining heavily outside.

FATHER LAURENCE (cont.)
Go hence. Be gone by the break of day.
Sojourn in Mantua. Give me thy hand.

Romeo embraces him.

ROMEO
Farewell.

INT. CAPULET MANSION. NIGHT.
Sobs echo through the house.
Dave Paris stands in the entrance hallway clutching a huge bunch of flowers.
Fulgencio Capulet stands beside him, whiskey glass in hand.
CUT TO: Gloria on the upper landing. There is a strange faraway quality about her as she descends to Dave and Capulet.

> GLORIA
> She'll not come down tonight.

Dave, an understanding smile.

> DAVE
> These times of woe afford no times to woo.

Capulet guides Dave into the house.

> CAPULET
> Look you, she loved her kinsman Tybalt dearly.
> GLORIA
> (joining)
> And so did I.
> CAPULET
> (a cold glance at Gloria)
> Well, we were born to die.

Capulet takes a large slug of whiskey. Gloria leans
  close to Dave.

> GLORIA
> I'll know her mind early tomorrow.
> Tonight she's mewed up to her heaviness.

As Gloria, Dave, and Capulet exit down the hallway
  we CRANE UP: toward Juliet's bedroom door.

INT. JULIET'S BEDROOM. NIGHT.
CLOSE ON: Juliet's face. Tears stream onto the pil-

low. Without warning a hand lightly touches her
cheek. Juliet's eyes dart up to discover Romeo
standing above her, soaked.

A still moment of disbelief. Leaning down, Romeo
kisses away the tears that fall from her dark, wide
eyes.

EXT. CAPULET MANSION. NIGHT.

Balthasar in his car listening to the radio in the rain.

INT. JULIET'S BEDROOM. NIGHT.

Romeo is soaked. Juliet helps him undress.
He is wounded. She tends to him.
They make love.

INT. SITTING ROOM. NIGHT.

Beneath an impressive gun cabinet, Capulet sits in
an armchair drinking. Dave and Gloria sit opposite as Capulet whips himself into a frenzy of
drunken excitement.

> CAPULET
> We'll keep no great ado, a friend or two.
> For, hark you, Tybalt being slain so late,
> It may be thought we held him carelessly,
> Being our kinsman if we revel much—
> But soft, what day is this?
> DAVE
> Monday, my lord.

CAPULET
Well, Wednesday is too soon—what say you to
   Thursday?

Gloria looks up alarmed; Dave is stunned.

DAVE
My lord, I . . .
      CAPULET
      (leaning close)
I will make a desperate tender of my child's love.
      (a drunken good humor)
I think she will be ruled in all respects by me;
      (exploding with hearty laughter)
                  Nay, more, I doubt it not!

CUT TO: Gloria; her face hardens.

CAPULET (cont.)
      (to Dave)
But what say you to Thursday?

Dave is trying to catch up.

DAVE
My lord, I . . .

CUT TO: Capulet eyes Dave intently.

DAVE (cont.)
I would that Thursday were tomorrow.

Delighted, Capulet jumps to his feet.

>   CAPULET
>   A Thursday let it be then!

Capulet holds out his glass in a toast. Dave and
    Gloria rise.

>   CAPULET
>   Wife, go you to Juliet ere you go to bed.
>   Tell her, a Thursday she shall be married
>   To this noble sir!

CLOSE ON: The glasses clink.

EXT. CAPULET ESTATE. DAWN.
A pink and gold dawn breaks over Capulet Mansion.

INT. JULIET'S BEDROOM. DAWN.
A tangle of young limbs.
Romeo and Juliet blissfully asleep. The dawn light
    creeps into the room.
CRANE DOWN: Toward the sleeping innocence of
    the faces.
HOLD: A shadow of fear passes across Romeo's fea-
    tures.
With a cry of panic, he sits bolt upright.

EXT. CAPULET ESTATE. DAWN.
Balthasar asleep in the car.

INT. JULIET'S BEDROOM. DAWN.
Wide awake, but disoriented, Romeo stares around
    the room—as Juliet stirs, he remembers where he
    is.
Slipping quietly from the bed, Romeo begins to
    dress.
CLOSE ON: Romeo. A pair of lips enter frame and
    find his neck. It is Juliet. She hugs herself to him.

> JULIET
> Wilt thou be gone? It is not yet near day.

Romeo turns—softly he strokes her cheek.

> ROMEO
> I must be gone and live, or stay and die.

Juliet kisses his fingertips.

> JULIET
> Yond light is not daylight,

And then his cheek . . .

> JULIET (cont.)
> I know it, I.
> It is some meteor that the sun exhales

To light thee on thy way to Mantua.
Therefore stay yet. Thou needest not to be gone.

Romeo, feverishly returning the kisses, throws himself on Juliet.

> ROMEO
> Let me be taken, let me be put to death.
> I have more care to stay than will to go.
> Come, death, and welcome! Juliet wills it so.

Juliet is suddenly still. Romeo kisses her gently.

> ROMEO (cont.)
> How is't, my soul? Let's talk. It is not day.

Juliet pulls Romeo to his feet.

> JULIET
> It is, it is! Hie hence, be gone, away!
> O, now be gone! More light and light it grows.

Frantically she helps him into his clothes.

> ROMEO
> More light and light: more dark and dark our
> woes.

There is an urgent knocking on the door. They
freeze.

> NURSE (O.S.)
Madam!
> JULIET
Nurse?
> NURSE (O.S.)
Your lady mother is coming to your chamber.
> JULIET
Then, window, let day in, and let life out.

Desperately Juliet pulls Romeo out onto the balcony.

EXT. BALCONY. DAWN.
The storm, now past, has left a morning achingly
   pure.

> ROMEO
Farewell, farewell. One kiss, and I'll descend.

Romeo climbs down from the balcony and into the
   shadows.

> JULIET
O, think'st thou we shall ever meet again?

Romeo smiles up at her.

> ROMEO
I doubt it not.

Juliet's face darkens.

JULIET
O God, I have an ill-divining soul.
Methinks I see thee, now thou art so low,
As one dead in the bottom of a tomb.

Romeo scrambles back up to the balcony.

ROMEO
Trust me, love, all these woes shall serve
For sweet discourses in our times to come.

From Juliet's bedroom comes the brittle sound of
Gloria Capulet's voice.

GLORIA
Ho daughter! Are you up?

Juliet spins around. Gloria has parted the curtains
and is staring directly at her daughter.

GLORIA
Well, well.

CUT TO: Romeo sheltered just below the lip of the
balcony.
FOLLOW: His hand, as it slowly reaches up and
touches Juliet's fingers hidden behind her back.
Gloria returns to the room. Juliet steals a glance
toward Romeo as he silently mouths:

ROMEO
Adieu, adieu!

As Romeo lowers himself silently into the dark waters of the pool, Juliet whispers a little prayer to herself.

> JULIET
> O Fortune, Fortune! Be fickle, Fortune,
> For then I hope thou wilt not keep him long
> But send him back.

INT. JULIET'S BEDROOM. DAWN.

Juliet is trying not to cry as she goes in to her mother. Gloria turns to her.

> GLORIA
> Thou hast a careful father, child:
> One who, to put thee from thy heaviness,
> Hath sorted out a sudden day of joy
> That thou expects not nor I looked not for.

Juliet plays along.

> JULIET
> Madam, in happy time. What day is that?

Gloria takes a deep breath.

> GLORIA
> Marry, my child, early next Thursday morn
> The gallant, young, and noble gentleman,
> Sir Paris, at Saint Peter's Church,
> Shall happily make thee there a joyful bride.

CLOSE ON: Juliet. She can barely speak.

>JULIET
>Now by Saint Peter's Church, and Peter too,
>He shall not make me there a joyful bride!

Fear passes across Gloria's face.

>GLORIA
>Here comes your father. Tell him so yourself.

Capulet, whiskey glass in hand, ebulliently bursts
into the room.

>CAPULET
>How now, wife?
>Have you delivered to her our decree?
>GLORIA
>Ay, sir. But she will none, she gives you thanks.
>I would the fool were married to her grave!

Capulet; a dangerous calm.

>CAPULET
>How? Will she none?
>Is she not proud? Doth she not count her blest,
>Unworthy as she is, that we have wrought
>So worthy a gentleman to be her bridegroom?
>JULIET
>Not proud you have, but thankful that you have.
>Proud can I never be of what I hate.

PAUSE: Capulet considers his daughter, then . . .
BAM! He hurls his glass against the wall, shattering
  it into a thousand pieces.

> CAPULET
> Thank me no thankings, nor proud me no
>   prouds,
> But fettle your fine joints 'gainst Thursday
>   next . . .

Capulet advances. Juliet, terrified, retreats into the
  hallway.

INT. LANDING. DAY.

> JULIET
> Hear me with patience but to speak a word . . .

The Nurse appears as Capulet picks his daughter up
  and shakes her like a rag doll.

> CAPULET
> Speak not, reply not, do not answer me!

He throws her to the floor, slapping her violently.

> GLORIA
> (screaming)
> Fie, fie! What, are you mad?

Gloria tries to restrain Capulet. He backhands her,
  sending her flying against the wall—bellowing insanely, he advances on his cowering daughter.

CAPULET
Hang thee, young baggage! Disobedient wretch.

The Nurse throws herself between Capulet and Juliet.

NURSE
God in heaven bless her!
You are to blame, my lord, to rate her so.

Furious, Capulet shunts her aside.

CAPULET
Peace, you mumbling fool!

Capulet yanks his daughter's face close to his.

CAPULET (cont.)
I tell thee what—get thee to church o' Thursday
Or never after look me in the face.
An you be mine, I'll give you to my friend.
An you be not, hang, beg, starve, die in the
    streets,
Trust to it. Bethink you. I'll not be forsworn.

Capulet storms off down the stairs.
CLOSE ON: Juliet. She huddles, shaking at the top
    of the stairs.

JULIET
O sweet my mother, cast me not away!
Delay this marriage for a month, a week.

Or if you do not, make the bridal bed
In that dim monument where Tybalt lies.

A trickle of blood issues from Gloria's cut lip. She
checks her appearance in the hall mirror.

>   GLORIA
> Talk not to me, for I'll not speak a word.
> Do as thou wilt, for I have done with thee.

Gloria leaves.

>   JULIET
> O God!—O Nurse, how shall this be prevented?

The Nurse doesn't reply.

>   JULIET (cont.)
> What sayest thou? Hast thou not a word of joy?
> Some comfort, Nurse.

A heavy silence.
The Nurse goes to Juliet and gently helps her up.
FOLLOW: As she guides her to her bedroom.

INT. JULIET'S BEDROOM. DAY.
>   NURSE
> Faith, here it is.
> I think it best you married with this Paris.
> O, he's a lovely gentleman!
> I think you are happy in this second match,

For it excels your first; or if it did not,
Your first is dead—or 'twere as good he were
As living here and you no use of him.

Juliet is very still.

> JULIET
> Speakest thou from thy heart?
> NURSE
> And from my soul too. Else beshrew them both.
> JULIET
> Amen.

Juliet ever so calmly turns toward the window.

> NURSE
> (unsure)
> What?

Juliet is matter-of-fact.

> JULIET
> Well, thou hast comforted me marvelous much.
> Go in; and tell my lady I am gone,
> Having displeased my father, to Friar Laurence,
> To make confession and to be absolved.

The old woman nods. She strokes Juliet's hair.

> NURSE
> This is wisely done.

The Nurse leaves.

Juliet does not look back. A disturbing choral chant
as we hold on Juliet's cold eyes, from which a
single tear falls.

EXT. CHURCH AERIAL. DAY.

DISSOLVE TO: An aerial of the church in the cold,
gray morning.

> DAVE (V.O.)
> Immoderately she weeps for Tybalt's death . . .

INT. CHURCH. DAY.

Sunlight pierces stained glass; the chant a sinister
underscoring.

Father Laurence and Dave Paris stand at the front of
the church.

> DAVE
> . . . Now, sir, her father counts it dangerous
> That she doth give her sorrow so much sway,
> And in his wisdom hastes our marriage
> To stop the inundation of her tears . . .

Father Laurence turns. Juliet stands framed in the
white glare of the doorway. Dave smiles.

> DAVE
> Happily met, my lady and my wife.

Juliet advances slowly, an icy calm, her gun barely
   concealed.

>   JULIET
> That may be, sir, when I may be a wife.
>   DAVE
> That "may be," must be, love, on Thursday next.

Juliet stares past Dave.

>   JULIET
> What must be, shall be.

Father Laurence; a forced cheerfulness.

>   FATHER LAURENCE
> That's a certain text.
>   DAVE
> Come you to make confession?

Juliet forces her face into a smile.

>   JULIET
> Are you at leisure, holy father, now?
> Or shall I come to you at evening mass?
>   FATHER LAURENCE
> My leisure serves me, pensive daughter, now.
>   (to Dave)
> We must entreat the time alone.
>   DAVE
> God shield I should disturb devotion!
> Juliet, on Thursday early will I rouse ye;

Dave bends.
CLOSE ON: Juliet; she stares stonily ahead as Dave
    kisses her cheek.

                DAVE (cont.)
    Till then, adieu, and keep this holy kiss.

Dave leaves.
TRACK WITH: Juliet; she runs for the sacristy.
The priest follows.

INT. SACRISTY. DAY.

                FATHER LAURENCE
    O Juliet, I already know thy grief.

Juliet pulls away.

                JULIET
    Tell me not, Father, that thou hearest of this,
    Unless thou tell me how I may prevent it.
                FATHER LAURENCE
    It strains me past the compass of my wits.
                JULIET
                (desperately)
    If in thy wisdom thou canst give no help
    Do thou but call my resolution wise,
    And with this . . .

Juliet desperately pulls out the gun. She points it
    toward herself.

> JULIET (cont.)
> I'll help it presently!

Horrified, Father Laurence moves to her.
Juliet, panicked, levels the gun at him.

> FATHER LAURENCE
> Hold, daughter!
> JULIET
> (through tears)
> Be not so long to speak. I long to die!

Father Laurence holds out a soothing hand.

> FATHER LAURENCE
> I do spy a kind of hope,
> Which craves as desperate an execution
> As that is desperate which we would prevent.
> If, rather than marry Paris,
> Thou hast the strength of will to slay thyself,
> Then it is likely thou wilt undertake
> A thing like death . . .

We hear the distended chords of Fauré's Requiem.

> FATHER LAURENCE (cont.)
> to chide away this shame . . .

It continues throughout as:

INT. GREENHOUSE WORKROOM. DAY.

PULL BACK: A drop of blue liquid fills a tiny glass vial held by Father Laurence.

> FATHER LAURENCE (cont.)
> No warmth, no breath shall testify thou livest.
> Each part, deprived of supple government,
> Shall stiff and stark and cold appear, like death.
> Now when the bridegroom in the morning
> Comes to rouse thee from thy bed, there art thou, dead.
> Thou shalt be borne to that same ancient vault
> Where all the kindred of the Capulets lie.
> In the meantime, against thou shalt awake,
> Shall Romeo by my letters know our drift,
> And hither shall he come. And that very
> Night shall Romeo bear thee hence to Mantua.

The priest cautiously hands Juliet the vial.

> FATHER LAURENCE (cont.)
> Take thou this vial, being then in bed,
> And this distilling liquor drink thou off.
> I'll send my letters to thy lord with speed to Mantua.

EXT. LOADING DOCK. DAY.

As Father Laurence speaks, the screen fills with an express envelope addressed "Romeo—Mantua." The envelope pulls away from the camera and falls into a canvas bag brimming with hundreds of like envelopes.

TRACK: With the canvas bag. It continues its journey into the back of an express delivery van.

Heavy double doors slam shut, filling the screen with the slogan "Post Post Haste."

The van pulls away.

DISSOLVE TO:

EXT. MANTUA. DAY.

A burning red sun is setting over an endless vista of ragged wasteland. Cutting across the bottom of the screen is the tiny image of the Post Post Haste van.

TIGHT ON: A weathered sign reads "Mantua." Behind it a vast colony of permanent trailer homes stretches into the distance.

The rap, rap, rap of knocking echoes through the park . . .

CUT TO: The source of the knocking. An express delivery man, envelope in hand, raps vigorously on the door of an unremarkable trailer.

INT. TRAILER. DAY.

TOPOGRAPHICAL SHOT: Romeo lies flat on a single bed in the cramped trailer.

The rap, rap, rap is very loud now. We move toward Romeo and realize he cannot hear the knocking because he has Walkman headphones on.

INT. JULIET'S BEDROOM. DAY.

The heraldic "Wedding Chimes" by J. S. Bach. Juliet stands resplendent in a radiant bridal gown.
   The image floats ethereally in a towering slab of
   mirror.

INT. TRAILER. DAY.

Romeo, still oblivious.

EXT. TRAILER. DAY.

Unsuccessful, the delivery man is filling out a "WE
   CALLED" card. He pushes it under the door.
DISSOLVE TO:

INT. JULIET'S BEDROOM. NIGHT.

Alone, sitting on her bed, Juliet stares at the small
   vial of blue liquid.

>   JULIET
>   (whispers)
> What if this mixture do not work at all?
> Shall I be married then tomorrow morning?

She cautiously begins to unscrew the tiny black lid.
   Suddenly, a knock at her door. Palming the vial,
   Juliet swings around to meet the arrival of her
   mother. Gloria probes her daughter's uneasiness.

GLORIA
What, are you busy, ho? Need you my help?
JULIET
(makes light of it)
No, madam. We have culled such necessaries
As are behoveful for our state tomorrow.
So please you, let me now be left alone,
And let the Nurse this night sit up with you.

Juliet begins to pull down the covers on her bed.

JULIET (cont.)
For I am sure you have your hands full all
In this so sudden business.

Gloria, sensing Juliet's distress, moves cautiously
toward her. Taking hold of the bedcovers, she
helps her daughter into bed.

GLORIA
Good night.

Juliet slides into bed. Gloria covers her with the
blanket.

GLORIA (cont.)
Get thee to bed, and rest, for thou hast need.

A brief moment between mother and daughter. Gloria, unable to cross that final barrier, moves to the
door; but she is stopped by the urgency in Juliet's
voice.

>   JULIET
> Farewell!

Gloria turns to Juliet.

>   JULIET (cont.)
> God knows when we shall meet again.

CLOSE ON: Gloria. A faint perplexity, and then, with an almost warm smile, she turns out the light and leaves.
The room is in darkness but for patterns of moonlight through windows.
Juliet brings the vial to her mouth.

>   JULIET (cont.)
> Come, vial. Romeo, I drink to thee.

Juliet drinks; a sudden violent convulsion. Her face contorts in fear.
CRANE UP: Into the air.

INT. CAPULETS' MANSION—JULIET'S BEDROOM. DAY.

TIME LAPSE: A cold early morning light emanates through the rain-streaked windows, throwing a pattern of tears on the walls of the room and across Juliet's lifeless body.
A dour-looking man in black stands near the bed. Father Laurence enters, closes the door, acknowl-

edges the man, kneels and hastily examines Juliet's
    pupils. He looks to the man in black.
DISSOLVE TO: Topographical shot: close-up of the
    empty glass vial being passed from one hand to
    another.
DISSOLVE TO: Father Laurence pocketing it. We
    are still topographical and hear the line,

> FATHER LAURENCE
> (to the man in black)
> As the custom is,
> In all her best array bear her to church.

The man in black allows two other dark-suited men
    into the room as we . . .
DISSOLVE TO:

INT. CHURCH. DAY.
Match topographical shot: Juliet laid out on her
    deathbed, enshrined in hundreds of lit candles.
TRACK THROUGH: Lines of Capulet mourners.
DISCOVER: Fulgencio and Gloria and Dave Paris.
SETTLE ON: the distressed face of Balthasar, who
    peers in through the door at the back of the
    church.

INT. CHURCH. DAY.
Balthasar is startled by a tug on his sleeve. He turns
    to find the SACRISTAN, who indicates to him to
    go inside.

Balthasar turns and makes a run for it.
HOLD ON: The bewildered Sacristan.

EXT. MANTUA. DAY.

WIDE SHOT: High above the wasteland that is
   Mantua. Beyond the trailer park stretches a long
   ribbon of black highway. From one direction the
   Post Post Haste van approaches, from the other,
   Balthasar's car.
They both turn off the highway and into the park.
CRANE DOWN: The express van pulls up at the
   front office. The driver alights and goes inside.
   Balthasar continues to Romeo's van.

EXT. TRAILER. DAY.

Romeo sits on the steps of the trailer. He is writing
   in his notebook.

> ROMEO (V.O.)
> And all this day an unaccustomed spirit
> Lifts me above the ground with cheerful thoughts.
> I dreamt my lady came and found me dead
> And breathed such life with kisses in my lips
> That I revived and was an emperor.
> Ah me, how sweet is love itself possessed
> When but love's shadows are so rich in joy.

He looks up to see Balthasar pull up.

ROMEO
(under his breath)
News from Verona!

An excited Romeo runs toward the car as we
PAN DOWN: To see the "WE CALLED" card lying trodden in the dust.

EXT. TRAILER PARK. DAY.
CRANE HIGH: Romeo sprints across open ground
to intercept Balthasar's car. In the background we
see the Post Post Haste messenger leaving the office and walking toward his van. Balthasar's car
skids to a halt and he jumps out.
Romeo yells joyously.

ROMEO
How now, Balthasar?

Balthasar cannot speak.

ROMEO (cont.)
Dost thou not bring me letters from the Priest?
How doth my lady? Is my father well?
How doth my lady Juliet? That I ask again,
For nothing can be ill if she be well.

Balthasar does not know how to say what he has
come to tell. He looks away.

BALTHASAR
Then she is well and nothing can be ill.
Her body sleeps in Capels' monument,
And her immortal part with angels lives.
I saw her laid low . . .
Oh pardon me for bringing these ill news.

For a long moment Romeo is profoundly still. When
he speaks, it is with a chilling calm.

ROMEO
Is it e'en so?

Balthasar nods.
Romeo turns and stares into the distant wasteland.
CLOSE ON: He speaks with bitter determination.

ROMEO
Then I defy you, stars!

Romeo moves to the car.

ROMEO
I will hence tonight.

Balthasar tries to restrain him.

BALTHASAR
Have patience . . .

Exploding with fury, Romeo throws Balthasar against
the vehicle.

ROMEO
Leave me!

CUT TO: The Post Post Haste messenger. He looks
up at the boys in the distance, then looks down
at the priest's undelivered envelope in his hand.
He reads the words "Romeo, Mantua," and begins to move tentatively toward them.
CUT TO: The boys.

BALTHASAR
(pleading)
Your looks are pale and wild and do import some
misadventure.
ROMEO
(with cold serenity)
Tush, thou art deceived.
Hast thou no letters to me from the Priest?

Balthasar shakes his head.
Romeo turns.

ROMEO (cont.)
No matter . . .

PAN: To see the Post Post Haste messenger approaching over the hood of the car.
PAN BACK: To see tears made gold by the fiery
light of the setting sun in the corners of Romeo's
eyes.
PUSH IN: To hear him silently whisper:

>>>>>>>>>>>>>>>>>>>>>>>>>>ROMEO (cont.)
Well, Juliet, I will lie with thee tonight.

Romeo turns and strides toward the car.

>>>>>>>>>>>>>>>>>>>>>>>>>>ROMEO (cont.)
I will hence tonight.

Romeo leaps into the driver's seat and starts up the
car; Balthasar slides into the passenger seat.
CUT TO: the messenger.
Balthasar's car roars through frame.
PUSH IN: On the messenger, then follow his gaze,
which goes after the boy's car, now a cloud of
dust on the horizon.

EXT. SYCAMORE GROVE ALLEY. NIGHT.
The golden arch of the old cinema with the words
SYCAMORE GROVE.
PULL OUT: Balthasar's car speeds through the
frame of the proscenium arch.
WHIP PAN: To the upstairs window at the back of
the pool hall. We hear the squealing halt of a car.
TILT DOWN: Balthasar's car is stopped below in
the shadows; the driver's door is open.
TILT UP: To the window.

**INT. APARTMENT REAR OF POOL HALL.
NIGHT.**
PUSH THROUGH: The window of the top floor.

Romeo runs into frame in front of us, bangs on the door.

PUSH: Past Romeo to the bespectacled eye that has appeared in the crack of the partly open doorway. It is Crusty, the owner of the pool hall. Below the face, the barrel of a shotgun protrudes menacingly.

CUT TO: Romeo in the dark, paint-peeling hallway.

> ROMEO
> Let me have a dram of poison, such soon-speeding gear
> As will disperse itself through all the veins
> That the life-weary taker may fall dead.

The eye considers, a voice rasps back.

> CRUSTY
> Such mortal drugs I have, but Verona's law
> Is death to any he that utters them.

Romeo speaks with fury.

> ROMEO
> The world is not thy friend, nor the world's law.
> Then be not poor, but break it and take this.

Romeo shoves a wad of money at Crusty's face.

BEAT. The rattle of a latch chain and the door swings open.

Standing in the doorway is Crusty.

>   CRUSTY
>   My poverty, but not my will consents.

CLOSE ON: Romeo.

>   ROMEO
>   I pay thy poverty and not thy will.

INT. BALTHASAR'S CAR. NIGHT.
The sound of an approaching vehicle catches Balthasar's attention and he turns sharply.
PAN with Balthasar's eyeline to DISCOVER a police patrol car cruising by. The cops stare back.

INT. COP CAR. NIGHT.
Cops' P.O.V., through the window of their moving vehicle, of Balthasar's car parked beneath Crusty's window.

INT. CRUSTY'S APARTMENT. NIGHT.
Crusty's apartment is filled with cats. Dozens of feline eyes glow in the dim room. As Romeo stands nervously, Crusty extracts a small chemist's vial from inside a statue-of-Our-Lady table lamp. He now speaks with cool professionalism.

>   CRUSTY
>   Drink it off and, if you had the strength
>   Of twenty men it would dispatch you straight.

Romeo takes the vial and hands over the money.

> ROMEO
> There is my gold, worse poison to men's souls
> Than these poor compounds that thou mayst not
> sell.

Romeo holds the vial of clear, yellow liquid up to
the light.

INT. COP CAR. NIGHT.
P.O.V. through the window as the car rounds on
Balthasar's parked car. Romeo, exiting the build-
ing, is caught in the headlights. He freezes momentarily. The patrolman barks into the radio
handset.

> PATROLMAN
> This is that banished Montague.

INT. CAPTAIN PRINCE'S OFFICE. NIGHT.
Captain Prince and two armed officers stand listening to the police radio receiver.

> CAPTAIN PRINCE
> Romeo! Hence in haste!

EXT. SYCAMORE GROVE ALLEY. NIGHT.
Tires screech as Romeo dives into the passenger seat

of Balthasar's moving vehicle. It roars away. Sirens blare; the police car gives chase.

INT. CHOPPER NIGHT.
TIGHT ON: Prince's face. He looks below as the chopper banks sharply.

INT. BALTHASAR'S CAR NIGHT.
WINDOW CAM: Romeo's P.O.V.: The car jumps the median strip onto the other side of the road and an underground tunnel is hurtling toward us.

INT. TUNNEL NIGHT.
In the strange yellow light of the tunnel, Balthasar's car skids to a halt.

INT. GREENHOUSE NIGHT.
Father Laurence speaks nervously into the phone.

FATHER LAURENCE
The letter was of dear import.

INT. POST POST HASTE OFFICE. NIGHT.
A clerk handles the undelivered letter.

CLERK
I could not send it
Nor get a messenger to bring it thee.

INT. GREENHOUSE NIGHT.
FATHER LAURENCE
The neglecting it
May do much damage.

EXT. TUNNEL NIGHT.
Romeo is out of the car. Balthasar attempts to stop
him.

ROMEO
Live, and be prosperous; and farewell, good fellow.

The sound of sirens is very close now. Balthasar's car
squeals off. Two police cars slash frame. Romeo
runs back out of the tunnel.

EXT. TUNNEL NIGHT.
Balthasar's car hits the chopper spotlight, the patrol
cars close behind.

EXT. CHURCH NIGHT.
The lit-up church towers into the sky.

WHIP PAN: To Romeo running toward the church up the street.

WHIP PAN: To patrol cars swerving to a halt at the end of the street behind him.

TRACK WITH: Romeo; he is almost at the church when a careening patrol car rounds the corner. He sidesteps it.

HOLD ON: The cops leap out.

TRACK WITH: Romeo scrambling up the steps.

WHIP PAN: To find the shocked sacristan as he scrambles from his chair.

CUT TO: Romeo halting suddenly, feet from the panicked sacristan. An unsure moment between them.

CUT TO: Cops leveling their rifles.

CUT TO: Romeo grabs the bewildered sacristan, jams his gun to his temple, and turns on the cops, screaming.

ROMEO
Tempt not a desperate man.

Romeo backs toward the doors.

CUT TO: The rifled cops' P.O.V.; hunting for a clean shot.

Romeo is almost at the door.

SUDDENLY: We hear a deafening thunder. The frame blows out in blinding white light.

TILT UP: Prince's chopper swoops down.

CUT TO: Romeo's P.O.V. of a harnessed marksman on the chopper taking aim at him.

MARKSMAN'S P.O.V.: Romeo caught in the glare
   of the burning arc light.
CUT TO: Romeo. Blinded, he raises his gun toward
   the chopper.

EXT. CHURCH. NIGHT.
Without hesitation the airborne marksman opens
fire.
BANG! A bullet slams into Romeo's shoulder,
   throwing him back into the church, freeing the
   sacristan.

INT. GREENHOUSE. NIGHT.
Father Laurence looks up sharply.

EXT. CHURCH NIGHT.
A bloodied Romeo fires back as he struggles with the
   huge brass doors of the church.

INT. CHURCH. NIGHT.
The police fire continues as Romeo, with a final
   gathering of strength, shoves the door and it rum-
   bles closed with a bang.

INT. CHOPPER. NIGHT.
Captain Prince bellows into the radio.

CAPTAIN PRINCE
Hold! Hold!

INT. CHURCH. NIGHT.
It is dark and silent. Struggling for breath, Romeo listens. The firing has stopped.

EXT. CHURCH.
CHOPPER P.O.V.: We follow the chopper's arc light as it scans the scene. The firing has ceased.
CUT TO: Prince. He motions to the pilot and they fly toward the church. We follow the arc light as it passes over the Madonna statue.

INT. CHURCH. NIGHT.
Romeo follows the moving sound of the chopper as it flies overhead.

INT. GREENHOUSE. NIGHT.
Father Laurence's face is suddenly bleached with the blinding white arc light as he looks up through the broken pane of glass above his head.

INT./EXT. GREENHOUSE. NIGHT.
Father Laurence's P.O.V. through the pane of glass. He can see, like an avenging angel above the Ma-

donna, Prince's chopper, its arc light streaming into the greenhouse from behind the statue.

INT. CHURCH. NIGHT.

Romeo, leaning against the brass doors, listens as the sound of the chopper recedes into the distance. A moment of relief, and then his consciousness settles upon the light that emanates through the gap between the inner doors of the church. The threat from outside begins to fade as Romeo, rising slowly, gun dangling from one hand, ever so delicately pushes the door open with the other. As the door opens, it reveals an image of unexpected beauty. The velvety black cavern of the church is glowing warm with hundreds of lit candles that converge around a towering tentlike shroud, through which the shadowy silhouette of a sleeping girl can be seen.

Romeo walks slowly down the aisle, each painful step bringing him closer and closer to the sleeping girl.

When he completes the journey, he gently pulls back the fine translucent cloth to reveal the unbearable vision of his wife's face, even more beautiful in seeming death. Romeo kneels close, as if not wanting to wake a sleeping child. Unconscious tears fall from his eyes as he whispers.

ROMEO
O my love, my wife,
Death, that hath sucked the honey of thy breath,

Hath had no power yet upon thy beauty,
Thou art not conquered. Beauty's ensign yet
Is crimson in thy lips and in thy cheeks,
And death's pale flag is not advanced there.

Romeo draws Juliet from the pedestal into his arms.
As he does, he becomes more confused by her
warm, seemingly alive body.

>   ROMEO (cont.)
> Ah, dear Juliet,
> Why art thou yet so fair?
> Shall I believe
> That unsubstantial death is amorous
> And keeps thee here in dark to be his paramour?

Romeo takes Juliet's wedding ring from around his
neck.

>   ROMEO (cont.)
> For fear of that
> I still will stay thee.
> Here, oh here will I set up my everlasting rest.

Romeo places the wedding ring on her finger, and
gently kisses it.
CLOSE ON: Juliet's hand with the ring on it. Ever
so slightly it moves. Romeo does not notice.

>   ROMEO (cont.)
> And shake the yoke of inauspicious stars
> From this world-wearied flesh. Eyes, look your

last. Arm, take your last embrace. And, lips, O
you the doors of breath seal with a righteous
kiss . . .

Gently Romeo kisses Juliet's lips. As he moves away,
Juliet's eyes open.
JULIET'S P.O.V.: A dreamlike image of her Romeo
against a halo of candlelight. Juliet ever so weakly
reaches out to touch him.

ROMEO
A dateless bargain to engrossing death.

Romeo brings the vial to his lips. Juliet's hand
comes into frame, almost touching his face. Ro-
meo drinks as Juliet's hand brushes against the
side of his cheek. Startled, Romeo drops the vial.
It smashes. He grabs her hand and looks at her.
CUT TO: the wide eyes of Juliet.
CUT TO: Romeo, an uncomprehending realization.
CUT TO: Juliet through a blurry consciousness.

JULIET
Romeo.

CLOSE ON: Romeo still clutching her hand; his
breath races and he shakes from the effects of the
drug. He fights to speak, convulses, collapsing in
Juliet's lap.
CUT TO: Juliet. Forcing herself up, she cradles his
head in her arms.

JULIET
Oh Romeo, what's here?

Romeo's clear wide eyes stare back. He is completely
still but for the sound of weak breaths desperately
drawn across motionless lips. Juliet finds the broken vial beside him.

JULIET (cont.)
Drunk all, and left no friendly drop to help me
after. I will kiss thy lips.
Haply some poison yet doth hang on them.

She delicately kisses Romeo's lips.

JULIET (cont.)
(a heartbroken whisper)
Thy lips are warm.

Desperately the lovers cling to each other. With all
his desire to stay alive, Romeo whispers:

ROMEO
Thus with a kiss I die.

There is no breath. He is still. Silence. Tears slip from
her eyes. Juliet hugs the lifeless Romeo to her.

JULIET
Romeo. O my true love, Romeo.

She looks to the gun resting nearby.

Ever so gently she takes it in her hand and, fighting
    through fear, turns the barrel toward herself.
Juliet's eyes are closed; she is almost serene.
TIGHT ON: Juliet's finger on the trigger.
Tears slip from her eyes.
PUSH IN: On her finger as it squeezes the trigger.
SUDDENLY: We hear:

> FATHER LAURENCE (V.O.)
> Come, daughter . . .

Juliet's eyes flash open. Standing in front of her is
    Father Laurence. He is completely still but for his
    outstretched hand. He waits for a moment; then,
    like a parent calming a frightened child, he whis-
    pers:

> FATHER LAURENCE (cont.)
> Come, daughter, away.
> A greater power than we can contradict
> Hath thwarted our intents.

CUT TO: Juliet. She contemplates his outstretched
    hand. Slowly she seems to soften.
Father Laurence edges ever so slowly closer.

> FATHER LAURENCE (cont.)
> Come, Juliet, come, come away.

FOLLOW: Juliet's eyes on the finger of the out-
    stretched hand of Father Laurence.

CUT TO: Father Laurence. His hand touches the gun.

CUT TO: Juliet. With painful resignation, she begins to release her grip.

CUT TO: Father Laurence. He has it almost in his hand.

SUDDENLY: A bang at the door. The lock is being worked.

CUT TO: Juliet. Startled, she looks to the door.

CUT TO: Father Laurence. He swings around, a look of terror.

CUT TO: The doors bursting open.

HOLD: On Father Laurence. We hear the clear click of the gun cocking.

In that instant he realizes what it is he has heard and, before he has time to turn back again, we hear the deafening sound of a gunshot echo through the church.

CUT TO: SLOW MOTION: The gun falling from Juliet's hand.

CUT TO: SLOW MOTION: The horrified face of Father Laurence.

CUT TO: SLOW MOTION: Captain Prince in the open doorway.

CUT TO: SLOW MOTION: Juliet's head settling on Romeo's chest. A wash of deep red blood floods across them both. We hold for a long beat.

CUT TO: Father Laurence.

CUT TO: Captain Prince.

TOPOGRAPHICAL SHOT: Of the two young lovers at peace, lying together in the deathbed, lit by a ring of candles. We crane higher and higher. As

we do we see the police rush in. Prince and Father Laurence stand with the dead youths between
them. We continue up, passing through the dome
of the church.

EXT. CHURCH. DAWN.
HOLD: On the Madonna statue.
Night slowly transforms to a cold gray morning. We
    track over the church and down to the front
    steps, scattered police cars, media vans, and as-
    sembled crowd. As we pass the open back door of
    a police car, a devastated Gloria Capulet and Car-
    oline Montague are being attended to. We move
    toward two covered stretchers being loaded into
    ambulances. As the doors close, we discover Cap-
    ulet and Montague. Their faces reveal all.
Captain Prince walks between them. The three men
    stand there with nothing to say.
Prince catches their gaze.
CLOSE ON: Captain Prince.

> CAPTAIN PRINCE
> See what a scourge is laid upon your hate,
> That heaven finds means to kill your joys with
>   love!
> And I, for winking at your discords too,
> Have lost a brace of kinsmen: all are punish'd.

As the ambulances pull away, the camera pulls high
    into the sky.
The cries of Gloria and Caroline mix with the

scratchy calls of police radios and television re-
porters.

The image pixelates into a television picture.

PULL OUT: As if on a TV screen, an
anchorwoman watches the image on a studio
monitor.

She turns:

ANCHORWOMAN
(to camera)

A glooming peace this morning with it brings:
The sun for sorrow will not show his head.
Go hence, to have more talk of these sad things.
Some shall be pardoned, some punished,
For never was a story of more woe
Than this of Juliet and her Romeo.

The anchorwoman changes beat to the next story;
but her dialogue fades, and her image gets smaller
as the television recedes into a black distance.

The music that reminds us most of these two lost
lives swells. When the television is very small it is
switched off.

BLACK SCREEN. HOLD A BEAT. END
CREDITS.

ROMEO AND JULIET

BY WILLIAM SHAKESPEARE

DRAMATIS PERSONAE

CHORUS.

ESCALUS, PRINCE of Verona.

PARIS, a young Count, kinsman of the Prince.

MONTAGUE, } heads of two houses at variance
CAPULET, } with each other.

OLD MAN, of the Capulet family.

ROMEO, son of Montague.

MERCUTIO, kinsman of the Prince, and friend to Romeo.

BENVOLIO, nephew of Montague, and friend to Romeo.

TYBALT, nephew of Lady Capulet.

PETRUCHIO, a Capulet.

FRIAR LAURENCE, } Franciscans.
FRIAR JOHN, }

SAMPSON, }
GREGORY, }
ANTHONY, } servants to Capulet.
POTPAN, }

ABRAHAM, servant to Montague.

BALTHASAR, servant to Romeo.

PETER, servant to Juliet's nurse.

APOTHECARY.

SIMON CATLING, }
HUGH REBECK, } musicians.
JAMES SOUNDPOST, }

PAGE to PARIS; another PAGE; OFFICER.

LADY MONTAGUE, wife of Montague.

LADY CAPULET, wife of Capulet.

JULIET, daughter of Capulet.

NURSE to Juliet.

CITIZENS of Verona; GENTLEMEN and GENTLEWOMEN
of both houses; MASKERS, TORCHBEARERS, GUARDS,
WATCHMEN, SERVANTS, and ATTENDANTS.

SCENE: Verona; Mantua.

PROLOGUE

Enter Chorus

CHORUS

Two households both alike in dignity,
In fair Verona where we lay our scene,
From ancient grudge break to new mutiny,
Where civil blood makes civil hands unclean.
From forth the fatal loins of these two foes,   5
A pair of star-crossed lovers take their life;
Whose misadventured piteous overthrows
Doth with their death bury their parents' strife.
The fearful passage of their death-marked love,
And the continuance of their parents' rage,   10
Which, but their children's end, naught could remove,
Is now the two hours' traffic of our stage;
The which if you with patient ears attend,
What here shall miss, our toil shall strive to mend.

[Exit.]

Notes on this play begin on p. 117.

ACT I

SCENE ONE.

Verona. A public place. Enter Sampson and Gregory with swords and bucklers.

SAMPSON

Gregory, on my word we'll not carry coals.

GREGORY

No, for then we should be colliers.

SAMPSON

I mean, an we be in choler, we'll draw.

GREGORY

Ay, while you live, draw your neck out of collar.   5

SAMPSON

I strike quickly being moved.

GREGORY

But thou art not quickly moved to strike.

SAMPSON

A dog of the house of Montague moves me.   10

GREGORY

To move is to stir, and to be valiant is to stand.
Therefore if thou art moved thou run'st away.

SAMPSON

A dog of that house shall move me to stand. I
will take the wall of any man or maid of Montague's.   15

GREGORY

That shows thee a weak slave, for the weakest goes to
the wall.

SAMPSON

'Tis true, and therefore women being the weaker
vessels are ever thrust to the wall. Therefore I will   20

push Montague's men from the wall, and thrust his
maids to the wall.

GREGORY

The quarrel is between our masters and us their men.

SAMPSON

'Tis all one. I will show myself a tyrant. When I   25
have fought with the men, I will be cruel with the
maids—I will cut off their heads.

GREGORY

The heads of the maids?

SAMPSON

Ay the heads of the maids, or their maidenheads   30
—take it in what sense thou wilt.

GREGORY

They must take it in sense that feel it.

SAMPSON

Me they shall feel while I am able to stand, and 'tis
known I am a pretty piece of flesh.   35

GREGORY

'Tis well thou art not fish; if thou hadst, thou hadst
been Poor-John. Draw thy tool, here comes two of the
house of Montagues.

[*Enter Abraham and Balthasar.*]

SAMPSON

My naked weapon is out; quarrel, I will back thee.   40

GREGORY

How, turn thy back and run?

SAMPSON

Fear me not.

GREGORY

No marry, I fear thee!

SAMPSON

Let us take the law of our sides, let them begin.   45

GREGORY

I will frown as I pass by, and let them take it as they
list.

SAMPSON

Nay, as they dare, I will bite my thumb at them, which
is a disgrace to them if they bear it.   50

ABRAHAM
Do you bite your thumb at us sir?
SAMPSON
I do bite my thumb sir.
ABRAHAM
Do you bite your thumb at us sir?
SAMPSON [aside to Gregory]
Is the law of our side if I say ay?   55
GREGORY [aside to Sampson]
No.
SAMPSON
No sir, I do not bite my thumb at you sir, but I bite
my thumb sir.
GREGORY
Do you quarrel sir?
ABRAHAM
Quarrel sir? No sir.   60
SAMPSON
But if you do sir, I am for you; I serve as good a man
as you.
ABRAHAM
No better.
SAMPSON
Well sir.

[Enter Benvolio.]
GREGORY [aside to Sampson]
Say better; here comes one of my master's kinsmen.   65
SAMPSON
Yes, better sir.
ABRAHAM
You lie.
SAMPSON
Draw if you be men. Gregory, remember thy swash-
ing blow.   [They fight].   70
BENVOLIO
Part fools, [Draws, and beats down their swords.]
Put up your swords, you know not what you do.
                                              [Enter Tybalt.]
TYBALT
What, art thou drawn among these heartless hinds?

Turn thee Benvolio, look upon thy death.
BENVOLIO
I do but keep the peace, put up thy sword,   75
Or manage it to part these men with me.
TYBALT
What, drawn and talk of peace? I hate the word,
As I hate hell, all Montagues, and thee.
Have at thee coward!   [*They fight.*]
    [*Enter Officer, and Citizens with clubs and
    partisans.*]
OFFICER
Clubs, bills, and partisans! Strike, beat them down.   80
CITIZENS
Down with the Capulets! Down with the Montagues!
    [*Enter Capulet in his gown, and Lady Capulet.*]
CAPULET
What noise is this? Give me my long sword, ho!
LADY CAPULET
A crutch, a crutch! Why call you for a sword?
    [*Enter Montague and Lady Montague.*]
CAPULET
My sword I say. Old Montague is come,
And flourishes his blade in spite of me.   85
MONTAGUE
Thou villain Capulet! Hold me not, let me go.
LADY MONTAGUE
Thou shalt not stir one foot to seek a foe.
               [*Enter Prince Escalus, attended.*]
PRINCE
Rebellious subjects, enemies to peace,
Profaners of this neighbour-stained steel—
Will they not hear? What ho, you men, you beasts,   90
That quench the fire of your pernicious rage
With purple fountains issuing from your veins—
On pain of torture, from those bloody hands
Throw your mistempered weapons to the ground,
And hear the sentence of your moved Prince.   95
Three civil brawls bred of an airy word,
By thee old Capulet, and Montague,

Have thrice disturbed the quiet of our streets,
And made Verona's ancient citizens
Cast by their grave beseeming ornaments,   100
To wield old partisans, in hands as old,
Cankered with peace, to part your cankered hate.
If ever you disturb our streets again,
Your lives shall pay the forfeit of the peace.
For this time, all the rest depart away.   105
You Capulet shall go along with me;
And Montague, come you this afternoon,
To know our farther pleasure in this case,
To old Freetown, our common judgement-place
Once more, on pain of death, all men depart.   110
    [*Exeunt all but Montague, Lady Montague, and
    Benvolio.*]
                MONTAGUE
Who set this ancient quarrel new abroach?
Speak nephew, were you by when it began?
                BENVOLIO
Here were the servants of your adversary,
And yours, close fighting ere I did approach.
I drew to part them, in the instant came   115
The fiery Tybalt, with his sword prepared,
Which as he breathed defiance to my ears,
He swung about his head and cut the winds,
Who nothing hurt withal hissed him in scorn.
While we were interchanging thrusts and blows,   120
Came more and more, and fought on part and part,
Till the Prince came, who parted either part.
                LADY MONTAGUE
O where is Romeo? Saw you him to-day?
Right glad I am he was not at this fray.
                BENVOLIO
Madam, an hour before the worshipped sun   125
Peered forth the golden window of the east,
A troubled mind drave me to walk abroad,
Where underneath the grove of sycamore,
That westward rooteth from this city side,
So early walking did I see your son.   130
Towards him I made, but he was ware of me,

And stole into the covert of the wood.
I, measuring his affections by my own,
Which then most sought where most might not be
    found,
Being one too many by my weary self,   135
Pursued my humour, not pursuing his,
And gladly shunned who gladly fled from me.
       MONTAGUE
Many a morning hath he there been seen,
With tears augmenting the fresh morning's dew,
Adding to clouds more clouds with his deep sighs.
But all so soon as the all-cheering sun   140
Should in the farthest east begin to draw
The shady curtains from Aurora's bed,
Away from light steals home my heavy son,
And private in his chamber pens himself,
Shuts up his windows, locks fair daylight out,   145
And makes himself an artificial night.
Black and portentous must this humour prove,
Unless good counsel may the cause remove.
       BENVOLIO
My noble uncle, do you know the cause?
       MONTAGUE
I neither know it, nor can learn of him.   150
       BENVOLIO
Have you importuned him by any means?
       MONTAGUE
Both by my self and many other friends.
But he, his own affections' counsellor,
Is to himself—I will not say how true—
But to himself so secret and so close,   155
So far from sounding and discovery,
As is the bud bit with an envious worm,
Ere he can spread his sweet leaves to the air,
Or dedicate his beauty to the sun.
Could we but learn from whence his sorrows grow,   160
We would as willingly give cure as know.
                    [*Enter Romeo.*]
       BENVOLIO
See where he comes, so please you step aside.

I'll know his grievance or be much denied.

MONTAGUE

I would thou wert so happy by thy stay
To hear true shrift. Come madam, let's away.   165

　　　　　　[Exeunt Montague and Lady Montague.]

BENVOLIO

Good morrow cousin.

ROMEO

　　　　　　　　　Is the day so young?

BENVOLIO

But new struck nine.

ROMEO

　　　　　　　Ay me, sad hours seem long.
Was that my father that went hence so fast?

BENVOLIO

It was. What sadness lengthens Romeo's hours?

ROMEO

Not having that which having makes them short.   170

BENVOLIO

In love?

ROMEO

Out—

BENVOLIO

Of love?

ROMEO

Out of her favour where I am in love.

BENVOLIO

Alas that love, so gentle in his view,   175
Should be so tyrannous and rough in proof!

ROMEO

Alas that love, whose view is muffled still,
Should without eyes see pathways to his will.
Where shall we dine? O me, what fray was here?
Yet tell me not, for I have heard it all.   180
Here's much to do with hate, but more with love.
Why then, o brawling love, a loving hate,
O any thing of nothing first create!
O heavy lightness, serious vanity,
Misshapen chaos of well-seeming forms,   185
Feather of lead, bright smoke, cold fire, sick health,

Still-waking sleep, that is not what it is!
This love feel I, that feel no love in this.
Dost thou not laugh?
> BENVOLIO
>> No coz, I rather weep.
> ROMEO
Good heart, at what?
> BENVOLIO
>> At thy good heart's oppression.   190
> ROMEO
Why such is love's transgression.
Griefs of mine own lie heavy in my breast,
Which thou wilt propagate to have it pressed
With more of thine; this love that thou hast shown,
Doth add more grief, to too much of mine own.   195
Love is a smoke raised with the fume of sighs;
Being purged, a fire sparkling in lovers' eyes;
Being vexed, a sea nourished with lovers' tears.
What is it else? A madness most discreet,
A choking gall, and a preserving sweet.   200
Farewell my coz.
> BENVOLIO
>> Soft, I will go along.
And if you leave me so, you do me wrong.
> ROMEO
Tut I have lost myself; I am not here.
This is not Romeo, he's some other where.
> BENVOLIO
Tell me in sadness, who is that you love.   205
> ROMEO
What, shall I groan and tell thee?
> BENVOLIO
>> Groan? Why no
But sadly tell me who.
> ROMEO
Bid a sick man in sadness make his will!
Ah word ill urged to one that is so ill.
In sadness cousin, I do love a woman.   210
> BENVOLIO
I aimed so near, when I supposed you loved.

ROMEO

A right good mark-man. And she's fair I love.

BENVOLIO

A right fair mark, fair coz, is soonest hit.

ROMEO

Well in that hit you miss, she'll not be hit
With Cupid's arrow. She hath Dian's wit,   215
And in strong proof of chastity well armed,
From love's weak childish bow she lives uncharmed.
She will not stay the siege of loving terms,
Nor bide th' encounter of assailing eyes,
Nor ope her lap to saint-seducing gold.   220
O she is rich in beauty, only poor,
That when she dies with beauty dies her store.

BENVOLIO

Then she hath sworn that she will still live chaste?

ROMEO

She hath, and in that sparing makes huge waste.
For beauty starved with her severity   225
Cuts beauty off from all posterity.
She is too fair, too wise; wisely too fair,
To merit bliss by making me despair.
She hath forsworn to love, and in that vow
Do I live dead that live to tell it now.   230

BENVOLIO

Be ruled by me, forget to think of her.

ROMEO

O teach me how I should forget to think.

BENVOLIO

By giving liberty unto thine eyes.
Examine other beauties.

ROMEO

                                   'Tis the way
To call hers, exquisite, in question more.   235
These happy masks that kiss fair ladies' brows,
Being black, put us in mind they hide the fair.
He that is strucken blind cannot forget
The precious treasure of his eyesight lost.
Show me a mistress that is passing fair,   240
What doth her beauty serve, but as a note

Where I may read who passed that passing fair?
Farewell, thou canst not teach me to forget.
                    BENVOLIO
I'll pay that doctrine, or else die in debt. [*Exeunt.*]

                    SCENE TWO.

                    The same. Enter Capulet,
                    Paris, and Servant.

          CAPULET
But Montague is bound as well as I,
In penalty alike; and 'tis not hard, I think,
For men so old as we to keep the peace.
          PARIS
Of honourable reckoning are you both,
And pity 'tis you lived at odds so long.
But now my lord, what say you to my suit?   5
          CAPULET
But saying o'er what I have said before.
My child is yet a stranger in the world,
She hath not seen the change of fourteen years.
Let two more summers wither in their pride   10
Ere we may think her ripe to be a bride.
          PARIS
Younger than she are happy mothers made.
          CAPULET
And too soon marred are those so early made.
Earth hath swallowed all my hopes but she:
She is the hopeful lady of my earth.   15
But woo her gentle Paris, get her heart,
My will to her consent is but a part.
An she agree, within her scope of choice
Lies my consent and fair according voice.
This night I hold an old accustomed feast,   20

Whereto I have invited many a guest,
Such as I love; and you among the store,
One more, most welcome, makes my number more.
At my poor house look to behold this night
Earth-treading stars that make dark heaven light.   25
Such comfort as do lusty young men feel,
When well-apparelled April on the heel
Of limping Winter treads, even such delight
Among fresh female buds shall you this night
Inherit at my house; hear all, all see,   30
And like her most whose merit most shall be:
Which on more view of many, mine being one
May stand in number, though in reckoning none.
Come go with me. [*To Servant, giving him a paper.*]
    Go sirrah, trudge about
Through fair Verona, find those persons out   35
Whose names are written there, and to them say,
My house and welcome on their pleasure stay.

                        [*Exeunt Capulet and Paris.*]
        SERVANT
Find them out whose names are written here! It
is written that the shoemaker should meddle with his
yard, and the tailor with his last, the fisher with his   40
pencil, and the painter with his nets. But I am
sent to find those persons whose names are here writ,
and can never find what names the writing person
hath here writ. I must to the learned, in good
time.   45

                        [*Enter Benvolio and Romeo.*]
        BENVOLIO
Tut man, one fire burns out another's burning,
One pain is lessened by another's anguish;
Turn giddy, and be holp by backward turning;
One desperate grief cures with another's languish.
Take thou some new infection to thy eye,   50
And the rank poison of the old will die.
        ROMEO
Your plantain leaf is excellent for that.
        BENVOLIO
For what I pray thee?

ROMEO
                    For your broken shin.

BENVOLIO
Why Romeo, art thou mad?

ROMEO
Not mad, but bound more than a madman is;   55
Shut up in prison, kept without my food,
Whipped and tormented, and—God-den good fellow.

SERVANT
God gi' god-den, I pray sir can you read?

ROMEO
Ay, mine own fortune in my misery.   60

SERVANT
Perhaps you have learned it without book. But I pray
can you read any thing you see?

ROMEO
Ay, if I know the letters and the language.

SERVANT
Ye say honestly, rest you merry.   65

ROMEO
Stay fellow, I can read.   [Reads the paper:]
    *Seigneur Martino, and his wife and daughters;
County Anselme and his beauteous sisters; the lady
widow of Vitruvio, Seigneur Placentio, and his lovely
nieces; Mercutio and his brother Valentine; mine*   70
*uncle Capulet, his wife and daughters; my fair niece
Rosaline, Livia, Seigneur Valentio, and his cousin
Tybalt; Lucio and the lively Helena.*
                            [Gives back the paper:]
A fair assembly: whither should they come?   75

SERVANT
Up.

ROMEO
Whither? To supper?

SERVANT
To our house.

ROMEO
Whose house?

SERVANT
My master's.   80

ROMEO
Indeed I should have asked you that before.
SERVANT
Now I'll tell you without asking. My master is the
great rich Capulet, and if you be not of the house of
Montagues, I pray come and crush a cup of wine.   85
Rest you merry.   [*Exit.*]
BENVOLIO
At this same ancient feast of Capulet's
Sups the fair Rosaline whom thou so loves,
With all the admired beauties of Verona.
Go thither, and with unattainted eye,   90
Compare her face with some that I shall show,
And I will make thee think thy swan a crow.
ROMEO
When the devout religion of mine eye
Maintains such falsehood, then turn tears to fires;
And these who often drowned could never die,   95
Transparent heretics, be burnt for liars.
One fairer than my love—the all-seeing sun
Ne'er saw her match, since first the world begun.
BENVOLIO
Tut you saw her fair, none else being by,
Herself poised with herself in either eye.   100
But in that crystal scales let there be weighed
Your lady's love against some other maid
That I will show you shining at this feast,
And she shall scant show well that now shows best.
ROMEO
I'll go along, no such sight to be shown,   105
But to rejoice in splendour of mine own.

[*Exeunt.*]

SCENE THREE.

Verona. Capulet's house.
Enter Lady Capulet and Nurse.

LADY CAPULET
Nurse, where's my daughter? Call her forth to me.
        NURSE
Now by my maidenhead—at twelve year old—I bade
her come. What lamb! What lady-bird! God forbid!
Where's this girl? What, Juliet!
                                    [*Enter Juliet.*]

        JULIET
How now? Who calls?
        NURSE
Your mother.
        JULIET
Madam, I am here, what is your will?   5
        LADY CAPULET
This is the matter—nurse, give leave awhile,
We must talk in secret. Nurse, come back again,
I have remembered me. Thou's hear our counsel.
Thou knowest my daughter's of a pretty age.   10
        NURSE
Faith I can tell her age unto an hour.
        LADY CAPULET
She's not fourteen.
        NURSE
I'll lay fourteen of my teeth, and yet to my teen be
it spoken, I have but four, she's not fourteen. How
long is it now to Lammas-tide?
        LADY CAPULET
A fortnight and odd days.   15
        NURSE
Even or odd, of all days in the year,
Come Lammas Eve at night shall she be fourteen.
Susan and she—God rest all Christian souls—

Were of an age. Well, Susan is with God,
She was too good for me. But as I said,   20
On Lammas Eve at night shall she be fourteen;
That shall she marry, I remember it well.
'Tis since the earthquake now eleven years,
And she was weaned—I never shall forget it—
Of all the days of the year, upon that day.   25
For I had then laid wormwood to my dug,
Sitting in the sun under the dove-house wall.
My lord and you were then at Mantua—
Nay I do bear a brain—but as I said,
When it did taste the wormwood on the nipple   30
Of my dug, and felt it bitter, pretty fool,
To see it tetchy and fall out with the dug!
Shake, quoth the dove-house; 'twas no need I trow
To bid me trudge.
And since that time it is eleven years,   35
For then she could stand high-lone; nay by th' rood,
She could have run and waddled all about;
For even the day before, she broke her brow,
And then my husband—God be with his soul,
'A was a merry man—took up the child.   40
Yea, quoth he, dost thou fall upon thy face?
Thou wilt fall backward when thou hast more wit,
Wilt thou not Jule? And by my holidame,
The pretty wretch left crying, and said ay.
To see now how a jest shall come about!   45
I warrant, an I should live a thousand years,
I never should forget it. Wilt thou not Jule, quoth he,
And pretty fool it stinted, and said ay.
        LADY CAPULET
Enough of this, I pray thee hold thy peace.
        NURSE
Yes madam, yet I cannot choose but laugh,   50
To think it should leave crying, and say ay.
And yet I warrant it had upon it brow
A bump as big as a young cockerel's stone.
A perilous knock, and it cried bitterly.
Yea, quoth my husband, fall'st upon thy face?   55
Thou wilt fall backward when thou comest to age;

Wilt thou not Jule? It stinted, and said ay.
    JULIET
And stint thou too, I pray thee nurse, say I.
    NURSE
Peace, I have done. God mark thee to his grace;
Thou wast the prettiest babe that e'er I nursed;   60
An I might live to see thee married once,
I have my wish.
    LADY CAPULET
Marry, that marry is the very theme
I came to talk of. Tell me daughter Juliet,
How stands your dispositions to be married?   65
    JULIET
It is an honour that I dream not of.
    NURSE
An honour? Were not I thine only nurse,
I would say thou hadst sucked wisdom from thy teat.
    LADY CAPULET
Well, think of marriage now. Younger than you,
Here in Verona, ladies of esteem,   70
Are made already mothers. By my count,
I was your mother much upon these years
That you are now a maid. Thus then in brief—
The valiant Paris seeks you for his love.
    NURSE
A man, young lady; lady, such a man   75
As all the world—why he's a man of wax.
    LADY CAPULET
Verona's summer hath not such a flower.
    NURSE
Nay he's a flower, in faith a very flower.
    LADY CAPULET
What say you, can you love the gentleman?
This night you shall behold him at our feast,   80
Read o'er the volume of young Paris' face,
And find delight writ there with beauty's pen;
Examine every married lineament,
And see how one another lends content;
And what obscured in this fair volume lies   85
Find written in the margent of his eyes.

This precious book of love, this unbound lover,
To beautify him only lacks a cover.
The fish lives in the sea, and 'tis much pride
For fair without the fair within to hide.   90
That book in many's eyes doth share the glory,
That in gold clasps locks in the golden story;
So shall you share all that he doth possess,
By having him, making yourself no less.

NURSE

No less, nay bigger; women grow by men.   95

LADY CAPULET

Speak briefly, can you like of Paris' love?

JULIET

I'll look to like, if looking liking move.
But no more deep will I endart mine eye
Than your consent gives strength to make it fly.

[Enter Servant.]

SERVANT

Madam the guests are come, supper served up, you   100
called, my young lady asked for, the nurse cursed in
the pantry, and every thing in extremity. I must hence
to wait; I beseech you follow straight.

LADY CAPULET

We follow thee. [Exit Servant.] Juliet, the County
stays.   105

NURSE

Go girl, seek happy nights to happy days.

[Exeunt.]

SCENE FOUR.

Verona. A street. Enter Romeo, Mercutio,
Benvolio, with other Maskers,
and Torchbearers.

ROMEO

What, shall this speech be spoke for our excuse?
Or shall we on without apology?

BENVOLIO

The date is out of such prolixity.
We'll have no Cupid hoodwinked with a scarf,
Bearing a Tartar's painted bow of lath,   5
Scaring the ladies like a crow-keeper;
Nor no without-book prologue, faintly spoke
After the prompter, for our entrance.
But let them measure us by what they will,
We'll measure them a measure, and be gone.   10

ROMEO

Give me a torch, I am not for this ambling;
Being but heavy, I will bear the light.

MERCUTIO

Nay gentle Romeo, we must have you dance.

ROMEO

Not I, believe me, you have dancing shoes
With nimble soles, I have a soul of lead   15
So stakes me to the ground I cannot move.

MERCUTIO

You are a lover, borrow Cupid's wings,
And soar with them above a common bound.

ROMEO

I am too sore enpierced with his shaft,
To soar with his light feathers; and so bound,   20
I cannot bound a pitch above dull woe.
Under love's heavy burden do I sink.

MERCUTIO

And to sink in it should you burden love;
Too great oppression for a tender thing.

ROMEO

Is love a tender thing? It is too rough,   25
Too rude, too boisterous, and it pricks like thorn.

MERCUTIO

If love be rough with you, be rough with love.
Prick love for pricking, and you beat love down.
Give me a case to put my visage in.
                                        [*Puts on a mask.*]
A visor for a visor. What care I   30
What curious eye doth quote deformities?
Here are the beetle brows shall blush for me.

BENVOLIO
Come knock and enter, and no sooner in,
But every man betake him to his legs.
ROMEO
A torch for me; let wantons light of heart   35
Tickle the senseless rushes with their heels.
For I am proverbed with a grandsire phrase—
I'll be a candle-holder and look on—
The game was ne'er so fair, and I am done.
MERCUTIO
Tut, dun's the mouse, the constable's own word.   40
If thou are Dun, we'll draw thee from the mire
Of this sir-reverence love, wherein thou stickest
Up to the ears. Come, we burn daylight, ho!
ROMEO
Nay that's not so.
MERCUTIO
                    I mean sir, in delay
We waste our lights in vain, like lamps by day.   45
Take our good meaning, for our judgment sits
Five times in that, ere once in our five wits.
ROMEO
And we mean well in going to this mask;
But 'tis no wit to go.
MERCUTIO
                    Why, may one ask?
ROMEO
I dreamt a dream to-night.
MERCUTIO
                              And so did I.   50
ROMEO
Well, what was yours?
MERCUTIO
                       That dreamers often lie.
ROMEO
In bed asleep while they do dream things true.
MERCUTIO
O then I see Queen Mab hath been with you.
She is the fairies' midwife, and she comes
In shape no bigger than an agate stone   55

On the forefinger of an alderman,
Drawn with a team of little atomies
Over men's noses as they lie asleep.
Her wagon-spokes made of long spinners' legs;
The cover, of the wings of grasshoppers;   60
Her traces, of the smallest spider web;
Her collars, of the moonshine's watery beams;
Her whip of cricket's bone; the lash of film;
Her wagoner, a small gray-coated gnat,
Not half so big as a round little worm,   65
Pricked from the lazy finger of a maid.
Her chariot is an empty hazel-nut,
Made by the joiner squirrel or old grub,
Time out a mind the fairies' coachmakers.
And in this state she gallops night by night   70
Through lovers' brains, and then they dream of love;
O'er courtiers' knees, that dream on curtsies straight;
O'er lawyers' fingers, who straight dream on fees;
O'er ladies' lips, who straight on kisses dream,
Which oft the angry Mab with blisters plagues,   75
Because their breaths with sweetmeats tainted are.
Sometime she gallops o'er a courtier's nose,
And then dreams he of smelling out a suit;
And sometime comes she with a tithe-pig's tail,
Tickling a parson's nose as 'a lies asleep,   80
Then he dreams of another benefice.
Sometime she driveth o'er a soldier's neck,
And then dreams he of cutting foreign throats,
Of breaches, ambuscadoes, Spanish blades,
Of healths five fathom deep; and then anon   85
Drums in his ear, at which he starts and wakes;
And being thus frighted, swears a prayer or two,
And sleeps again. This is that very Mab
That plats the manes of horses in the night,
And bakes the elf-locks in foul sluttish hairs.   90
Which once untangled, much misfortune bodes.
This is the hag, when maids lie on their backs,
That presses them and learns them first to bear,
Making them women of good carriage.
This is she—

ROMEO

            Peace, peace, Mercutio, peace.   95
Thou talk'st of nothing.

MERCUTIO

                True, I talk of dreams;
Which are the children of an idle brain,
Begot of nothing but vain fantasy;
Which is as thin of substance as the air,
And more inconstant than the wind who wooes   100
Even now the frozen bosom of the north,
And being angered puffs away from thence,
Turning his side to the dew-dropping south.

BENVOLIO

This wind you talk of blows us from ourselves.
Supper is done, and we shall come too late.   105

ROMEO

I fear, too early; for my mind misgives
Some consequence, yet hanging in the stars,
Shall bitterly begin his fearful date
With this night's revels, and expire the term
Of a despised life closed in my breast,   110
By some vile forfeit of untimely death.
But he that hath the steerage of my course
Direct my sail. On lusty gentlemen.

BENVOLIO

Strike drum.

        [They march about the stage, and exeunt.]

SCENE FIVE.

*Verona. A hall in Capulet's house.
Enter Musicians, and two Servants
with napkins.*

FIRST SERVANT

Where's Potpan, that he helps not to take away?
He shift a trencher? He scrape a trencher?

SECOND SERVANT

When good manners shall lie all in one or two men's
hands, and they unwashed too, 'tis a foul thing.   5

FIRST SERVANT

Away with the joint-stools, remove the court-cupboard,
look to the plate. Good thou, save me a piece of
marchpane, and as thou loves me, let the porter let in
Susan Grindstone and Nell.   10

[Exit Second Servant.]

Anthony and Potpan!

[Enter Anthony and Potpan.]

ANTHONY

Ay boy, ready.

FIRST SERVANT

You are looked for, and called for, asked for, and
sought for in the great chamber.

POTPAN

We cannot be here and there too. Cheerly boys, be   15
brisk awhile, and the longer liver take all.

[They retire.]

[Enter the Maskers at one door, and at the
other Capulet, Lady Capulet, Juliet, Nurse,
Tybalt, and others of the house and Guests,
meeting.]

CAPULET

Welcome gentlemen. Ladies that have their toes
Unplagued with corns will walk a bout with you.
Ah ha, my mistresses, which of you all   20
Will now deny to dance? She that makes dainty,
She I'll swear hath corns. Am I come near ye now?
Welcome gentlemen. I have seen the day
That I have worn a visor and could tell
A whispering tale in a fair lady's ear,   25
Such as would please. 'Tis gone, 'tis gone, 'tis gone.
You are welcome, gentlemen. Come, musicians play.
A hall, a hall, give room, and foot it girls.

[Music plays, and they dance.]

More light you knaves, and turn the tables up;
And quench the fire, the room is grown too hot.   30
Ah sirrah, this unlooked for sport comes well.
Nay sit, nay sit, good cousin Capulet,
For you and I are past our dancing days.
How long is't now since last yourself and I
Were in a mask?

>   SECOND CAPULET
>   By'r lady, thirty years.   35

>   CAPULET
What man, 'tis not so much, 'tis not so much;
'Tis since the nuptial of Lucentio,
Come Pentecost as quickly as it will,
Some five and twenty years, and then we masked.

>   SECOND CAPULET
'Tis more, 'tis more, his son is elder sir;   40
His son is thirty.

>   CAPULET
>   Will you tell me that?
His son was but a ward two years ago.

>   ROMEO [to a Servant]
What lady's that which doth enrich the hand
Of yonder knight?

>   SERVANT
I know not sir.   45

>   ROMEO
O she doth teach the torches to burn bright.
It seems she hangs upon the cheek of night
As a rich jewel in an Ethiop's ear;
Beauty too rich for use, for earth too dear.
So shows a snowy dove trooping with crows,   50
As yonder lady o'er her fellows shows.
The measure done, I'll watch her place of stand,
And touching hers make blessed my rude hand.
Did my heart love till now? Forswear it sight,
For I ne'er saw true beauty till this night.   55

>   TYBALT
This by his voice should be a Montague.
Fetch me my rapier, boy. What dares the slave
Come hither covered with an antic face,

To fleer and scorn at our solemnity?   60
Now by the stock and honour of my kin,
To strike him dead I hold it not a sin.
    C A P U L E T
Why how now kinsman, wherefore storm you so?
     T Y B A L T
Uncle, this is a Montague, our foe;
A villain that is hither come in spite,
To scorn at our solemnity this night.   65
    C A P U L E T
Young Romeo is it?
     T Y B A L T
             'Tis he, that villain Romeo.
    C A P U L E T
Content thee gentle coz, let him alone.
'A bears him like a portly gentleman;
And to say truth, Verona brags of him
To be a virtuous and well governed youth.   70
I would not for the wealth of all this town
Here in my house do him disparagement.
Therefore be patient, take no note of him;
It is my will, the which if thou respect,
Show a fair presence, and put off these frowns,   75
An ill-beseeming semblance for a feast.
     T Y B A L T
It fits when such a villain is a guest.
I'll not endure him.
    C A P U L E T
          He shall be endured.
What goodman boy, I say he shall; go to,
Am I the master here or you? Go to.   80
You'll not endure him? God shall mend my soul,
You'll make a mutiny among my guests?
You will set cock-a-hoop, you'll be the man?
     T Y B A L T
Why uncle, 'tis a shame—
    C A P U L E T
          Go to, go to,
You are a saucy boy. Is't so indeed?   85
This trick may chance to scathe you, I know what.

You must contrary me? Marry 'tis time.
Well said my hearts! You are a princox, go;
Be quiet, or—more light, more light! For shame!
I'll make you quiet. What, cheerly my hearts!   90
    TYBALT
Patience perforce with wilful choler meeting
Makes my flesh tremble in their different greeting.
I will withdraw, but this intrusion shall,
Now seeming sweet, convert to bitt'rest gall.

                                        [Exit.]
    ROMEO [to Juliet]
If I profane with my unworthiest hand   95
This holy shrine, the gentle sin is this,
My lips two blushing pilgrims ready stand
To smooth that rough touch with a tender kiss.
    JULIET
Good pilgrim, you do wrong your hand too much,
Which mannerly devotion shows in this;   100
For saints have hands that pilgrims' hands do touch,
And palm to palm is holy palmers' kiss.
    ROMEO
Have not saints lips, and holy palmers too?
    JULIET
Ay pilgrim, lips that they must use in prayer.
    ROMEO
O then dear saint, let lips do what hands do.   105
They pray; grant thou, lest faith turn to despair.
    JULIET
Saints do not move, though grant for prayers' sake.
    ROMEO
Then move not while my prayer's effect I take.
Thus from my lips, by thine, my sin is purged.
    JULIET
Then have my lips the sin that they have took.   110
    ROMEO
Sin from my lips? O trespass sweetly urged.
Give me my sin again.
    JULIET
                    You kiss by th' book.

NURSE
Madam, your mother craves a word with you.
ROMEO
What is her mother?
NURSE
                    Marry bachelor,
Her mother is the lady of the house,   115
And a good lady, and a wise and virtuous.
I nursed her daughter that you talked withal.
I tell you, he that can lay hold of her
Shall have the chinks.
ROMEO
                    Is she a Capulet?
O dear account, my life is my foe's debt.   120
BENVOLIO
Away, be gone; the sport is at the best.
ROMEO
Ay, so I fear, the more is my unrest.
CAPULET
Nay gentlemen, prepare not to be gone;
We have a trifling foolish banquet towards.
Is it e'en so? Why then I thank you all.   125
I thank you, honest gentlemen; good night.
More torches here! Come on, then, let's to bed.
[To second Capulet.] Ah sirrah, by my fay, it waxes
    late.
I'll to my rest. [Exeunt all but Juliet and Nurse.]
JULIET
Come hither nurse. What is yond gentleman?   130
NURSE
The son and heir of old Tiberio.
JULIET
What's he that now is going out of door?
NURSE
Marry that I think be young Petruchio.
JULIET
What's he that follows here that would not dance?
NURSE   135
I know not.

JULIET
Go ask his name—if he be married,
My grave is like to be my wedding-bed.
        NURSE
His name is Romeo, and a Montague;
The only son of your great enemy.
        JULIET
My only love sprung from my only hate,   140
Too early seen unknown, and known too late!
Prodigious birth of love it is to me,
That I must love a loathed enemy.
        NURSE
What's this, what's this?
        JULIET
                          A rhyme I learned even now
Of one I danced withal.   [A call within, Juliet.]
        NURSE
                          Anon, anon!   145
Come let's away, the strangers all are gone.
                                        [Exeunt.]

ACT II

PROLOGUE

Enter Chorus.

Now old desire doth in his death-bed lie,
And young affection gapes to be his heir;
That fair for which love groaned for and would die,
With tender Juliet matched, is now not fair.
Now Romeo is beloved, and loves again,   5
Alike bewitched by the charm of looks;
But to his foe supposed he must complain,
And she steal love's sweet bait from fearful hooks.
Being held a foe, he may not have access
To breathe such vows as lovers use to swear;   10
And she as much in love, her means much less
To meet her new beloved any where.
But passion lends them power, time means, to meet,
Temp'ring extremities with extreme sweet.   [*Exit.*]

SCENE ONE.

*Verona. Capulet's walled orchard and a
lane by it. Enter Romeo in the lane.*

ROMEO
Can I go forward when my heart is here?

Turn back, dull earth, and find thy centre out.
> [*Climbs over the orchard wall. Enter Benvolio and Mercutio in the lane.*]

BENVOLIO

Romeo! My cousin Romeo! Romeo!

MERCUTIO

                              He is wise,
And on my life hath stolen him home to bed.

BENVOLIO

He ran this way and leaped this orchard wall.   5
Call, good Mercutio.

MERCUTIO

               Nay I'll conjure too.
Romeo! Humours! Madman! Passion! Lover!
Appear thou in the likeness of a sigh,
Speak but one rhyme and I am satisfied;
Cry but, ay me, pronounce but love and dove;   10
Speak to my gossip Venus one fair word,
One nickname for her purblind son and heir,
Young Abraham Cupid, he that shot so true,
When King Cophetua loved the beggar-maid.
He heareth not, he stirreth not, he moveth not;   15
The ape is dead, and I must conjure him.
I conjure thee by Rosaline's bright eyes,
By her high forehead, and her scarlet lip,
By her fine foot, straight leg, and quivering thigh,
And the demesnes that there adjacent lie,   20
That in thy likeness thou appear to us.

BENVOLIO

An if he hear thee thou wilt anger him.

MERCUTIO

This cannot anger him; 'twould anger him
To raise a spirit in his mistress' circle
Of some strange nature, letting it there stand   25
Till she had laid it and conjured it down;
That were some spite. My invocation
Is fair and honest; in his mistress' name
I conjure only but to raise up him.

BENVOLIO

Come, he hath hid himself among these trees   30

To be consorted with the humorous night.
Blind is his love, and best befits the dark.
MERCUTIO
If love be blind, love cannot hit the mark.
Now will he sit under a medlar tree,
And wish his mistress were that kind of fruit   35
As maids call medlars, when they laugh alone.
O Romeo that she were, o that she were
An open et cetera, thou a poperin pear.
Romeo good night, I'll to my truckle bed;
This field-bed is too cold for me to sleep.   40
Come, shall we go?
        BENVOLIO
                    Go then, for 'tis in vain
To seek him here that means not to be found.
                    [Exeunt Benvolio and Mercutio.]

SCENE TWO.

The same.

ROMEO [*comes forward*]
He jests at scars that never felt a wound.
                    [*Enter Juliet above.*]
But soft, what light through yonder window breaks?
It is the East, and Juliet is the sun.
Arise fair sun and kill the envious moon,
Who is already sick and pale with grief,   5
That thou her maid art far more fair than she.
Be not her maid since she is envious,
Her vestal livery is but sick and green,
And none but fools do wear it; cast it off.
It is my lady, o it is my love.   10
O that she knew she were.
She speaks, yet she says nothing; what of that?

Her eye discourses, I will answer it.
I am too bold, 'tis not to me she speaks.
Two of the fairest stars in all the heaven,   15
Having some business, do entreat her eyes
To twinkle in their spheres till they return.
What if her eyes were there, they in her head?
The brightness of her cheek would shame those stars,
As daylight doth a lamp; her eyes in heaven   20
Would through the airy region stream so bright,
That birds would sing, and think it were not night.
See how she leans her cheek upon her hand.
O that I were a glove upon that hand,
That I might touch that cheek.

    JULIET

                     Ay me!

    ROMEO

                             She speaks.   25
O speak again bright angel, for thou art
As glorious to this night being o'er my head,
As is a winged messenger of heaven
Unto the white-upturned wond'ring eyes
Of mortals that fall back to gaze on him,   30
When he bestrides the lazy pacing clouds,
And sails upon the bosom of the air.

    JULIET

O Romeo, Romeo, wherefore art thou Romeo?
Deny thy father, and refuse thy name.
Or if thou wilt not, be but sworn my love,   35
And I'll no longer be a Capulet.

    ROMEO

Shall I hear more, or shall I speak at this?

    JULIET

'Tis but thy name that is my enemy.
Thou art thyself, though not a Montague.
What's Montague? It is nor hand nor foot,   40
Nor arm nor face, nor any other part
Belonging to a man. O be some other name.
What's in a name? That which we call a rose
By any other word would smell as sweet;
So Romeo would, were he not Romeo called,   45

Retain that dear perfection which he owes
Without that title. Romeo doff thy name,
And for thy name which is no part of thee,
Take all myself.

ROMEO

          I take thee at thy word.
Call me but love, and I'll be new baptized;   50
Henceforth I never will be Romeo.

JULIET

What man art thou, that thus bescreened in night
So stumblest on my counsel?

ROMEO

             By a name
I know not how to tell thee who I am.
My name, dear saint, is hateful to myself,   55
Because it is an enemy to thee.
Had I it written, I would tear the word.

JULIET

My ears have not yet drunk a hundred words
Of thy tongue's uttering, yet I know the sound.
Art thou not Romeo, and a Montague?   60

ROMEO

Neither, fair maid, if either thee dislike.

JULIET

How cam'st thou hither, tell me, and wherefore?
The orchard walls are high and hard to climb,
And the place death, considering who thou art,
If any of my kinsmen find thee here.   65

ROMEO

With love's light wings did I o'er-perch these walls,
For stony limits cannot hold love out,
And what love can do, that dares love attempt.
Therefore thy kinsmen are no stop to me.

JULIET

If they do see thee, they will murder thee.   70

ROMEO

Alack there lies more peril in thine eye
Than twenty of their swords; look thou but sweet,
And I am proof against their enmity.

JULIET

I would not for the world they saw thee here.

ROMEO

I have night's cloak to hide me from their eyes.   75
And but thou love me, let them find me here.
My life were better ended by their hate,
Than death prorogued, wanting of thy love.

JULIET

By whose direction found'st thou out this place?

ROMEO

By love that first did prompt me to enquire;   80
He lent me counsel, and I lent him eyes.
I am no pilot, yet wert thou as far
As that vast shore washed with the farthest sea,
I should adventure for such merchandise.

JULIET

Thou knowest the mask of night is on my face,   85
Else would a maiden blush bepaint my cheek,
For that which thou hast heard me speak tonight.
Fain would I dwell on form, fain, fain, deny
What I have spoke; but farewell compliment.
Dost thou love me? I know thou wilt say ay,   90
And I will take thy word; yet if thou swear'st,
Thou mayst prove false; at lovers' perjuries
They say Jove laughs. O gentle Romeo,
If thou dost love, pronounce it faithfully.
Or if thou thinkest I am too quickly won,   95
I'll frown and be perverse, and say thee nay,
So thou wilt woo; but else not for the world.
In truth fair Montague I am too fond;
And therefore thou mayst think my haviour light.
But trust me gentleman, I'll prove more true   100
Than those that have more cunning to be strange.
I should have been more strange, I must confess,
But that thou overheard'st, ere I was ware,
My true love's passion; therefore pardon me,
And not impute this yielding to light love,   105
Which the dark night hath so discovered.

ROMEO

Lady, by yonder blessed moon I vow,

That tips with silver all these fruit tree tops—
JULIET
O swear not by the moon, th' inconstant moon,
That monthly changes in her circled orb,   110
Lest that thy love prove likewise variable.
ROMEO
What shall I swear by?
JULIET
                Do not swear at all.
Or if thou wilt, swear by thy gracious self,
Which is the god of my idolatry,
And I'll believe thee.
ROMEO
              If my heart's dear love—   115
JULIET
Well do not swear. Although I joy in thee,
I have no joy of this contract to-night,
It is too rash, too unadvised, too sudden,
Too like the lightning, which doth cease to be
Ere one can say, it lightens. Sweet, good night.   120
This bud of love by summer's ripening breath
May prove a beauteous flower when next we meet.
Good night, good night. As sweet repose and rest
Come to thy heart as that within my breast.
ROMEO
O wilt thou leave me so unsatisfied?   125
JULIET
What satisfaction canst thou have to-night?
ROMEO
Th' exchange of thy love's faithful vow for mine.
JULIET
I gave thee mine before thou didst request it.
And yet I would it were to give again.
ROMEO
Wouldst thou withdraw it? For what purpose, love?   130
JULIET
But to be frank and give it thee again;
And yet I wish but for the thing I have.
My bounty is as boundless as the sea,
My love as deep; the more I give to thee

The more I have, for both are infinite.   135
                              [*Nurse calls within.*]
I hear some noise within; dear love adieu.
Anon good nurse! Sweet Montague, be true.
Stay but a little, I will come again.   [*Exit above.*]
       ROMEO
O blessed, blessed night! I am afeard,
Being in night, all this is but a dream,   140
Too flattering-sweet to be substantial.
                          [*Re-enter Juliet above.*]
       JULIET
Three words, dear Romeo, and good night indeed.
If that thy bent of love be honourable,
Thy purpose marriage, send me word to-morrow.
By one that I'll procure to come to thee,   145
Where and what time thou wilt perform the rite;
And all my fortunes at thy foot I'll lay,
And follow thee my lord throughout the world.
       NURSE [*within*]
Madam!
       JULIET
I come, anon.—But if thou meanest not well,   150
I do beseech thee—
       NURSE [*within*]
Madam!
       JULIET
                By and by, I come.—
To cease thy strife, and leave me to my grief.
To-morrow will I send.
       ROMEO
                So thrive my soul—
       JULIET
A thousand times good night.   [*Exit above.*]   155
       ROMEO
A thousand times the worse, to want thy light.
Love goes toward love as schoolboys from their books,
But love from love, toward school with heavy looks.
                              [*Re-enter Juliet.*]
       JULIET
Hist, Romeo, hist! O for a falconer's voice,

To lure this tassel-gentle back again.   160
Bondage is hoarse, and may not speak aloud,
Else would I tear the cave where Echo lies,
And make her airy tongue more hoarse than mine,
With repetition of my Romeo's name.
Romeo!

    ROMEO
It is my soul that calls upon my name.   165
How silver-sweet sound lovers' tongues by night,
Like softest music to attending ears.

    JULIET
Romeo!

    ROMEO
    My sweet.

    JULIET
              At what a clock to-morrow
Shall I send to thee?

    ROMEO
              By the hour of nine.

    JULIET
I will not fail; 'tis twenty years till then.   170
I have forgot why I did call thee back.

    ROMEO
Let me stand here till thou remember it.

    JULIET
I shall forget, to have thee still stand there,
Remembering how I love thy company.

    ROMEO
And I'll still stay, to have thee still forget,   175
Forgetting any other home but this.

    JULIET
'Tis almost morning; I would have thee gone,
And yet no farther than a wanton's bird,
That lets it hop a little from her hand,
Like a poor prisoner in his twisted gyves,   180
And with a silken thread plucks it back again,
So loving-jealous of his liberty.

    ROMEO
I would I were thy bird.

JULIET

Sweet, so would I;
Yet I should kill thee with much cherishing.
Good night, good night. Parting is such sweet sorrow,   185
That I shall say good night till it be morrow.

[*Exit above.*]

ROMEO

Sleep dwell upon thine eyes, peace in thy breast.
Would I were sleep and peace, so sweet to rest.
Hence will I to my ghostly father's cell,
His help to crave, and my dear hap to tell.   190

[*Exit*]

SCENE THREE.

Verona. Friar Laurence's cell.
Enter Friar Laurence, with a basket.

FRIAR LAURENCE

The gray-eyed morn smiles on the frowning night,
Check'ring the eastern clouds with streaks of light;
And fleckeled darkness like a drunkard reels
From forth day's path and Titan's fiery wheels.
Now ere the sun advance his burning eye,   5
The day to cheer, and night's dank dew to dry.
I must up-fill this osier-cage of ours
With baleful weeds and precious-juiced flowers.
The earth that's nature's mother is her tomb;
What is her burying grave, that is her womb.   10
And from her womb children of divers kind
We sucking on her natural bosom find;
Many for many virtues excellent,
None but for some, and yet all different.
O mickle is the powerful grace that lies   15
In plants, herbs, stones, and their true qualities.
For naught so vile that on the earth doth live,
But to the earth some special good doth give;

Nor aught so good, but strained from that fair use,
Revolts from true birth, stumbling on abuse.   20
Virtue itself turns vice being misapplied,
And vice sometime's by action dignified.
　　　　　[Enter Romeo and stands by the door.]
Within the infant rind of this weak flower
Poison hath residence, and medicine power;
For this being smelt with that part cheers each part;   25
Being tasted, slays all senses with the heart.
Two such opposed kings encamp them still
In man as well as herbs—grace and rude will;
And where the worser is predominant,
Full soon the canker death eats up that plant.   30
　　ROMEO *[advances]*
Good morrow father.
　　FRIAR LAURENCE
　　　　　Benedicite!
What early tongue so sweet saluteth me?
Young son, it argues a distempered head
So soon to bid good morrow to thy bed.
Care keeps his watch in every old man's eye,   35
And where care lodges, sleep will never lie;
But where unbruised youth with unstuffed brain
Doth couch his limbs, there golden sleep doth reign.
Therefore thy earliness doth me assure
Thou art up-roused by some distemperature;   40
Or if not so, then here I hit it right,
Our Romeo hath not been in bed to-night.
　　ROMEO
That last is true; the sweeter rest was mine.
　　FRIAR LAURENCE
God pardon sin, wast thou with Rosaline?
　　ROMEO
With Rosaline, my ghostly father, no.   45
I have forgot that name, and that name's woe.
　　FRIAR LAURENCE
That's my good son; but where hast thou been then?
　　ROMEO
I'll tell thee ere thou ask it me again.
I have been feasting with mine enemy,

Where on a sudden one hath wounded me,   50
That's by me wounded; both our remedies
Within thy help and holy physic lies.
I bear no hatred, blessed man; for lo,
My intercession likewise steads my foe.

FRIAR LAURENCE
Be plain good son, and homely in thy drift;   55
Riddling confession finds but riddling shrift.

ROMEO
Then plainly know my heart's dear love is set
On the fair daughter of rich Capulet.
As mine on hers, so hers is set on mine,
And all combined, save what thou must combine   60
By holy marriage. When, and where, and how,
We met, we wooed, and made exchange of vow.
I'll tell thee as we pass, but this I pray,
That thou consent to marry us to-day.

FRIAR LAURENCE
Holy Saint Francis, what a change is here!   65
Is Rosaline that thou didst love so dear
So soon forsaken? Young men's love then lies
Not truly in their hearts, but in their eyes.
Jesu Maria, what a deal of brine
Hath washed thy sallow cheeks for Rosaline!   70
How much salt water thrown away in waste,
To season love, that of it doth not taste!
The sun not yet thy sighs from heaven clears,
Thy old groans yet ring in mine ancient ears.
Lo here upon thy cheek the stain doth sit   75
Of an old tear that is not washed off yet.
If e'er thou wast thyself, and these woes thine,
Thou and these woes were all for Rosaline.
And art thou changed? Pronounce this sentence then,
Women may fall, when there's no strength in men.   80

ROMEO
Thou chid'st me oft for loving Rosaline.

FRIAR LAURENCE
For doting, not for loving, pupil mine.

ROMEO
And bad'st me bury love.

FRIAR LAURENCE
                            Not in a grave,
To lay one in another out to have.
ROMEO
I pray thee chide me not, her I love now   85
Doth grace for grace, and love for love allow.
The other did not so.
FRIAR LAURENCE
                            Oh she knew well
Thy love did read by rote, that could not spell.
But come young waverer, come go with me,
In one respect I'll thy assistant be;   90
For this alliance may so happy prove,
To turn your households' rancour to pure love.
ROMEO
O let us hence, I stand on sudden haste.
FRIAR LAURENCE
Wisely and slow, they stumble that run fast.
                                    [*Exeunt.*]

SCENE FOUR.

*Verona. A street. Enter Benvolio
and Mercutio.*

MERCUTIO
Where the devil should this Romeo be?
Came he not home to-night?
BENVOLIO
Not to his father's; I spoke with his man.
MERCUTIO
Why that same pale hard-hearted wench, that Rosaline,
Torments him so, that he will sure run mad.   5
BENVOLIO
Tybalt, the kinsman to old Capulet,

Hath sent a letter to his father's house.
MERCUTIO
A challenge, on my life.
BENVOLIO
Romeo will answer it.
MERCUTIO
Any man that can write may answer a letter.   10
BENVOLIO
Nay, he will answer the letter's master, how he dares
being dared.
MERCUTIO
Alas poor Romeo, he is already dead, stabbed with a
white wench's black eye, run through the ear with a
love-song, the very pin of his heart cleft with the   15
blind bow-boy's butt-shaft; and is he a man to en-
counter Tybalt?
BENVOLIO
Why what is Tybalt?
MERCUTIO
More than Prince of Cats. O he's the courageous   20
captain of compliments. He fights as you sing prick-
song, keeps time, distance, and proportion; he rests his
minim rests, one, two, and the third in your bosom;
the very butcher of a silk button, a duellist, a duellist;
a gentleman of the very first house, of the first and   25
second cause. Ah the immortal passado, the punto reverso, the hay!
BENVOLIO
The what?
MERCUTIO
The pox of such antic lisping affecting fantasticoes,
these new tuners of accent! By Jesu a very good   30
blade—a very tall man—a very good whore! Why,
is not this a lamentable thing, grandsire, that we
should be thus afflicted with these strange flies, these
fashion-mongers, these pardon-me's, who stand so
much on the new form that they cannot sit at ease   35
on the old bench? O their bones, their bones!
[Enter Romeo.]

BENVOLIO
Here comes Romeo, here comes Romeo.

MERCUTIO
Without his roe, like a dried herring. O flesh, flesh,
how art thou fishified! Now is he for the numbers
that Petrarch flowed in; Laura to his lady was a
kitchen-wench, marry she had a better love to be-
rhyme her; Dido a dowdy, Cleopatra a gipsy, Helen
and Hero, hildings and harlots; Thisbe a gray eye or
so, but not to the purpose—Signior Romeo, bon jour.   45
There's a French salutation to your French slop. You
gave us the counterfeit fairly last night.

ROMEO
Good morrow to you both. What counterfeit did I
give you?   50

MERCUTIO
The slip sir, the slip, can you not conceive?

ROMEO
Pardon good Mercutio, my business was great, and
in such a case as mine a man may strain courtesy.   55

MERCUTIO
That's as much as to say, such a case as yours
constrains a man to bow in the hams.

ROMEO
Meaning to curtsy.

MERCUTIO
Thou hast most kindly hit it.

ROMEO
A most courteous exposition.   60

MERCUTIO
Nay I am the very pink of courtesy.

ROMEO
Pink for flower.

MERCUTIO
Right.

ROMEO
Why then is my pump well flowered.

MERCUTIO
Sure wit. Follow me this jest now, till thou hast   65

worn out thy pump, that when the single sole of
it is worn, the jest may remain after the wearing
solely singular.

ROMEO

O single-soled jest, solely singular for the single-
ness.   70

MERCUTIO

Come between us good Benvolio; my wits faints.

ROMEO

Switch and spurs, switch and spurs; or I'll cry a
match.

MERCUTIO

Nay, if our wits run the wild-goose chase, I am   75
done; for thou hast more of the wild goose in one
of thy wits than I am sure I have in my whole five.
Was I with you there for the goose?

ROMEO

Thou wast never with me for anything, when thou
wast not there for the goose.   80

MERCUTIO

I will bite thee by the ear for that jest.

ROMEO

Nay good goose, bite not.

MERCUTIO

Thy wit is very bitter sweeting, it is most sharp
sauce.

ROMEO

And is it not then well served in to a sweet goose?   85

MERCUTIO

O here's a wit of cheveril, that stretches from an inch
narrow to an ell broad.

ROMEO

I stretch it out for that word broad, which added to
the goose proves thee far and wide a broad goose.   90

MERCUTIO

Why, is not this better now than groaning for love?
Now art thou sociable, now art thou Romeo; now
art thou what thou art, by art as well as by nature, for
this drivelling love is like a great natural that runs   95
lolling up and down to hide his bauble in a hole.

BENVOLIO
Stop there, stop there.

MERCUTIO
Thou desirest me to stop in my tale against the hair.   100

BENVOLIO
Thou wouldest else have made thy tale large.

MERCUTIO
O thou art deceived; I would have made it short, for
I was come to the whole depth of my tale, and meant
indeed to occupy the argument no longer.   105

[Enter Nurse and Peter.]

ROMEO
Here's goodly gear! A sail, a sail!

MERCUTIO
Two, two; a shirt and a smock.

NURSE
Peter.   110

PETER
Anon.

NURSE
My fan Peter.

MERCUTIO
Good Peter, to hide her face, for her fan's the fairer
face.

NURSE
God ye good morrow gentlemen.   115

MERCUTIO
God ye good den fair gentlewoman.

NURSE
Is it good den?

MERCUTIO
'Tis no less, I tell ye, for the bawdy hand of the dial
is now upon the prick of noon.

NURSE
Out upon you, what a man are you!   120

ROMEO
One, gentlewoman, that God hath made for himself
to mar.

NURSE
By my troth it is well said, for himself to mar quoth

'a? Gentlemen, can any of you tell me where I may
find the young Romeo?   125

NURSE

ROMEO

I can tell you, but young Romeo will be older when
you have found him than he was when you sought
him. I am the youngest of that name, for fault of a
worse.

NURSE

You say well.   130

MERCUTIO

Yea, is the worst well? Very well took, i' faith, wisely,
wisely.

NURSE

If you be he sir, I desire some confidence with you.

BENVOLIO

She will indite him to some supper.   135

MERCUTIO

A bawd, a bawd, a bawd! So ho!

ROMEO

What hast thou found?

MERCUTIO

No hare sir, unless a hare sir, in a Lenten pie, that
is something stale and hoar ere it be spent.

[Sings.] 140

An old hare hoar,
And an old hare hoar,
Is very good meat in Lent.
But a hare that is hoar
Is too much for a score,   145
When it hoars ere it be spent.

Romeo, will you come to your father's? We'll to
dinner thither.

ROMEO

I will follow you.

MERCUTIO

Farewell ancient lady; farewell, [sings] Lady, lady,   150
lady.

[Exeunt Mercutio and Benvolio.]

NURSE
I pray you sir, what saucy merchant was this that was
so full of his ropery?

ROMEO
A gentleman, nurse, that loves to hear himself talk,   155
and will speak more in a minute than he will stand to
in a month.

NURSE
An 'a speak any thing against me, I'll take him down,
an 'a were lustier than he is, and twenty such Jacks;
and if I cannot, I'll find those that shall. Scurvy   160
knave, I am none of his flirt-gills, I am none of his
skains-mates. [*To Peter.*] And thou must stand by
too and suffer every knave to use me at his pleasure?

PETER
I saw no man use you at his pleasure; if I had, my   165
weapon should quickly have been out, I warrant you:
I dare draw as soon as another man, if I see occasion
in a good quarrel, and the law on my side.

NURSE
Now afore God I am so vexed, that every part   170
about me quivers. Scurvy knave! Pray you sir a
word: and as I told you, my young lady bid me
enquire you out; what she bid me say, I will keep
to myself; but first let me tell ye, if ye should lead
her in a fool's paradise, as they say, it were a very   175
gross kind of behaviour, as they say; for the gentlewoman is young; and therefore, if you should deal
double with her, truly it were an ill thing to be offered
to any gentlewoman, and very weak dealing.   180

ROMEO
Nurse, commend me to thy lady and mistress. I protest
unto thee—

NURSE
Good heart, and i' faith I will tell her as much. Lord,
lord, she will be a joyful woman.   185

ROMEO
What wilt thou tell her, nurse? Thou dost not mark
me.

NURSE

I will tell her sir, that you do protest, which as I take
it is a gentlemanlike offer.   190

ROMEO

Bid her devise
Some means to come to shrift this afternoon,
And there she shall at Friar Laurence' cell
Be shrived and married. Here is for thy pains.

NURSE

No truly sir, not a penny.   195

ROMEO

Go to, I say you shall.

NURSE

This afternoon sir? Well, she shall be there.

ROMEO

And stay good nurse behind the abbey wall,
Within this hour my man shall be with thee,   200
And bring thee cords made like a tackled stair,
Which to the high top-gallant of my joy
Must be my convoy in the secret night.
Farewell; be trusty, and I'll quit thy pains.
Farewell, commend me to thy mistress.   205

NURSE

Now God in heaven bless thee. Hark you sir.

ROMEO

What sayst thou my dear nurse?

NURSE

Is your man secret? Did you ne'er hear say,
Two may keep counsel, putting one away?

ROMEO

I warrant thee my man's as true as steel.   210

NURSE

Well sir, my mistress is the sweetest lady. Lord, lord,
when 'twas a little prating thing. O there is a nobleman
in town, one Paris, that would fain lay knife aboard;
but she good soul had as lief see a toad, a very toad,
as see him. I anger her sometimes, and tell her that   215
Paris is the properer man, but I'll warrant you, when
I say so, she looks as pale as any clout in the versal

world. Doth not rosemary and Romeo begin both
with a letter?   220
    ROMEO
Ay nurse, what of that? Both with an R.
    NURSE
Ah mocker, that's the dog's name; R is for the—
no, I know it begins with some other letter. And she
hath the prettiest sententious of it, of you and rose-   225
mary, that it would do you good to hear it.
    ROMEO
Commend me to thy lady.
    NURSE
Ay, a thousand times. [*Exit Romeo.*] Peter!   230
    PETER
Anon.
    NURSE [*gives him her fan to carry*]
Before, and apace.   [*Exeunt.*]

SCENE FIVE.

Verona. Capulet's orchard.
Enter Juliet.

    JULIET
The clock struck nine when I did send the nurse;
In half an hour she promised to return.
Perchance she cannot meet him—that's not so—
O she is lame, love's heralds should be thoughts,
Which ten times faster glide than the sun's beams,   5
Driving back shadows over louring hills.
Therefore do nimble-pinioned doves draw love,
And therefore hath the wind-swift Cupid wings.
Now is the sun upon the highmost hill

Of this day's journey, and from nine till twelve   10
Is three long hours, yet she is not come.
Had she affections and warm youthful blood,
She would be as swift in motion as a ball;
My words would bandy her to my sweet love,
And his to me.   15
But old folks, many feign as they were dead,
Unwieldy, slow, heavy and pale as lead.

                              [Enter Nurse and Peter.]

O God she comes! O honey nurse what news?
Hast thou met with him? Send thy man away.

        NURSE

Peter, stay at the gate.   *[Exit Peter.]*   20

        JULIET

Now good sweet nurse—o lord, why look'st thou sad?
Though news be sad, yet tell them merrily.
If good, thou sham'st the music of sweet news,
By playing it to me with so sour a face.

        NURSE

I am aweary, give me leave awhile.   25
Fie how my bones ache, what a jaunce have I had!

        JULIET

I would thou hadst my bones, and I thy news.
Nay come I pray thee speak, good, good nurse speak.

        NURSE

Jesu, what haste! Can you not stay awhile?
Do you not see that I am out of breath?   30

        JULIET

How art thou out of breath, when thou hast breath
To say to me that thou art out of breath?
The excuse that thou dost make in this delay
Is longer than the tale thou dost excuse.
Is thy news good or bad? Answer to that.   35
Say either, and I'll stay the circumstance.
Let me be satisfied, is't good or bad?

        NURSE

Well, you have made a simple choice, you know
not how to choose a man. Romeo? No, not he, though
his face be better than any man's, yet his leg excels   40
all men's; and for a hand and a foot and a body,

though they be not to be talked on, yet they are past
compare. He is not the flower of courtesy, but I'll
warrant him, as gentle as a lamb. Go thy ways wench,
serve God. What, have you dined at home?   45
  JULIET
No, no. But all this did I know before.
What says he of our marriage, what of that?
  NURSE
Lord how my head aches, what a head have I!
It beats as it would fall in twenty pieces.   50
My back a tother side, ah my back, my back!
Beshrew your heart for sending me about
To catch my death with jauncing up and down.
  JULIET
I' faith I am sorry that thou art not well.
Sweet, sweet, sweet nurse, tell me what says my love?   55
  NURSE
Your love says, like an honest gentleman, and a
courteous, and a kind, and a handsome, and I warrant
a virtuous—where is your mother?
  JULIET
Where is my mother? Why she is within,   60
Where should she be? How oddly thou repliest!
Your love says like an honest gentleman,
Where is your mother?
  NURSE
     O God's lady dear,
Are you so hot? Marry come up I trow,
Is this the poultice for my aching bones?   65
Henceforward do your messages yourself.
  JULIET
Here's such a coil. Come, what says Romeo?
  NURSE
Have you got leave to go to shrift to-day?
  JULIET
I have.
  NURSE
Then hie you hence to Friar Laurence' cell,   70
There stays a husband to make you a wife.
Now comes the wanton blood up in your cheeks,

They'll be in scarlet straight at any news.
Hie you to church. I must another way,
To fetch a ladder by the which your love   75
Must climb a bird's nest soon when it is dark.
I am the drudge, and toil in your delight.
But you shall bear the burden soon at night.
Go. I'll to dinner. Hie you to the cell.
                    JULIET
Hie to high fortune! Honest nurse farewell.   80
                                        [*Exeunt.*]

SCENE SIX.

Verona. Friar Laurence's cell.
Enter Friar Laurence and Romeo.

        FRIAR LAURENCE
So smile the heavens upon this holy act,
That after-hours with sorrow chide us not.
        ROMEO
Amen, amen, but come what sorrow can,
It cannot countervail the exchange of joy
That one short minute gives me in her sight.   5
Do thou but close our hands with holy words,
Then love-devouring death do what he dare,
It is enough I may but call her mine.
        FRIAR LAURENCE
These violent delights have violent ends,
And in their triumph die; like fire and powder,   10
Which as they kiss consume. The sweetest honey
Is loathsome in his own deliciousness,
And in the taste confounds the appetite.
Therefore love moderately, long love doth so;
Too swift arrives as tardy as too slow. [*Enter Juliet.*] 15
Here comes the lady. O so light a foot
Will ne'er wear out the everlasting flint.
A lover may bestride the gossamers

That idles in the wanton summer air,
And yet not fall; so light is vanity.   20

    JULIET

Good even to my ghostly confessor.

    FRIAR LAURENCE

Romeo shall thank thee daughter for us both.

    JULIET

As much to him, else is his thanks too much.

    ROMEO

Ah, Juliet, if the measure of thy joy
Be heaped like mine, and that thy skill be more   25
To blazon it, then sweeten with thy breath
This neighbour air, and let rich music's tongue
Unfold the imagined happiness that both
Receive in either by this dear encounter.

    JULIET

Conceit, more rich in matter than in words,   30
Brags of his substance, not of ornament.
They are but beggars that can count their worth.
But my true love is grown to such excess,
I cannot sum up sum of half my wealth.

    FRIAR LAURENCE

Come, come with me, and we will make short work.   35
For by your leaves, you shall not stay alone,
Till holy Church incorporate two in one.   [*Exeunt.*]

ACT III

SCENE ONE.

Verona. A public place. Enter Mercutio,
Benvolio, Page, and Servants.

BENVOLIO

I pray thee good Mercutio, let's retire.
The day is hot, the Capulets abroad;
And if we meet we shall not 'scape a brawl,
For now these hot days, is the mad blood stirring.

MERCUTIO

Thou art like one of these fellows that when he enters   5
the confines of a tavern claps me his sword upon the
table, and says, God send me no need of thee; and by
the operation of the second cup draws him on the
drawer, when indeed there is no need.   10

BENVOLIO

Am I like such a fellow?

MERCUTIO

Come, come, thou art as hot a Jack in thy mood
as any in Italy; and as soon moved to be moody, and
as soon moody to be moved.

BENVOLIO

And what to?   15

MERCUTIO

Nay an there were two such we should have none
shortly, for one would kill the other. Thou? Why thou
wilt quarrel with a man that hath a hair more, or a
hair less, in his beard than thou hast; thou wilt quarrel
with a man for cracking nuts, having no other reason   20

but because thou hast hazel eyes; what eye, but such
an eye, would spy out such a quarrel? Thy head is
as full of quarrels as an egg is full of meat, and yet
thy head hath been beaten as addle as an egg for   25
quarrelling. Thou hast quarrelled with a man for
coughing in the street, because he hath wakened thy
dog that hath lain asleep in the sun. Didst thou not
fall out with a tailor for wearing his new doublet   30
before Easter? With another for tying his new shoes
with old riband? And yet thou wilt tutor me from
quarrelling.

BENVOLIO

An I were so apt to quarrel as thou art, any man
should buy the fee-simple of my life for an hour and   35
a quarter.

MERCUTIO

The fee-simple? O simple!

[*Enter Tybalt, Petruchio, and other Capulets.*]

BENVOLIO

By my head, here comes the Capulets.

MERCUTIO

By my heel, I care not.

TYBALT

Follow me close, for I will speak to them. Gentle-   40
men, good den; a word with one of you.

MERCUTIO

And but one word with one of us? Couple it with
something, make it a word and a blow.

TYBALT

You shall find me apt enough to that sir, an you will
give me occasion.   45

MERCUTIO

Could you not take some occasion without giving?

TYBALT

Mercutio, thou consortest with Romeo.

MERCUTIO

Consort? What, dost thou make us minstrels? An
thou make minstrels of us, look to hear nothing but   50
discords. Here's my fiddlestick, here's that shall make
you dance. Zounds, consort!

BENVOLIO

We talk here in the public haunt of men.
Either withdraw unto some private place,
Or reason coldly of your grievances,   55
Or else depart; here all eyes gaze on us.

MERCUTIO

Men's eyes were made to look, and let them gaze.
I will not budge for no man's pleasure, I.

[*Enter Romeo.*]

TYBALT

Well, peace be with you sir, here comes my man.

MERCUTIO

But I'll be hanged sir, if he wear your livery.   60
Marry go before to field, he'll be your follower;
Your worship in that sense may call him man.

TYBALT

Romeo, the love I bear thee can afford
No better term than this—thou art a villain.

ROMEO

Tybalt, the reason that I have to love thee   65
Doth much excuse the appertaining rage
To such a greeting—villain am I none.
Therefore farewell, I see thou knowest me not.

TYBALT

Boy, this shall not excuse the injuries
That thou hast done me, therefore turn and draw. 70

ROMEO

I do protest I never injured thee,
But love thee better than thou canst devise,
Till thou shalt know the reason of my love.
And so good Capulet, which name I tender
As dearly as mine own, be satisfied.   75

MERCUTIO

O calm, dishonourable, vile submission!
Alla stoccata carries it away.   [*Draws.*]
Tybalt, you rat-catcher, will you walk?

TYBALT

What wouldst thou have with me?

MERCUTIO

Good King of Cats, nothing but one of your nine   80

lives, that I mean to make bold withal, and as you
shall use me hereafter dry-beat the rest of the eight.
Will you pluck your sword out of his pilcher by
the ears? Make haste, lest mine be about your ears
ere it be out.   85

TYBALT
I am for you.   [Draws.]

ROMEO
Gentle Mercutio, put thy rapier up.

MERCUTIO
Come sir, your passado.   [They fight.]

ROMEO
Draw Benvolio, beat down their weapons.
Gentlemen, for shame, forbear this outrage.   90
Tybalt, Mercutio, the Prince expressly hath
Forbid this bandying in Verona streets.
Hold Tybalt. Good Mercutio—
          [Tybalt thrusts Mercutio, and exits with other
          Capulets.]

MERCUTIO
                                        I am hurt.
A plague a both your houses, I am sped.
Is he gone and hath nothing?

BENVOLIO
                                        What, art thou hurt?   95

MERCUTIO
Ay, ay, a scratch, a scratch; marry 'tis enough.
Where is my page? Go villain, fetch a surgeon.
                                        [Exit Page.]

ROMEO
Courage man, the hurt cannot be much.

MERCUTIO
No 'tis not so deep as a well, nor so wide as a church
door, but 'tis enough, 'twill serve. Ask for me to-   100
morrow, and you shall find me a grave man. I am
peppered, I warrant, for this world. A plague a both
your houses! Zounds, a dog, a rat, a mouse, a cat, to
scratch a man to death! A braggart, a rogue, a villain,
that fights by the book of arithmetic! Why the devil   105

came you between us? I was hurt under your arm.
ROMEO
I thought it all for the best.
MERCUTIO
Help me into some house Benvolio,   110
Or I shall faint. A plague a both your houses!
They have made worms' meat of me. I have it,
And soundly too. Your houses!
     [Exit, led by Benvolio and Servants.]
ROMEO
This gentleman, the Prince's near ally,
My very friend, hath got this mortal hurt   115
In my behalf; my reputation stained
With Tybalt's slander, Tybalt that an hour
Hath been my cousin. O sweet Juliet,
Thy beauty hath made me effeminate,
And in my temper softened valour's steel.   120
      [Enter Benvolio.]
BENVOLIO
O Romeo, Romeo, brave Mercutio is dead.
That gallant spirit hath aspired the clouds,
Which too untimely here did scorn the earth.
ROMEO
This day's black fate on more days doth depend,
This but begins the woe others must end.   125
      [Enter Tybalt.]
BENVOLIO
Here comes the furious Tybalt back again.
ROMEO
Again? In triumph! And Mercutio slain.
Away to heaven respective lenity,
And fire-eyed fury be my conduct now
Now Tybalt take the villain back again   130
That late thou gavest me, for Mercutio's soul
Is but a little way above our heads,
Staying for thine to keep him company.
Either thou or I, or both, must go with him.
TYBALT
Thou wretched boy, that didst consort him here,   135
Shalt with him hence.

ROMEO

>This shall determine that.
>>[*They fight; Tybalt falls.*]

BENVOLIO

Romeo away, be gone.
The citizens are up, and Tybalt slain.
Stand not amazed, the Prince will doom thee death,
If thou art taken. Hence, be gone, away.   140

ROMEO

O I am fortune's fool!

BENVOLIO

>Why dost thou stay?
>>[*Exit Romeo. Enter citizens.*]

CITIZEN

Which way ran he that killed Mercutio?
Tybalt, that murderer, which way ran he?

BENVOLIO

There lies that Tybalt.

CITIZEN

>Up sir, go with me.
I charge thee in the Prince's name obey.   145
>[*Enter Prince, Montague, Capulet, Lady Mon-
>tague and Lady Capulet, attended.*]

PRINCE

Where are the vile beginners of this fray?

BENVOLIO

O noble Prince, I can discover all
The unlucky manage of this fatal brawl.
There lies the man, slain by young Romeo,
That slew thy kinsman, brave Mercutio.   150

LADY CAPULET

Tybalt, my cousin, o my brother's child!
O Prince, o cousin, husband! O the blood is spilt
Of my dear kinsman! Prince, as thou art true,
For blood of ours shed blood of Montague.
O cousin, cousin!   155

PRINCE

Benvolio, who began this bloody fray?

BENVOLIO

Tybalt here slain, whom Romeo's hand did slay.

Romeo, that spoke him fair, bid him bethink
How nice the quarrel was, and urged withal
Your high displeasure. All this, uttered   160
With gentle breath, calm look, knees humbly bowed,
Could not take truce with the unruly spleen
Of Tybalt deaf to peace, but that he tilts
With piercing steel at bold Mercutio's breast;
Who, all as hot, turns deadly point to point,   165
And with a martial scorn, with one hand beats
Cold death aside, and with the other sends
It back to Tybalt, whose dexterity
Retorts it. Romeo he cries aloud,
Hold friends, friends part, and swifter than his tongue,   170
His agile arm beats down their fatal points,
And 'twixt them rushes; underneath whose arm
An envious thrust from Tybalt hit the life
Of stout Mercutio, and then Tybalt fled;
But by and by comes back to Romeo,   175
Who had but newly entertained revenge,
And to't they go like lightning, for ere I
Could draw to part them was stout Tybalt slain.
And as he fell, did Romeo turn and fly.
This is the truth, or let Benvolio die.   180
    LADY CAPULET
He is a kinsman to the Montague;
Affection makes him false, he speaks not true.
Some twenty of them fought in this black strife,
And all those twenty could but kill one life.
I beg for justice, which thou, Prince, must give.   185
Romeo slew Tybalt, Romeo must not live.
    PRINCE
Romeo slew him, he slew Mercutio.
Who now the price of his dear blood doth owe?
    MONTAGUE
Not Romeo, Prince, he was Mercutio's friend;
His fault concludes but what the law should end,   190
The life of Tybalt.
    PRINCE
            And for that offence
Immediately we do exile him hence.

I have an interest in your hate's proceeding:
My blood for your rude brawls doth lie a-bleeding.
But I'll amerce you with so strong a fine,   195
That you shall all repent the loss of mine.
I will be deaf to pleading and excuses,
Nor tears nor prayers shall purchase out abuses.
Therefore use none. Let Romeo hence in haste,
Else, when he is found, that hour is his last.   200
Bear hence this body, and attend our will.
Mercy but murders, pardoning those that kill.
                                            [*Exeunt.*]

SCENE TWO.

Verona. Capulet's orchard. Enter Juliet.

JULIET

Gallop apace, you fiery-footed steeds,
Towards Phoebus' lodging; such a wagoner
As Phaethon would whip you to the west,
And bring in cloudy night immediately.
Spread thy close curtain, love-performing night,   5
That runaway's eyes may wink, and Romeo
Leap to these arms, untalked of and unseen.
Lovers can see to do their amorous rites,
And by their own beauties; or if love be blind,
It best agrees with night. Come civil night,   10
Thou sober-suited matron all in black,
And learn me how to lose a winning match,
Played for a pair of stainless maidenhoods.
Hood my unmanned blood bating in my cheeks
With thy black mantle, till strange love grow bold,   15
Think true love acted simple modesty.
Come night, come Romeo, come thou day in night;
For thou wilt lie upon the wings of night,
Whiter than new snow upon a raven's back.
Come gentle night, come loving black-browed night,   20
Give me my Romeo, and when he shall die,

Take him and cut him out in little stars,
And he will make the face of heaven so fine,
That all the world will be in love with night,
And pay no worship to the garish sun.   25
O I have brought the mansion of a love,
But not possessed it, and though I am sold,
Not yet enjoyed. So tedious is this day,
As is the night before some festival
To an impatient child that hath new robes   30
And may not wear them.

> [*Enter Nurse with ladder of cords.*]
>   O here comes my nurse.

And she brings news; and every tongue that speaks
But Romeo's name speaks heavenly eloquence.
Now nurse, what news? What, hast thou there the cords
That Romeo bid thee fetch?

    NURSE

                Ay, ay, the cords.   35
                [*Throws them down.*]

    JULIET

Ay me, what news? Why dost thou wring thy hands?

    NURSE

Ah weladay, he's dead, he's dead, he's dead.
We are undone lady, we are undone.
Alack the day, he's gone, he's killed, he's dead.

    JULIET

Can heaven be so envious?

    NURSE

                Romeo can,   40
Though heaven cannot. O Romeo, Romeo,
Who ever would have thought it? Romeo!

    JULIET

What devil art thou, that dost torment me thus?
This torture should be roared in dismal hell.
Hath Romeo slain himself? Say thou but ay,   45
And that bare vowel I shall poison more
Than the death-darting eye of cockatrice.
I am not I, if there be such an I;
Or those eyes shut that makes thee answer ay.

If he be slain, say ay, or if not, no,   50
Brief sounds determine of my weal or woe.
   NURSE
I saw the wound, I saw it with mine eyes—
God save the mark—here on his manly breast.
A piteous corse, a bloody piteous corse,
Pale, pale as ashes, all bedaubed in blood,   55
All in gore-blood. I swounded at the sight.
   JULIET
O break, my heart, poor bankrupt, break at once.
To prison eyes, ne'er look on liberty.
Vile earth, to earth resign; end motion here;
And thou and Romeo press one heavy bier.   60
   NURSE
O Tybalt, Tybalt, the best friend I had,
O courteous Tybalt, honest gentleman,
That ever I should live to see thee dead!
   JULIET
What storm is this that blows so contrary?
Is Romeo slaughtered? And is Tybalt dead?   65
My dearest cousin, and my dearer lord?
Then dreadful trumpet, sound the general doom,
For who is living, if those two are gone?
   NURSE
Tybalt is gone, and Romeo banished.
Romeo that killed him, he is banished.   70
   JULIET
O God, did Romeo's hand shed Tybalt's blood?
   NURSE
It did, it did, alas the day, it did!
   JULIET
O serpent heart, hid with a flow'ring face!
Did ever dragon keep so fair a cave?
Beautiful tyrant, fiend angelical,   75
Dove-feathered raven, wolvish-ravening lamb,
Despised substance of divinest show,
Just opposite to what thou justly seem'st,
A damned saint, an honourable villain!
O nature, what hadst thou to do in hell,   80
When thou didst bower the spirit of a fiend

In mortal paradise of such sweet flesh?
Was ever book containing such vile matter
So fairly bound? O that deceit should dwell
In such a gorgeous palace!

NURSE

               There's no trust,   85
No faith, no honesty in men; all perjured,
All forsworn, all naught, all dissemblers.
Ah, where's my man? Give me some aqua-vitae.
These griefs, these woes, these sorrows make me old.
Shame come to Romeo.

JULIET

               Blistered be thy tongue   90
For such a wish. He was not born to shame.
Upon his brow shame is ashamed to sit;
For 'tis a throne where honour may be crowned
Sole monarch of the universal earth.
O what a beast was I to chide at him!   95

NURSE

Will you speak well of him that killed your cousin?

JULIET

Shall I speak ill of him that is my husband?
Ah poor my lord, what tongue shall smooth thy name,
When I thy three-hours wife have mangled it?
But wherefore, villain, didst thou kill my cousin?   100
That villain cousin would have killed my husband.
Back foolish tears, back to your native spring,
Your tributary drops belong to woe,
Which you mistaking offer up to joy.
My husband lives, that Tybalt would have slain,   105
And Tybalt's dead, that would have slain my husband.
All this is comfort, wherefore weep I then?
Some word there was, worser than Tybalt's death,
That murdered me, I would forget it fain;
But o it presses to my memory,   110
Like damned guilty deeds to sinners' minds.
Tybalt is dead and Romeo banished.
That banished, that one word banished.
Hath slain ten thousand Tybalts. Tybalt's death
Was woe enough if it had ended there.   115

Or, if sour woe delights in fellowship,
And needly will be ranked with other griefs,
Why followed not, when she said Tybalt's dead,
Thy father or thy mother, nay or both,
Which modern lamentation might have moved?   120
But with a rearward following Tybalt's death,
Romeo is banished—to speak that word,
Is father, mother, Tybalt, Romeo, Juliet,
All slain, all dead. Romeo is banished.
There is no end, no limit, measure, bound,   125
In that word's death; no words can that woe sound.
Where is my father and my mother, nurse?

    N U R S E
Weeping and wailing over Tybalt's corse.
Will you go to them? I will bring you thither.

    J U L I E T
Wash they his wounds with tears? Mine shall be spent,   130
When theirs are dry, for Romeo's banishment.
Take up those cords. Poor ropes you are beguiled,
Both you and I, for Romeo is exiled.
He made you for a highway to my bed,
But I a maid die maiden-widowed.   135
Come cords, come nurse, I'll to my wedding-bed,
And death, not Romeo, take my maidenhead.

    N U R S E
Hie to your chamber, I'll find Romeo
To comfort you. I wot well where he is.
Hark ye, your Romeo will be here at night.   140
I'll to him, he is hid at Laurence' cell.

    J U L I E T
O find him, give this ring to my true knight,
And bid him come, to take his last farewell.

                                        [Exeunt.]

SCENE THREE.

Verona. Friar Laurence's cell.
Enter Friar Laurence.

FRIAR LAURENCE
Romeo come forth, come forth thou fearful man.
Affliction is enamoured of thy parts,
And thou art wedded to calamity.   [*Enter Romeo.*]

ROMEO
Father what news? What is the Prince's doom?
What sorrow craves acquaintance at my hand,   5
That I yet know not?
　　FRIAR LAURENCE
　　　　　　Too familiar
Is my dear son with such sour company.
I bring thee tidings of the Prince's doom.
　　ROMEO
What less than doomsday is the Prince's doom?
　　FRIAR LAURENCE
A gentler judgement vanished from his lips;   10
Not body's death, but body's banishment.
　　ROMEO
Ha, banishment? Be merciful, say death;
For exile hath more terror in his look,
Much more than death. Do not say banishment.
　　FRIAR LAURENCE
Hence from Verona art thou banished.   15
Be patient, for the world is broad and wide.
　　ROMEO
There is no world without Verona walls,
But purgatory, torture, hell itself.
Hence banished is banished from the world,
And world's exile is death. Then banished   20
Is death mis-termed. Calling death banished,
Thou cut'st my head off with a golden axe,
And smilest upon the stroke that murders me.
　　FRIAR LAURENCE
O deadly sin, o rude unthankfulness!

Thy fault our law calls death, but the kind Prince   25
Taking thy part hath rushed aside the law,
And turned that black word death to banishment.
This is dear mercy, and thou seest it not.
   ROMEO
'Tis torture and not mercy; heaven is here
Where Juliet lives; and every cat and dog,   30
And little mouse, every unworthy thing,
Live here in heaven, and may look on her,
But Romeo may not. More validity,
More honourable state, more courtship lives
In carrion flies than Romeo; they may seize   35
On the white wonder of dear Juliet's hand,
And steal immortal blessing from her lips,
Who even in pure and vestal modesty
Still blush, as thinking their own kisses sin.*
But Romeo may not, he is banished.   40
Flies may do this, but I from this must fly;
They are freemen, but I am banished.
Hadst thou no poison mixed, no sharp-ground knife,
No sudden mean of death, though ne'er so mean,   45
But—banished—to kill me? Banished?
O friar, the damned use that word in hell;
Howling attends it. How hast thou the heart,
Being a divine, a ghostly confessor,
A sin-absolver, and my friend professed,   50
To mangle me with that word banished?
This may flies do, when I from this must fly,
And sayest thou yet, that exile is not death?
   FRIAR LAURENCE
Thou fond mad man, hear me a little speak.
   ROMEO
O thou wilt speak again of banishment.
   FRIAR LAURENCE
I'll give thee armour to keep off that word,
Adversity's sweet milk, philosophy,   55
To comfort thee though thou art banished.

---

*Lines deleted in rewriting:

ROMEO

Yet banished? Hang up philosophy,
Unless philosophy can make a Juliet,
Displant a town, reverse a Prince's doom,
It helps not, it prevails not. Talk no more.   60

FRIAR LAURENCE

O then I see that mad men have no ears.

ROMEO

How should they when that wise men have no eyes?

FRIAR LAURENCE

Let me dispute with thee of thy estate.

ROMEO

Thou canst not speak of that thou dost not feel.
Wert thou as young as I, Juliet thy love,   65
An hour but married, Tybalt murdered,
Doting like me, and like me banished,
Then mightst thou speak, then mightst thou tear thy
    hair,
And fall upon the ground, as I do now,
Taking the measure of an unmade grave.   70

[*Nurse within knocks.*]

FRIAR LAURENCE

Arise. One knocks; good Romeo hide thyself.

ROMEO

Not I, unless the breath of heart-sick groans
Mist-like infold me from the search of eyes.

[*She knocks again.*]

FRIAR LAURENCE

Hark how they knock.—Who's there?—Romeo arise;
Thou wilt be taken.—Stay awhile.—Stand up.   75

[*Knock.*]

Run to my study.—By and by.—God's will,
What simpleness is this!—I come, I come.

[*Knock.*]

Who knocks so hard? Whence come you? What's your
    will?

NURSE [*within*]

Let me come in, and you shall know my errand.
I come from Lady Juliet.

FRIAR LAURENCE
                    Welcome then.   80
                                        [*Enter Nurse.*]

NURSE
O holy friar, o tell me holy friar,
Where's my lady's lord, where's Romeo?
FRIAR LAURENCE
There on the ground, with his own tears made drunk.
NURSE
O he is even in my mistress' case,
Just in her case. O woeful sympathy,   85
Piteous predicament! Even so lies she,
Blubbering and weeping, weeping and blubbering.
Stand up, stand up; stand an you be a man.
For Juliet's sake, for her sake rise and stand.
Why should you fall into so deep an O?   90
                                        [*He rises.*]

ROMEO
Nurse—
NURSE
Ah, sir, ah sir, death's the end of all.
ROMEO
Spakest thou of Juliet? How is it with her?
Doth not she think me an old murderer,
Now I have stained the childhood of our joy   95
With blood removed but little from her own?
Where is she? And how doth she? And what says
My concealed lady to our cancelled love?
NURSE
O she says nothing sir, but weeps and weeps,
And now falls on her bed, and then starts up,   100
And Tybalt calls, and then on Romeo cries,
And then down falls again.
ROMEO
                    As if that name,
Shot from the deadly level of a gun,
Did murder her; as that name's cursed hand
Murdered her kinsman. O tell me friar, tell me,   105
In what vile part of this anatomy

Doth my name lodge? Tell me, that I may sack
The hateful mansion.   [*Draws his dagger.*]
   FRIAR LAURENCE
                Hold thy desperate hand.
Art thou a man? Thy form cries out thou art.
Thy tears are womanish, thy wild acts denote   110
The unreasonable fury of a beast.
Unseemly woman in a seeming man,
Or ill-beseeming beast in seeming both!
Thou hast amazed me. By my holy order,
I thought thy disposition better tempered.   115
Hast thou slain Tybalt? Wilt thou slay thyself,
And slay thy lady that in thy life lives,
By doing damned hate upon thyself?
Why railest thou on thy birth, the heaven, and earth,
Since birth, and heaven, and earth, all three do meet   120
In thee at once; which thou at once wouldst lose?
Fie, fie, thou shamest thy shape, thy love, thy wit,
Which like a usurer abound'st in all,
And usest none in that true use indeed
Which should bedeck thy shape, thy love, thy wit.   125
Thy noble shape is but a form of wax,
Digressing from the valour of a man;
Thy dear love sworn but hollow perjury,
Killing that love which thou hast vowed to cherish;
Thy wit, that ornament to shape and love,   130
Misshapen in the conduct of them both,
Like powder in a skilless soldier's flask,
Is set afire by thine own ignorance,
And thou dismembered with thine own defence.
What, rouse thee man, thy Juliet is alive,   135
For whose dear sake thou wast but lately dead.
There art thou happy. Tybalt would kill thee,
But thou slewest Tybalt; there art thou happy too.
The law that threatened death becomes thy friend,
And turns it to exile; there art thou happy.   140
A pack of blessings light upon thy back,
Happiness courts thee in her best array,
But like a misbehaved and sullen wench,

Thou pouts upon thy fortune and thy love.
Take heed, take heed, for such die miserable.   145
Go get thee to thy love as was decreed,
Ascend her chamber, hence and comfort her;
But look thou stay not till the watch be set,
For then thou canst not pass to Mantua,
Where thou shalt live till we can find a time   150
To blaze your marriage, reconcile your friends,
Beg pardon of the Prince, and call thee back,
With twenty hundred thousand times more joy
Than thou went'st forth in lamentation.
Go before nurse, commend me to thy lady,   155
And bid her hasten all the house to bed,
Which heavy sorrow makes them apt unto.
Romeo is coming.

                    NURSE
O lord, I could have stayed here all the night
To hear good counsel. O what learning is!   160
My lord, I'll tell my lady you will come.

                    ROMEO
Do so, and bid my sweet prepare to chide.

                    NURSE
Here sir, a ring she bid me give you, sir.
Hie you, make haste, for it grows very late.   [Exit.]

                    ROMEO
How well my comfort is revived by this!   165

              FRIAR LAURENCE
Go hence; good night; and here stands all your state—
Either be gone before the watch be set,
Or by the break of day disguised from hence.
Sojourn in Mantua; I'll find out your man,
And he shall signify from time to time   170
Every good hap to you that chances here.
Give me thy hand, 'tis late. Farewell; good night.

                    ROMEO
But that a joy past joy calls out on me,
It were a grief, so brief to part with thee.
Farewell.   [Exeunt.] 175

SCENE FOUR.

Verona. A hall in Capulet's house.
Enter Capulet, Lady Capulet, and Paris.

CAPULET
Things have fall'n out sir so unluckily,
That we have had no time to move our daughter.
Look you, she loved her kinsman Tybalt dearly,
And so did I. Well, we were born to die.
'Tis very late, she'll not come down to-night.   5
I promise you, but for your company,
I would have been abed an hour ago.
    PARIS
These times of woe afford no time to woo.
Madam good night, commend me to your daughter.
    LADY CAPULET
I will, and know her mind early to-morrow;   10
To-night she's mewed up to her heaviness.
    CAPULET
Sir Paris, I will make a desperate tender
Of my child's love. I think she will be ruled
In all respects by me; nay more, I doubt it not.
Wife, go you to her ere you go to bed,   15
Acquaint her here of my son Paris' love,
And bid her, mark you me, on Wednesday next—
But soft, what day is this?
    PARIS
                        Monday my lord.
    CAPULET
Monday? Ha, ha, well Wednesday is too soon.
A Thursday let it be, a Thursday, tell her,   20
She shall be married to this noble earl.
Will you be ready? Do you like this haste?
We'll keep no great ado—a friend or two.
For hark you, Tybalt being slain so late,
It may be thought we held him carelessly,   25

Being our kinsman, if we revel much.
Therefore we'll have some half a dozen friends,
And there an end. But what say you to Thursday?
    PARIS
My lord, I would that Thursday were to-morrow.
    CAPULET
Well get you gone, a Thursday be it then.   30
Go you to Juliet ere you go to bed;
Prepare her, wife, against this wedding-day.
Farewell my lord. Light to my chamber ho!
Afore me, it is so very late, that we
May call it early by and by. Good night.   35
                                        [*Exeunt.*]

SCENE FIVE.

Verona. Juliet's chamber.
Enter Romeo and Juliet above.

    JULIET
Wilt thou be gone? It is not yet near day.
It was the nightingale, and not the lark,
That pierced the fearful hollow of thine ear;
Nightly she sings on yond pomegranate tree.
Believe me love, it was the nightingale.   5
    ROMEO
It was the lark, the herald of the morn,
No nightingale. Look love, what envious streaks
Do lace the severing clouds in yonder east.
Night's candles are burnt out, and jocund day   10
Stands tiptoe on the misty mountain tops.
I must be gone and live, or stay and die.
    JULIET
Yond light is not day-light, I know it, I.
It is some meteor that the sun exhales,
To be to thee this night a torchbearer,

And light thee on thy way to Mantua.   15
Therefore stay yet, thou need'st not to be gone.
    R O M E O
Let me be ta'en, let me be put to death;
I am content, so thou wilt have it so.
I'll say yon gray is not the morning's eye,
'Tis but the pale reflex of Cynthia's brow.   20
Nor that is not the lark whose notes do beat
The vaulty heaven so high above our heads;
I have more care to stay than will to go.
Come death, and welcome, Juliet wills it so.
How is't my soul? Let's talk; it is not day.   25
    J U L I E T
It is, it is, hie hence, be gone, away!
It is the lark that sings so out of tune,
Straining harsh discords, and unpleasing sharps.
Some say the lark makes sweet division;
This doth not so, for she divideth us.   30
Some say the lark and loathed toad change eyes,
O now I would they had changed voices too,
Since arm from arm that voice doth us affray,
Hunting thee hence with hunt's-up to the day.
O now be gone; more light and light it grows.   35
    R O M E O
More light and light, more dark and dark our woes.
                     [*Enter Nurse.*]
    N U R S E
Madam.
    J U L I E T
Nurse.
    N U R S E
Your lady mother is coming to your chamber.
The day is broke, be wary, look about.   [*Exit.*]   40
    J U L I E T
Then window let day in, and let life out.
    R O M E O
Farewell, farewell. One kiss, and I'll descend.
               [*Goes down by the ladder.*]

JULIET

Art thou gone so, love, lord, ay husband, friend?
I must hear from thee every day in the hour,
For in a minute there are many days.   45
O by this count I shall be much in years,
Ere I again behold my Romeo.

ROMEO

Farewell.
I will omit no opportunity
That may convey my greetings, love, to thee.   50

JULIET

O think'st thou we shall ever meet again?

ROMEO

I doubt it not, and all these woes shall serve
For sweet discourses in our times to come.

JULIET

O God, I have an ill-divining soul.
Methinks I see thee now thou art so low,   55
As one dead in the bottom of a tomb.
Either my eyesight fails, or thou lookest pale.

ROMEO

And trust me love, in my eye so do you.
Dry sorrow drinks our blood. Adieu, adieu.
                                                  [Exit.]

JULIET

O fortune, fortune, all men call thee fickle;   60
If thou art fickle, what dost thou with him
That is renowned for faith? Be fickle, fortune;
For then I hope thou wilt not keep him long,
But send him back.

LADY CAPULET [within]
                    Ho daughter, are you up?   65

JULIET

Who is't that calls? It is my lady mother.
Is she not down so late, or up so early?
What unaccustomed cause procures her hither?
                              [Enter Lady Capulet.]

LADY CAPULET
Why how now Juliet?
    JULIET
                Madam I am not well.
    LADY CAPULET
Evermore weeping for your cousin's death?   70
What, wilt thou wash him from his grave with tears?
An if thou couldst, thou couldst not make him live.
Therefore have done; some grief shows much of love,
But much of grief shows still some want of wit.
    JULIET
Yet let me weep for such a feeling loss.   75
    LADY CAPULET
So shall you feel the loss, but not the friend
Which you weep for.
    JULIET
                Feeling so the loss,
I cannot choose but ever weep the friend.
    LADY CAPULET
Well girl, thou weep'st not so much for his death,
As that the villain lives which slaughtered him.   80
    JULIET
What villain madam?
    LADY CAPULET
                That same villain Romeo.
    JULIET [*aside*]
Villain and he be many miles asunder.—
God pardon him; I do with all my heart.
And yet no man like he doth grieve my heart.
    LADY CAPULET
That is because the traitor murderer lives.   85
    JULIET
Ay madam, from the reach of these my hands.
Would none but I might venge my cousin's death.
    LADY CAPULET
We will have vengeance for it, fear thou not,
Then weep no more. I'll send to one in Mantua,
Where that same banished runagate doth live,   90
Shall give him such an unaccustomed dram,

That he shall soon keep Tybalt company.
And then I hope thou wilt be satisfied.
    JULIET
Indeed I never shall be satisfied
With Romeo, till I behold him—dead—   95
Is my poor heart so for a kinsman vexed.
Madam, if you could find out but a man
To bear a poison, I would temper it,
That Romeo should upon receipt thereof
Soon sleep in quiet. O how my heart abhors   100
To hear him named—and cannot come to him—
To wreak the love I bore my cousin
Upon his body that hath slaughtered him.
    LADY CAPULET
Find thou the means, and I'll find such a man.
But now I'll tell thee joyful tidings girl.   105
    JULIET
And joy comes well in such a needy time.
What are they, beseech your ladyship?
    LADY CAPULET
Well, well, thou hast a careful father child,
One who to put thee from thy heaviness
Hath sorted out a sudden day of joy,   110
That thou expects not, nor I looked not for.
    JULIET
Madam, in happy time, what day is that?
    LADY CAPULET
Marry my child, early next Thursday morn,
The gallant, young, and noble gentleman,
The County Paris, at Saint Peter's Church,   115
Shall happily make thee there a joyful bride.
    JULIET
Now by Saint Peter's Church, and Peter too,
He shall not make me there a joyful bride.
I wonder at this haste, that I must wed
Ere he that should be husband comes to woo.   120
I pray you tell my lord and father, madam,
I will not marry yet, and when I do, I swear
It shall be Romeo, whom you know I hate,

Rather than Paris. These are news indeed.
LADY CAPULET
Here comes your father, tell him so yourself;   125
And see how he will take it at your hands.

                                  [Enter Capulet and Nurse.]
CAPULET
When the sun sets, the earth doth drizzle dew;
But for the sunset of my brother's son
It rains downright.
How now, a conduit, girl? What, still in tears?   130
Evermore showering? In one little body
Thou counterfeits a bark, a sea, a wind.
For still thy eyes, which I may call the sea,
Do ebb and flow with tears; the bark thy body is,
Sailing in this salt flood; the winds, thy sighs,   135
Who, raging with thy tears, and they with them,
Without a sudden calm, will overset
Thy tempest-tossed body. How now wife,
Have you delivered to her our decree?
LADY CAPULET
Ay sir, but she will none, she gives you thanks.   140
I would the fool were married to her grave.
CAPULET
Soft, take me with you, take me with you wife.
How will she none? Doth she not give us thanks?
Is she not proud? Doth she not count her blessed,
Unworthy as she is, that we have wrought   145
So worthy a gentleman to be her bridegroom?
JULIET
Not proud you have, but thankful that you have.
Proud can I never be of what I hate,
But thankful even for hate, that is meant love.
CAPULET
How, how, how, how, chop-logic, what is this?   150
Proud, and, I thank you, and, I thank you not;
And yet, not proud—mistress minion you,
Thank me no thankings, nor proud me no prouds,
But fettle your fine joints 'gainst Thursday next,
To go with Paris to Saint Peter's Church;   155
Or I will drag thee on a hurdle thither.

Out you green-sickness carrion, out you baggage,
You tallow-face!
    LADY CAPULET
                Fie, fie, what, are you mad?
    JULIET
Good father, I beseech you on my knees,
Hear me with patience, but to speak a word.   160
    CAPULET
Hang thee young baggage, disobedient wretch!
I tell thee what, get thee to church a Thursday,
Or never after look me in the face.
Speak not, reply not, do not answer me.
My fingers itch. Wife, we scarce thought us blessed,   165
That God had lent us but this only child;
But now I see this one is one too much,
And that we have a curse in having her.
Out on her, hilding!
    NURSE
                God in heaven bless her.
You are to blame my lord to rate her so.   170
    CAPULET
And why, my lady wisdom? Hold your tongue.
Good Prudence, smatter with your gossips, go.
    NURSE
I speak no treason.
    CAPULET
              O God ye god-den.
    NURSE
May not one speak?
    CAPULET
              Peace you mumbling fool.
Utter your gravity o'er a gossip's bowl,   175
For here we need it not.
    LADY CAPULET
              You are too hot.
    CAPULET
God's bread, it makes me mad.
Day, night, hour; tide, time; work, play;
Alone, in company; still my care hath been
To have her matched; and having now provided   180

A gentleman of princely parentage,
Of fair demesnes, youthful and nobly trained,
Stuffed as they say with honourable parts,
Proportioned as one's thought would wish a man—
And then to have a wretched puling fool,   185
A whining mammet, in her fortune's tender,
To answer, I'll not wed, I cannot love,
I am too young, I pray you pardon me—
But an you will not wed, I'll pardon you.
Graze where you will, you shall not house with me.   190
Look to't, think on't, I do not use to jest.
Thursday is near, lay hand on heart, advise.
An you be mine, I'll give you to my friend;
An you be not, hang, beg, starve, die in the streets,
For by my soul, I'll ne'er acknowledge thee,   195
Nor what is mine shall never do thee good.
Trust to't, bethink you. I'll not be forsworn.

                                             [*Exit.*]

    JULIET
Is there no pity sitting in the clouds,
That sees into the bottom of my grief?
O sweet my mother cast me not away.   200
Delay this marriage for a month, a week,
Or if you do not, make the bridal bed
In that dim monument where Tybalt lies.
        LADY CAPULET
Talk not to me, for I'll not speak a word.
Do as thou wilt, for I have done with thee.   205

                                             [*Exit.*]
    JULIET
O God! O nurse, how shall this be prevented?
My husband is on earth, my faith in heaven;
How shall that faith return again to earth,
Unless that husband send it me from heaven,
By leaving earth? Comfort me, counsel me.   210
Alack, alack, that heaven should practise stratagems
Upon so soft a subject as myself.
What sayst thou, hast thou not a word of joy?
Some comfort, nurse.

NURSE
           Faith here it is. Romeo
Is banished; and all the world to nothing,   215
That he dares ne'er come back to challenge you;
Or if he do, it needs must be by stealth.
Then since the case so stands as now it doth,
I think it best you married with the county.
O he's a lovely gentleman.   220
Romeo's a dishclout to him; an eagle, madam,
Hath not so green, so quick, so fair an eye
As Paris hath. Beshrew my very heart,
I think you are happy in this second match,
For it excels your first; or if it did not,   225
Your first is dead, or 'twere as good he were,
As living here, and you no use of him.
JULIET
Speak'st thou from thy heart?
NURSE
And from my soul too, else beshrew them both.
JULIET
Amen.
NURSE
What?
JULIET
Well thou hast comforted me marvellous much.   230
Go in, and tell my lady I am gone,
Having displeased my father, to Laurence' cell,
To make confession, and to be absolved.
NURSE
Marry I will, and this is wisely done.   [*Exit.*]
JULIET
Ancient damnation, o most wicked fiend!   235
Is it more sin to wish me thus forsworn,
Or to dispraise my lord with that same tongue
Which she hath praised him with above compare
So many thousand times? Go counsellor;
Thou and my bosom henceforth shall be twain.   240
I'll to the friar to know his remedy.
If all else fail, myself have power to die.   [*Exit.*]

ACT IV

SCENE ONE.

Verona. Friar Laurence's cell.
Enter Friar Laurence and Paris.

FRIAR LAURENCE
On Thursday sir? The time is very short.
　　PARIS
My father Capulet will have it so,
And I am nothing slow to slack his haste.
　　FRIAR LAURENCE
You say you do not know the lady's mind.
Uneven is the course, I like it not.　　　　　　　　　　5
　　PARIS
Immoderately she weeps for Tybalt's death,
And therefore have I little talked of love,
For Venus smiles not in a house of tears.
Now sir, her father counts it dangerous
That she do give her sorrow so much sway;　　　　　　10
And in his wisdom hastes our marriage,
To stop the inundation of her tears;
Which too much minded by herself alone,
May be put from her by society.
Now do you know the reason of this haste.　　　　　　15
　　FRIAR LAURENCE [*aside*]
I would I knew not why it should be slowed.

　　　　　　　　　　　　　　　　　[*Enter Juliet.*]
Look sir, here comes the lady toward my cell.
　　PARIS
Happily met, my lady and my wife.

JULIET
That may be sir, when I may be a wife.
PARIS
That may be, must be, love, on Thursday next.   20
JULIET
What must be shall be.
FRIAR LAURENCE
                        That's a certain text.
PARIS
Come you to make confession to this father?
JULIET
To answer that, I should confess to you.
PARIS
Do not deny to him that you love me.
JULIET
I will confess to you that I love him.   25
PARIS
So will ye, I am sure, that you love me.
JULIET
If I do so, it will be of more price,
Being spoke behind your back, than to your face.
PARIS
Pour soul, thy face is much abused with tears.
JULIET
The tears have got small victory by that,   30
For it was bad enough before their spite.
PARIS
Thou wrong'st it more than tears with that report.
JULIET
That is no slander sir, which is a truth,
And what I spake, I spake it to my face.
PARIS
Thy face is mine, and thou hast slandered it.   35
JULIET
It may be so, for it is not mine own.
Are you at leisure, holy father, now,
Or shall I come to you at evening mass?
FRIAR LAURENCE
My leisure serves me pensive daughter now.
My lord, we must entreat the time alone.   40

PARIS
God shield I should disturb devotion.
Juliet, on Thursday early will I rouse ye.
Till then adieu, and keep this holy kiss.   [*Exit.*]
    JULIET
O shut the door, and when thou hast done so,
Come weep with me, past hope, past cure, past help.   45
    FRIAR LAURENCE
O Juliet I already know thy grief,
It strains me past the compass of my wits.
I hear thou must, and nothing may prorogue it,
On Thursday next be married to this county.
    JULIET
Tell me not friar, that thou hearest of this,   50
Unless thou tell me how I may prevent it.
If in thy wisdom thou canst give no help,
Do thou but call my resolution wise,
And with this knife I'll help it presently.
God joined my heart and Romeo's, thou our hands;   55
And ere this hand, by thee to Romeo's sealed,
Shall be the label to another deed,
Or my true heart with treacherous revolt
Turn to another, this shall slay them both.
Therefore out of thy long-experienced time,   60
Give me some present counsel, or behold
'Twixt my extremes and me this bloody knife
Shall play the umpire, arbitrating that
Which the commission of thy years and art
Could to no issue of true honour bring.   65
Be not so long to speak; I long to die,
If what thou speak'st speak not of remedy.
    FRIAR LAURENCE
Hold daughter, I do spy a kind of hope,
Which craves as desperate an execution,
As that is desperate which we would prevent.   70
If rather than to marry County Paris
Thou hast the strength of will to slay thyself,
Then is it likely thou wilt undertake
A thing like death to chide away this shame,
That cop'st with death himself to 'scape from it;   75

And if thou darest, I'll give thee remedy.
JULIET
O bid me leap, rather than marry Paris,
From off the battlements of any tower,
Or walk in thievish ways, or bid me lurk
Where serpents are; chain me with roaring bears,   80
Or hide me nightly in a charnel house,
O'er-covered quite with dead men's rattling bones,
With reeky shanks and yellow chapless skulls.
Or bid me go into a new-made grave,
And hide me with a dead man in his shroud,   85
Things that to hear them told have made me tremble;
And I will do it without fear or doubt,
To live an unstained wife to my sweet love.
FRIAR LAURENCE
Hold then, go home, be merry, give consent
To marry Paris. Wednesday is to-morrow;   90
To-morrow night look that thou lie alone,
Let not thy nurse lie with thee in thy chamber.
Take thou this vial, being then in bed,
And this distilling liquor drink thou off,
When presently through all thy veins shall run   95
A cold and drowsy humour; for no pulse
Shall keep his native progress, but surcease;
No warmth, no breath, shall testify thou livest,
The roses in thy lips and cheeks shall fade
To waned ashes, thy eyes' windows fall,   100
Like death, when he shuts up the day of life.
Each part deprived of supple government,
Shall stiff and stark and cold appear like death,
And in this borrowed likeness of shrunk death
Thou shalt continue two and forty hours,   105
And then awake as from a pleasant sleep.
Now when the bridegroom in the morning comes
To rouse thee from thy bed, there art thou dead;
Then as the manner of our country is,
In thy best robes, uncovered, on the bier,   110
Thou shalt be borne to that same ancient vault,
Where all the kindred of the Capulets lie.
In the mean time, against thou shalt awake,

Shall Romeo by my letters know our drift,
And hither shall he come, and he and I   115
Will watch thy waking, and that very night
Shall Romeo bear thee hence to Mantua.
And this shall free thee from this present shame,
If no inconstant toy, nor womanish fear,
Abate thy valour in the acting it.   120
    JULIET
Give me, give me, o tell not me of fear.
    FRIAR LAURENCE
Hold. Get you gone, be strong and prosperous
In this resolve; I'll send a friar with speed
To Mantua, with my letters to thy lord.
    JULIET
Love give me strength, and strength shall help afford.   125
Farewell dear father.   [Exeunt.]

SCENE TWO.

Verona. A hall in Capulet's house.
Enter Capulet, Lady Capulet,
Nurse, and Servants.

    CAPULET
So many guests invite as here are writ.
                 [Exit First Servant.]
Sirrah, go hire me twenty cunning cooks.
    SECOND SERVANT
You shall have none ill sir, for I'll try if they can lick
their fingers.
    CAPULET
How canst thou try them so?   5
    SECOND SERVANT
Marry sir, 'tis an ill cook that cannot lick his own

fingers; therefore he that cannot lick his fingers goes
not with me.
                    CAPULET
Go, be gone.   [*Exit Second Servant.*]
We shall be much unfurnished for this time.   10
What, is my daughter gone to Friar Laurence?
                    NURSE
Ay forsooth.
                    CAPULET
Well, he may chance to do some good on her;
A peevish self-willed harlotry it is.
                                        [*Enter Juliet.*]
                    NURSE
See where she comes from shrift with merry look.   15
                    CAPULET
How now my headstrong, where have you been
    gadding?
                    JULIET
Where I have learned me to repent the sin
Of disobedient opposition
To you and your behests, and am enjoined
By holy Laurence to fall prostrate here,   20
And beg your pardon. [*Kneels.*] Pardon I beseech you,
Henceforward I am ever ruled by you.
                    CAPULET
Send for the county, go tell him of this.
I'll have this knot knit up to-morrow morning.
                    JULIET
I met the youthful lord at Laurence' cell,   25
And gave him what becomed love I might,
Not stepping o'er the bounds of modesty.
                    CAPULET
Why I am glad on't; this is well. Stand up.
This is as't should be. Let me see the county.
Ay marry go I say, and fetch him hither.   30
Now afore God, this reverend holy friar,
All our whole city is much bound to him.
                    JULIET
Nurse, will you go with me into my closet,

To help me sort such needful ornaments
As you think fit to furnish me to-morrow?   35
                LADY CAPULET
No, not till Thursday, there is time enough.
                CAPULET
Go nurse, go with her; we'll to church to-morrow.
                        [*Exeunt Juliet and Nurse.*]
                LADY CAPULET
We shall be short in our provision;
'Tis now near night.
                CAPULET
                Tush, I will stir about,
And all things shall be well, I warrant thee wife.   40
Go thou to Juliet, help to deck up her;
I'll not to bed to-night, let me alone.
I'll play the housewife for this once. What ho!
They are all forth. Well, I will walk myself
To County Paris, to prepare up him   45
Against to-morrow. My heart is wondrous light,
Since this same wayward girl is so reclaimed.
                                    [*Exeunt.*]

SCENE THREE.

Verona. Juliet's chamber.
Enter Juliet and Nurse.

                JULIET
Ay, those attires are best; but gentle nurse,
I pray thee leave me to myself to-night.
For I have need of many orisons,
To move the heavens to smile upon my state,
Which well thou knowest is cross and full of sin.   5
                        [*Enter Lady Capulet.*]

LADY CAPULET

What, are you busy, ho? Need you my help?

JULIET

No madam, we have culled such necessaries
As are behoveful for our state to-morrow.
So please you, let me now be left alone,
And let the nurse this night sit up with you;   10
For I am sure you have your hands full all,
In this so sudden business.

LADY CAPULET

              Good night.
Get thee to bed and rest, for thou hast need.

[Exeunt Lady Capulet and Nurse.]

JULIET

Farewell. God knows when we shall meet again.
I have a faint cold fear thrills through my veins   15
That almost freezes up the heat of life.
I'll call them back again to comfort me.
Nurse! What should she do here?
My dismal scene I needs must act alone.
Come vial.   20
What if this mixture do not work at all?
Shall I be married then to-morrow morning?
No, no, this shall forbid it. Lie thou there.

[Lays down her dagger.]

What if it be a poison which the friar
Subtly hath ministered to have me dead,   25
Lest in this marriage he should be dishonoured,
Because he married me before to Romeo?
I fear it is, and yet methinks it should not,
For he hath still been tried a holy man.
How if when I am laid into the tomb,   30
I wake before the time that Romeo
Come to redeem me—there's a fearful point.
Shall I not then be stifled in the vault,
To whose foul mouth no healthsome air breathes in,
And there die strangled ere my Romeo comes?   35
Or if I live, is it not very like,
The horrible conceit of death and night,

Together with the terror of the place—
As in a vault, an ancient receptacle,
Where for this many hundred years the bones   40
Of all my buried ancestors are packed,
Where bloody Tybalt yet but green in earth
Lies festering in his shroud, where as they say,
At some hours in the night spirits resort—
Alack, alack, is it not like that I,   45
So early waking—what with loathsome smells,
And shrieks like mandrakes torn out of the earth,
That living mortals hearing them run mad—
O if I wake, shall I not be distraught,
Environed with all these hideous fears,   50
And madly play with my forefathers' joints,
And pluck the mangled Tybalt from his shroud,
And in this rage, with some great kinsman's bone,
As with a club, dash out my desperate brains?
O look, methinks I see my cousin's ghost,   55
Seeking out Romeo that did spit his body
Upon a rapier's point—stay Tybalt, stay!
Romeo! Romeo! Romeo! I drink to thee.
       [*Drinks and falls on her bed. The curtains
       close.*]

SCENE FOUR.

Verona. A hall in Capulet's house.
Enter Lady Capulet and Nurse.

    LADY CAPULET
Hold, take these keys, and fetch more spices, nurse.
    NURSE
They call for dates and quinces in the pastry.
                    [*Enter Capulet.*]
    CAPULET
Come, stir, stir, stir, the second cock hath crowed,
The curfew bell hath rung, 'tis three a clock.

Look to the baked meats, good Angelica,   5
Spare not for cost.
              NURSE
                        Go you cot-quean, go,
Get you to bed; faith you'll be sick to-morrow
For this night's watching.
              CAPULET
No, not a whit; what, I have watched ere now
All night for lesser cause, and ne'er been sick.   10
        LADY CAPULET
Ay you have been a mouse-hunt in your time,
But I will watch you from such watching now.
                        [*Exeunt Lady Capulet and Nurse.*]
              CAPULET
A jealous-hood, a jealous-hood.
        [*Enter Servants with spits, and logs, and
        baskets.*]
                                        Now fellow,
What is there?
        FIRST SERVANT
Things for the cook, sir, but I know not what.
              CAPULET
Make haste, make haste. [*Exit First Servant.*] Sirrah
    fetch drier logs.   15
Call Peter, he will show thee where they are.
        SECOND SERVANT
I have a head sir, that will find out logs,
And never trouble Peter for the matter.
              CAPULET
Mass and well said, a merry whoreson, ha!
Thou shall be logger-head. [*Exeunt Servants.*] God
    Father, 'tis day.   20
The county will be here with music straight,
For so he said he would. [*Music.*] I hear him near.
Nurse! Wife! What ho! What, nurse I say!
                              [*Enter Nurse.*]
Go waken Juliet, go and trim her up.
I'll go and chat with Paris. Hie, make haste,   25
Make haste; the bridegroom he is come already.
Make haste I say.   [*Exeunt.*]

SCENE FIVE.

Verona. Juliet's chamber. Enter Nurse.

NURSE [*draws curtains*]
Mistress! What, mistress! Juliet! Fast, I warrant her.
    She—
Why lamb, why lady—fie you slug-a-bed!
Why love I say! Madam! Sweetheart! Why bride!
What, not a word? You take your pennyworths now.
Sleep for a week; for the next night I warrant   5
The County Paris hath set up his rest
That you shall rest but little, God forgive me.
Marry, and amen. How sound is she asleep!
I needs must wake her. Madam, madam, madam!
Ay, let the county take you in your bed,   10
He'll fright you up i' faith. Will it not be?
What, dressed, and in your clothes, and down again?
I must needs wake you. Lady, lady, lady!
Alas, alas, help, help, my lady's dead!
O, weladay that ever I was born!   15
Some aqua-vitae ho! My lord! My lady!
                                        [*Enter Lady Capulet.*]
        LADY CAPULET
What noise is here?
        NURSE
                    O lamentable day.
        LADY CAPULET
What is the matter?
        NURSE
                    Look, look, o heavy day.
        LADY CAPULET
O me, o me, my child, my only life.

Revive, look up, or I will die with thee.   20
Help, help! Call help.

                              [*Enter Capulet.*]

    CAPULET
For shame, bring Juliet forth; her lord is come.
    NURSE
She's dead, deceased, she's dead, alack the day!
    LADY CAPULET
Alack the day, she's dead, she's dead, she's dead!
    CAPULET
Ha! Let me see her. Out alas she's cold,   25
Her blood is settled, and her joints are stiff.
Life and these lips have long been separated.
Death lies on her like an untimely frost
Upon the sweetest flower of all the field.
    NURSE
O lamentable day.
    LADY CAPULET
               O woeful time.   30
    CAPULET
Death that hath ta'en her hence to make me wail,
Ties up my tongue, and will not let me speak.
    [*Enter Friar Laurence and Paris, with
    Catling, Rebeck, and Soundpost.*]
    FRIAR LAURENCE
Come, is the bride ready to go to church?
    CAPULET
Ready to go, but never to return.
O son, the night before thy wedding-day   35
Hath Death lain with thy wife; there she lies,
Flower as she was, deflowered by him.
Death is my son-in-law, Death is my heir,
My daughter he hath wedded. I will die,
And leave him all; life, living, all is Death's.   40
    PARIS
Have I thought, love, to see this morning's face,
And doth it give me such a sight as this?
    LADY CAPULET
Accursed, unhappy, wretched, hateful day,

Most miserable hour that e'er time saw
In lasting labour of his pilgrimage!   45
But one, poor one, one poor and loving child,
But one thing to rejoice and solace in,
And cruel Death hath catched it from my sight.

NURSE

O woe, o woeful, woeful, woeful day,
Most lamentable day, most woeful day   50
That ever, ever, I did yet behold!
O day, o day, o day, o hateful day,
Never was seen so black a day as this.
O woeful day, o woeful day!

PARIS

Beguiled, divorced, wronged, spited, slain,   55
Most detestable Death, by thee beguiled,
By cruel, cruel thee, quite overthrown!
O life, o life; not life, but love in death.

CAPULET

Despised, distressed, hated, martyred, killed!
Uncomfortable time, why cam'st thou now   60
To murder, murder, our solemnity?
O child, o child, my soul and not my child,
Dead art thou, alack my child is dead,
And with my child my joys are buried.

FRIAR LAURENCE

Peace ho for shame! Confusion's cure lives not   65
In these confusions. Heaven and yourself
Had part in this fair maid, now heaven hath all,
And all the better is it for the maid.
Your part in her you could not keep from death,
But heaven keeps his part in eternal life.   70
The most you sought was her promotion,
For 'twas your heaven she should be advanced
And weep ye now, seeing she is advanced
Above the clouds, as high as heaven itself?
O in this love, you love your child so ill,   75
That you run mad, seeing that she is well.
She's not well married that lives married long,
But she's best married that dies married young.
Dry up your tears, and stick your rosemary

On this fair corse; and as the custom is,   80
All in her best array bear her to church.
For though fond nature bids us all lament,
Yet nature's tears are reason's merriment.
              CAPULET
All things that we ordained festival
Turn from their office to black funeral;   85
Our instruments to melancholy bells,
Our wedding cheer to a sad burial feast;
Our solemn hymns to sullen dirges change,
Our bridal flowers serve for a buried corse,
And all things change them to the contrary.   90
              FRIAR LAURENCE
Sir, go you in, and madam, go with him,
And go Sir Paris; every one prepare
To follow this fair corse unto her grave.
The heavens do lour upon you for some ill;
Move them no more, by crossing their high will.   95
        [*Exeunt. Nurse, Catling, Rebeck, and Sound-
        post remain.*]
              CATLING
Faith we may put up our pipes and be gone.
              NURSE
Honest good fellows, ah put up, put up,
For well you know this is a pitiful case.   [*Exit.*]
              CATLING
Ay by my troth, the case may be amended.   100
                            [*Enter Peter.*]
              PETER
Musicians, o musicians, heart's ease, heart's ease.
O an you will have me live, play heart's ease.
              CATLING
Why heart's ease?   105
              PETER
O musicians, because my heart itself plays, my heart
is full. O play me some merry dump to comfort me.
              CATLING
Not a dump we, 'tis no time to play now.   110
              PETER
You will not then?

CATLING

No.

PETER

I will then give it you soundly.

CATLING

What will you give us?

PETER

No money on my faith, but the gleek. I will give 115
you the minstrel.

CATLING

Then will I give you the serving-creature.

PETER

Then will I lay the serving-creature's dagger on your
pate. I will carry no crochets. I'll re you, I'll fa you, 120
do you note me?

CATLING

And you re us and fa us, you note us.

REBECK

Pray you, put up your dagger, and put out your wit.

PETER

Then have at you with my wit. I will dry-beat you 125
with an iron wit, and put up my iron dagger. Answer
me like men. [Sings.]

    When griping grief the heart doth wound,
    And doleful dumps the mind oppress,
    Then music with her silver sound— 130
why silver sound, why music with her silver sound?
What say you Simon Catling?

CATLING

Marry sir, because silver hath a sweet sound.

PETER

Pretty. What say you Hugh Rebeck? 135

REBECK

I say, silver sound, because musicians sound for silver.

PETER

Pretty too. What say you James Soundpost?

SOUNDPOST

Faith I know not what to say. 140

PETER

O I cry you mercy; you are the singer. I will say for

you, it is music with her silver sound, because musicians have no gold for sounding.   [*Sings.*]

    Then music with her silver sound   145
    With speedy help doth lend redress.   [*Exit.*]

    C A T L I N G
What a pestilent knave is this same!

    R E B E C K
Hang him, Jack! Come we'll in here, tarry for the
mourners, and stay dinner.   [*Exeunt.*]   150

ACT V

SCENE ONE.

Mantua. A street. Enter Romeo.

ROMEO
If I may trust the flattering truth of sleep,
My dreams presage some joyful news at hand.
My bosom's lord sits lightly in his throne;
And all this day an unaccustomed spirit
Lifts me above the ground with cheerful thoughts.   5
I dreamt my lady came and found me dead—
Strange dream that gives a dead man leave to think—
And breathed such life with kisses in my lips,
That I revived and was an emperor.
Ah me, how sweet is love itself possessed,   10
When but love's shadows are so rich in joy.
                              [*Enter Balthasar.*]
News from Verona. How now Balthasar,
Dost thou not bring me letters from the friar?
How doth my lady? Is my father well?
How fares my Juliet? That I ask again,   15
For nothing can be ill if she be well.

BALTHASAR
Then she is well and nothing can be ill.
Her body sleeps in Capels' monument,
And her immortal part with angels lives.
I saw her laid low in her kindred's vault,   20
And presently took post to tell it you.
O pardon me for bringing these ill news,
Since you did leave it for my office sir.

ROMEO

Is it even so? Then I defy you, stars.
Thou knowest my lodging, get me ink and paper,   25
And hire post-horses; I will hence to-night.

BALTHASAR

I do beseech you sir, have patience.
Your looks are pale and wild, and do import
Some misadventure.

ROMEO

     Tush, thou art deceived.
Leave me, and do the thing I bid thee do.   30
Hast thou no letters to me from the friar?

BALTHASAR

No my good lord.

ROMEO

    No matter. Get thee gone,
And hire those horses; I'll be with thee straight.

           [*Exit Balthasar.*]

Well Juliet, I will lie with thee to-night.
Let's see for means. O mischief, thou art swift   35
To enter in the thoughts of desperate men.
I do remember an apothecary—
And hereabouts 'a dwells—which late I noted,
In tattered weeds, with overwhelming brows,
Culling of simples; meagre were his looks,   40
Sharp misery had worn him to the bones;
And in his needy shop a tortoise hung,
An alligator stuffed, and other skins
Of ill-shaped fishes, and about his shelves
A beggarly account of empty boxes,   45
Green earthen pots, bladders, and musty seeds,
Remnants of packthread, and old cakes of roses,
Were thinly scattered, to make up a show.
Noting this penury, to myself I said,
An if a man did need a poison now,   50
Whose sale is present death in Mantua,
Here lives a caitiff wretch would sell it him.
O this same thought did but forerun my need,
And this same needy man must sell it me.

As I remember, this should be the house.   55
Being holiday, the beggar's shop is shut.
What ho apothecary!

                                 [Enter Apothecary.]

APOTHECARY
              Who calls so loud?
ROMEO
Come hither man. I see that thou art poor.
Hold, there is forty ducats, let me have
A dram of poison, such soon-speeding gear   60
As will disperse itself through all the veins,
That the life-weary taker may fall dead,
And that the trunk may be discharged of breath,
As violently as hasty powder fired
Doth hurry from the fatal cannon's womb.   65
APOTHECARY
Such mortal drugs I have, but Mantua's law
Is death to any he that utters them.
ROMEO
Art thou so bare and full of wretchedness,
And fearest to die? Famine is in thy cheeks,
Need and oppression starveth in thy eyes,   70
Contempt and beggary hangs upon thy back.
The world is not thy friend, nor the world's law,
The world affords no law to make thee rich;
Then be not poor, but break it, and take this.
APOTHECARY
My poverty, but not my will consents.   75
ROMEO
I pay thy poverty and not thy will.
APOTHECARY
Put this in any liquid thing you will
And drink it off, and if you had the strength
Of twenty men, it would dispatch you straight.
ROMEO
There is thy gold, worse poison to men's souls, 80
Doing more murder in this loathsome world,
Than these poor compounds that thou mayst not sell.
I sell thee poison, thou hast sold me none.

Farewell, buy food, and get thyself in flesh.
Come cordial, and not poison, go with me.   85
To Juliet's grave, for there must I use thee.

                                        [*Exeunt.*]

SCENE TWO.

Verona. Friar Laurence's cell.
Enter Friar John.

FRIAR JOHN
Holy Franciscan friar, brother, ho!
                        [*Enter Friar Laurence.*]
    FRIAR LAURENCE
This same should be the voice of Friar John.
Welcome from Mantua. What says Romeo?
Or if his mind be writ, give me his letter.
    FRIAR JOHN
Going to find a barefoot brother out,   5
One of our order, to associate me,
Here in this city visiting the sick,
And finding him, the searchers of the town,
Suspecting that we both were in a house
Where the infectious pestilence did reign,   10
Sealed up the doors, and would not let us forth,
So that my speed to Mantua there was stayed.
    FRIAR LAURENCE
Who bare my letter then to Romeo?
    FRIAR JOHN
I could not send it, here it is again—
Nor get a messenger to bring it thee,   15
So fearful were they of infection.
    FRIAR LAURENCE
Unhappy fortune! By my brotherhood,
The letter was not nice, but full of charge
Of dear import; and the neglecting it

May do much danger. Friar John, go hence,   20
Get me an iron crow and bring it straight
Unto my cell.

    FRIAR JOHN
Brother I'll go and bring it thee.   *[Exit.]*

    FRIAR LAURENCE
Now must I to the monument alone;
Within this three hours will fair Juliet wake.
She will beshrew me much that Romeo   25
Hath had no notice of these accidents.
But I will write again to Mantua,
And keep her at my cell till Romeo come—
Poor living corse closed in a dead man's tomb.

                       [Exit.]

SCENE THREE.

Verona. A churchyard; the monument of the Capulets. Enter Paris and Page.

    PARIS
Give me thy torch boy; hence, and stand aloof.
Yet put it out, for I would not be seen.
Under yond yew trees lay thee all along,
Holding thy ear close to the hollow ground;
So shall no foot upon the churchyard tread—   5
Being loose, unfirm with digging up of graves—
But thou shalt hear it; whistle then to me,
As signal that thou hearest something approach.
Give me those flowers. Do as I bid thee, go.

    PAGE
I am almost afraid to stand alone,   10
Here in the churchyard, yet I will adventure.

                       [Retires.]

    PARIS
Sweet flower, with flowers thy bridal bed I strew.

O woe, thy canopy is dust and stones.
Which with sweet water nightly I will dew,
Or wanting that, with tears distilled by moans.   15
The obsequies that I for thee will keep,
Nightly shall be to strew thy grave and weep.
                                    [Page whistles.]
The boy gives warning something doth approach.
What cursed foot wanders this way to-night,
To cross my obsequies and true love's rite?   20
What, with a torch! Muffle me night awhile.
              [Retires. Enter Romeo and Balthasar.]
          ROMEO
Give me that mattock and the wrenching iron.
Hold, take this letter; early in the morning
See thou deliver it to my lord and father.
Give me the light. Upon thy life I charge thee,   25
Whate'er thou hearest or seest, stand all aloof,
And do not interrupt me in my course.
Why I descend into this bed of death,
Is partly to behold my lady's face;
But chiefly to take thence from her dead finger   30
A precious ring—a ring that I must use
In dear employment. Therefore hence, be gone.
But if thou, jealous, dost return to pry
In what I farther shall intend to do,
By heaven I will tear thee joint by joint,   35
And strew this hungry churchyard with thy limbs.
The time and my intents are savage-wild,
More fierce and more inexorable far,
Than empty tigers, or the roaring sea.
          BALTHASAR
I will be gone sir, and not trouble you.   40
          ROMEO
So shalt thou show me friendship. Take thou that.
Live and be prosperous, and farewell good fellow.
          BALTHASAR [aside]
For all this same, I'll hide me hereabout.
His looks I fear, and his intents I doubt.   [Retires.]
          ROMEO
Thou detestable maw, thou womb of death,   45

What said my man, when my betossed soul
Did not attend him as we rode? I think
He told me Paris should have married Juliet.
Said he not so? Or did I dream it so?
Or am I mad, hearing him talk of Juliet,   80
To think it was so? O give me thy hand,
One writ with me in sour misfortune's book.
I'll bury thee in a triumphant grave.
A grave? O no, a lantern, slaughtered youth.
For here lies Juliet, and her beauty makes   85
This vault a feasting presence full of light.
Death, lie thou there, by a dead man interred.
                            [*Lays Paris in the tomb.*]
How oft when men are at the point of death
Have they been merry, which their keepers call
A lightning before death. O how may I   90
Call this a lightning? O my love, O my wife!
Death that hath sucked the honey of thy breath,
Hath had no power yet upon thy beauty.
Thou art not conquered; beauty's ensign yet
Is crimson in thy lips and in thy cheeks,   95
And death's pale flag is not advanced there.
Tybalt, liest thou there in thy bloody sheet?
O what more favour can I do to thee,
Than with that hand that cut thy youth in twain
To sunder his that was thine enemy?   100
Forgive me cousin. Ah dear Juliet,
Why art thou yet so fair? Shall I believe
That unsubstantial Death is amorous,
And that the lean abhorred monster keeps
Thee here in dark to be his paramour?   105
For fear of that, I still will stay with thee,
And never from this palace of dim night*
Depart again. Here, here will I remain,
Depart again, come lie thou in my arm,
Here's to thy health, where'er thou tumblest in.
O true apothecary!

Lines deleted in rewriting:

Gorged with the dearest morsel of the earth,
Thus I enforce thy rotten jaws to open,
                              [*Opens the tomb.*]
And in despite I'll cram thee with more food.
    PARIS
This is that banished haughty Montague,
That murdered my love's cousin, with which grief   50
It is supposed that fair creature died,
And here is come to do some villainous shame
To the dead bodies. I will apprehend him.
Stop thy unhallowed toil vile Montague.
Can vengeance be pursued further than death?   55
Condemned villain, I do apprehend thee.
Obey and go with me, for thou must die.
    ROMEO
I must indeed, and therefore came I hither.
Good gentle youth, tempt not a desperate man;
Fly hence and leave me. Think upon these gone,   60
Let them affright thee. I beseech thee youth,
Put not another sin upon my head,
By urging me to fury. O be gone.
By heaven, I love thee better than myself,
For I come hither armed against myself.   65
Stay not, be gone, live, and hereafter say,
A madman's mercy bid thee run away.
    PARIS
I do defy thy conjurations,
And apprehend thee for a felon here.
    ROMEO
Wilt thou provoke me? Then have at thee boy.   70
                              [*They fight.*]
    PAGE
O lord, they fight, I will go call the watch.   [*Exit.*]
    PARIS
O I am slain! If thou be merciful,
Open the tomb, lay me with Juliet.   [*Dies.*]
    ROMEO
In faith I will. Let me peruse this face.
Mercutio's kinsman, noble County Paris!   75

Thy drugs are quick. Thus with a kiss I die.
With worms that are thy chamber-maids. O here
Will I set up my everlasting rest;   110
And shake the yoke of inauspicious stars
From this world-wearied flesh. Eyes look your last.
Arms, take your last embrace. And lips, o you
The doors of breath, seal with a righteous kiss
A dateless bargain to engrossing death.   115
Come bitter conduct, come unsavoury guide,
Thou desperate pilot, now at once run on
The dashing rocks thy sea-sick weary bark.
Here's to my love! O true apothecary!
Thy drugs are quick. Thus with a kiss I die.   120
        [*Enter Friar Laurence, with lantern, crow, and
        spade.*]
        FRIAR LAURENCE
Saint Francis be my speed. How oft to-night
Have my old feet stumbled at graves. Who's there?
        BALTHASAR
Here's one, a friend, and one that knows you well.
        FRIAR LAURENCE
Bliss be upon you. Tell me good my friend,
What torch is yond, that vainly lends his light   125
To grubs and eyeless skulls? As I discern,
It burneth in the Capels' monument.
        BALTHASAR
It doth so holy sir, and there's my master,
One that you love.
        FRIAR LAURENCE
                Who is it?
        BALTHASAR
                        Romeo.
        FRIAR LAURENCE
How long hath he been there?
        BALTHASAR
                        Full half an hour.   130
        FRIAR LAURENCE
Go with me to the vault.
        BALTHASAR
                I dare not sir.

My master knows not but I am gone hence,
And fearfully did menace me with death
If I did stay to look on his intents.

FRIAR LAURENCE
Stay then, I'll go alone. Fear comes upon me.   135
O much I fear some ill unlucky thing.

BALTHASAR
As I did sleep under this yew tree here,
I dreamt my master and another fought,
And that my master slew him.

FRIAR LAURENCE
                              Romeo!
Alack, alack, what blood is this which stains   140
The stony entrance of this sepulchre?
What mean these masterless and gory swords
To lie discoloured by this place of peace?
                              [Enters the tomb.]
Romeo! O, pale! Who else? What, Paris too?
And steeped in blood? Ah what an unkind hour   145
Is guilty of this lamentable chance!
The lady stirs.

JULIET
O comfortable friar, where is my lord?
I do remember well where I should be,
And there I am. Where is my Romeo? [Noise within.]   150

FRIAR LAURENCE
I hear some noise. Lady, come from that nest
Of death, contagion, and unnatural sleep.
A greater power than we can contradict
Hath thwarted our intents. Come, come away.
Thy husband in thy bosom there lies dead;   155
And Paris too. Come I'll dispose of thee
Among a sisterhood of holy nuns.
Stay not to question, for the watch is coming;
Come, go good Juliet, I dare no longer stay.
                              [Exit.]

JULIET
Go get thee hence, for I will not away.   160
What's here? A cup closed in my true love's hand?
Poison I see hath been his timeless end.

O churl, drunk all; and left no friendly drop
To help me after? I will kiss thy lips;
Haply some poison yet doth hang on them,   165
To make me die with a restorative.
Thy lips are warm.
      CHIEF WATCHMAN [within]
Lead boy. Which way?
      JULIET
Yea, noise? Then I'll be brief. O happy dagger!
                [Draws Romeo's dagger.]
This is thy sheath; there rust, and let me die.   170
          [Stabs herself. Enter Watch, with Page.]
      PAGE
This is the place; there where the torch doth burn.
      CHIEF WATCHMAN
The ground is bloody, search about the churchyard.
Go some of you, whoe'er you find attach.
            [Exeunt some of the Watch.]
Pitiful sight! Here lies the county slain,
And Juliet bleeding, warm, and newly dead,   175
Who here hath lain this two days buried.
Go tell the Prince, run to the Capulets,
Raise up the Montagues, some others search.
We see the ground whereon these woes do lie,
But the true ground of all these piteous woes   180
We cannot without circumstance descry.
        [Enter some of the Watch, with Balthasar.]
      SECOND WATCHMAN
Here's Romeo's man, we found him in the churchyard.
      CHIEF WATCHMAN
Hold him in safety, till the Prince come hither.
      [Enter Friar Laurence, and another Watchman.]
      THIRD WATCHMAN
Here is a friar that trembles, sighs, and weeps.
We took this mattock and this spade from him,   185
As he was coming from this churchyard's side.
      CHIEF WATCHMAN
A great suspicion. Stay the friar too.
           [Enter Prince and attendants.]

PRINCE
What misadventure is so early up,
That calls our person from our morning rest?
[*Enter Capulet and Lady Capulet.*]
CAPULET
What should it be that is so shrieked abroad? 190
LADY CAPULET
The people in the street cry Romeo,
Some Juliet, and some Paris, and all run
With open outcry toward our monument.
PRINCE
What fear is this which startles in your ears?
CHIEF WATCHMAN
Sovereign, here lies the County Paris slain, 195
And Romeo dead, and Juliet, dead before,
Warm and new killed.
PRINCE
Search, seek, and know how this foul murder comes.
CHIEF WATCHMAN
Here is a friar, and slaughtered Romeo's man,
With instruments upon them, fit to open 200
These dead men's tombs.
CAPULET
O heavens! O wife, look how our daughter bleeds.
This dagger hath mista'en, for lo his house
Is empty on the back of Montague,
And it mis-sheathed in my daughter's bosom. 205
LADY CAPULET
O me, this sight of death is as a bell,
That warns my old age to a sepulchre.
[*Enter Montague.*]
PRINCE
Come Montague, for thou art early up,
To see thy son and heir more early down.
MONTAGUE
Alas my liege, my wife is dead to-night; 210
Grief of my son's exile hath stopped her breath.
What further woe conspires against mine age?
PRINCE
Look and thou shalt see.

MONTAGUE

O thou untaught, what manners is in this,
To press before thy father to a grave?   215

PRINCE

Seal up the mouth of outrage for a while,
Till we can clear these ambiguities,
And know their spring, their head, their true descent;
And then will I be general of your woes,
And lead you even to death. Meantime forbear,   220
And let mischance be slave to patience.
Bring forth the parties of suspicion.

FRIAR LAURENCE

I am the greatest, able to do least,
Yet most suspected, as the time and place
Doth make against me, of this direful murder.   225
And here I stand both to impeach and purge
Myself condemned, and myself excused.

PRINCE

Then say at once what thou dost know in this.

FRIAR LAURENCE

I will be brief, for my short date of breath
Is not so long as is a tedious tale.   230
Romeo, there dead, was husband to that Juliet,
And she, there dead, that Romeo's faithful wife.
I married them, and their stolen marriage day
Was Tybalt's doomsday, whose untimely death
Banished the new-made bridegroom from this city;   235
For whom, and not for Tybalt, Juliet pined.
You, to remove that siege of grief from her,
Betrothed, and would have married her perforce,
To County Paris. Then comes she to me,
And with wild looks bid me devise some mean   240
To rid her from this second marriage,
Or in my cell there would she kill herself.
Then gave I her, so tutored by my art,
A sleeping potion; which so took effect
As I intended, for it wrought on her   245
The form of death. Meantime I writ to Romeo,
That he should hither come as this dire night,
To help to take her from her borrowed grave,

Being the time the potion's force should cease.
But he which bore my letter, Friar John,   250
Was stayed by accident, and yesternight
Returned my letter back. Then all alone
At the prefixed hour of her waking,
Came I to take her from her kindred's vault,
Meaning to keep her closely at my cell,   255
Till I conveniently could send to Romeo.
But when I came, some minute ere the time
Of her awakening, here untimely lay
The noble Paris and true Romeo dead.
She wakes, and I entreated her come forth,   260
And bear this work of heaven with patience.
But then a noise did scare me from the tomb,
And she, too desperate, would not go with me,
But as it seems, did violence on herself.
All this I know, and to the marriage   265
Her nurse is privy; and if aught in this
Miscarried by my fault, let my old life
Be sacrificed some hour before his time,
Unto the rigour of severest law.
              PRINCE
We still have known thee for a holy man.   270
Where's Romeo's man? What can he say to this?
              BALTHASAR
I brought my master news of Juliet's death,
And then in post he came from Mantua,
To this same place, to this same monument.
This letter he early bid me give his father,   275
And threatened me with death, going in the vault,
If I departed not, and left him there.
              PRINCE
Give me the letter, I will look on it.
Where is the county's page that raised the watch?
Sirrah, what made your master in this place?   280
              PAGE
He came with flowers to strew his lady's grave,
And bid me stand aloof, and so I did.
Anon comes one with light to ope the tomb,
And by and by my master drew on him,

And then I ran away to call the watch.   285
    PRINCE
This letter doth make good the friar's words,
Their course of love, the tidings of her death;
And here he writes, that he did buy poison
Of a poor pothecary, and therewithal
Came to this vault, to die, and lie with Juliet.   290
Where be these enemies? Capulet, Montague,
See what a scourge is laid upon your hate,
That heaven finds means to kill your joys with love.
And I for winking at your discords too
Have lost a brace of kinsmen; all are punished.   295
    CAPULET
O brother Montague, give me thy hand.
This is my daughter's jointure, for no more
Can I demand.
    MONTAGUE
            But I can give thee more,
For I will raise her statue in pure gold,
That while Verona by that name is known,   300
There shall no figure at such rate be set
As that of true and faithful Juliet.
    CAPULET
As rich shall Romeo's by his lady's lie,
Poor sacrifices of our enmity.
    PRINCE
A glooming peace this morning with it brings;   305
The sun, for sorrow, will not show his head.
Go hence, to have more talk of these sad things;
Some shall be pardoned, and some punished.
For never was a story of more woe,
Than this of Juliet and her Romeo.   [*Exeunt.*]   310

NOTES TO "ROMEO AND JULIET"

Prologue: Enter Chorus. Many Elizabethan dramatists used a chorus as a sort of narrator for the play. The idea was based on the choruses from the classical Greek drama. The Greek chorus, however, was much more complicated, and involved many people. In his later plays, Shakespeare abandoned the practice of using a chorus.

4 *civil blood makes civil hands unclean:* civil in the sense of "civil war": Citizens make their hands unclean by spilling the blood of fellow citizens.

6 *star-crossed:* Star-crossed lovers were lovers born under an unfavorable star, hence destined to destruction. The play contains many references to destiny, fate, and the stars. Generally, Elizabethans believed that heavenly bodies could influence the lives of men. Most of them also believed in the idea of Divine Providence guiding men. Many were able to reconcile the two beliefs.

9 *passage:* progress.

12 *two hours' traffic of our stage:* Shakespeare's plays must have been acted at a very rapid pace. The almost bare, open, outdoor stage and the continuous flow of action, as well as the rapid delivery of lines contributed to the speed of playing.

ACT ONE, SCENE ONE

2 *carry coals:* A coal hauler was one of the dirtiest and lowest of professions; hence a man who carried coals was one who put up with all kinds of insults.

3 *colliers:* coal carriers, who were regarded as shiftless workers or cheats.

4 *an:* if; *choler:* anger.

5 *collar:* a halter or hangman's noose.

2–5 *coals . . . colliers . . . choler . . . collar:* These four words comprise the first play on words, or pun, in the play, which abounds in such puns. To fully appreciate the pun, it is necessary to pronounce "coals" as the Elizabethans did, as though it were "cowls." The pun runs thus: ". . . we'll not carry coals [bear insults] . . . we should be colliers [lazy cheats] . . . I mean be in choler [anger] . . . draw your neck out of the collar [noose]."

10–11 *moves . . . to move:* "moves" (to incite) played off against "to move" (run).

15 *take the wall:* take the position farthest from the street, an act of discourtesy. Even today when a man and woman walk down the street, the man gives the woman, as a matter of courtesy, the position next to the wall. In Shakespeare's day any person of rank or dignity was always given this position. The custom probably grew out of the fact that streets were muddy and often contained drainage ditches down their center. The person who took the wall was protected from unpleasant splashing.

17–18 *The weakest goes to the wall:* from an old proverb meaning "the weakest is shoved to the rear." Again note Gregory's pun.

37 *Poor-John:* salted and dried fish (hake). It was considered dull food; *tool:* sword, but also a pun on the masculine genital organ. Gregory puns here to top Sampson's vulgar bragging about his prowess as a fighter and as a seducer of women. This play has many phrases with two or more meanings that are often bawdy or obscene.

43 *fear:* mistrust.

44 *marry:* indeed; originally an oath, "By the Virgin Mary." *I fear thee:* I have no faith in you. Gregory is not at all sure that Sampson will not run when the fighting starts.

45 *take the law:* Much as is the case today, the one starting the fight was considered wrong. The other could claim self-defense.

47 *list:* please.

49 *bite my thumb:* an insulting gesture similar to the present day "thumbing your nose". The gesture was made by placing the thumbnail under the teeth.

61 *I am for you:* I'm your match or I'm ready to fight you.

65 *Say better; here comes one of my master's kinsmen.* Gregory sees Tybalt approaching and grows bold.

70 *swashing:* slashing, swaggering.

73 *heartless hinds:* weak-spirited servants. Tybalt puns on the hart and the hind, the male and female red deer.

79 *Have at thee:* I shall attack; be on guard.

80 *Clubs, bills, and partisans:* a rallying cry for help in the Elizabethan streets. The clubs were carried by apprentices. Military men and the watch would carry bills and partisans, both of which were kinds of long spears with a cutting edge.

82 *long sword:* Prominent citizens often carried short swords for dress or ceremony. Servants would accompany them with their long swords, which they used in fights. Most young men of Shakespeare's day had abandoned the long sword for the rapier.

83 *A crutch:* A crutch would be better for a man your age.

85 *spite:* to spite me; in defiance of me.

89 *neighbor-stained steel:* steel, or sword, stained with neighbor's blood.

94 *mistempered:* ill-used, with a pun on the tempering of steel.

102 *Cankered . . . cankered:* Again a pun. The first "cankered" is "rusted"; the second is "malignant" or "rankling."

104 *forfeit:* penalty for breaking the peace.

109 *Freetown:* Shakespeare took the basis of his story from a poem by Arthur Brooke, called *Romeus and Juliet.* In that poem the house of the Capulets is called Freetown, Brooke's translation of the Italian *Villa Blanca.*

111 *Who set this ancient quarrel new abroach:* Who gave this old fight a new start?

119 *nothing hurt withal:* not at all hurt by this.

121 *part and part:* either side.

127 *drave:* drove.

128 *sycamore:* a tree symbolic of unhappy lovers.

131 *ware:* aware, wary.

132 *covert:* a hidden place in the woods, such as a thicket.

133 *affections:* feelings.

134 *Which . . . found:* Benvolio says that he too sought to be alone at that time.

135 *humour:* desire, inclination.

142 *Aurora's:* Aurora is the goddess of dawn; hence Romeo has stayed out till dawn.

143 *heavy:* unhappy, as we still use the word in "heavy heart."

147 *humour:* Here the word has more the sense of "mood." Actually physicians of the Middle Ages believed that four fluids, or humours, made up the human body and mind. An improper balance of these fluids caused mental and physical illness.

151 *importuned:* asked repeatedly or begged. The line means, "Have you begged an explanation of him in any way?"

153 *affections' counsellor:* feelings' adviser. In other words, Romeo kept his feelings to himself.

155 *close:* secret. He was close-mouthed.

156 *sounding:* investigation. We still use the phrase, "sound the depths."

157 *envious:* malicious or hateful.

158 *he:* it.

161 *We . . . know:* We are as eager to help him as we are to know what's wrong.

163 *much denied:* greatly refused. "He'll have to refuse me many times before I quit."

164 *happy by thy stay:* lucky in your waiting.

165 *shrift:* confession, especially as one confesses to a priest.

166 *morrow:* morning; *cousin:* term used for any relation other than immediate family; hence Romeo and Benvolio are kinsmen.

175 *view:* appearance.

176 *in proof:* in fact or action.

177 *whose view is muffled still:* whose sight is covered always. Love, or Cupid, was often depicted as wearing a blindfold. Even today we still use the expression, "Love is blind."

178 *will:* desire, i.e., lovemaking.

177–82 This speech contains many couplings of contradictory terms, or paradoxes; e.g., brawling love, loving hate, heavy lightness, serious vanity, cold fire, etc. The technical name for this figure of speech is oxymoron. By use of such figures, Romeo expresses his recognition of the contradictory elements that exist in love and the confusion these elements present to the lover. The signs of the fight remind him that love and hate are opposites of the same drive.

191 *transgression:* offense or crime.

193 *propagate:* increase; *pressed:* oppressed or burdened.

196 *fume:* mist.

197 *Being purged:* Being cleared of smoke and mist.

202 *Soft:* Wait.

205 *sadness:* seriousness.

207 *sadly:* seriously.

209 *ill urged:* badly advised. It is not a good idea to talk to a sick man about making his will.

212 *mark-man:* a pun: "marksman" and "point, man."

213 *fair:* clear. Here the pun is on the previous line's *fair,* meaning "beautiful."

215 *Dian's wit:* Diana was the goddess of chastity. Rosaline had her wit, or intelligence, in defending her virtue.

216 *proof:* tested armor.

218 *stay:* heed.

220 *ope her lap to saint-seducing gold:* In Greek mythology, Danae, the mother of Perseus, was seduced by Zeus in the form of a shower of gold.

223 *still:* always.

225 *starved:* starved to death.

227–8 *wisely too fair . . . despair:* She is too fair (honorable) to earn heaven by making me lose hope (despair). But this, of course, is what Rosaline has done. In modern terms the phrase is something like this: She is too good to do this to me.

235 *to call . . . question more:* "to call in question" is "to examine" or "consider"; hence, when Benvolio tells Romeo to examine other beauties, Romeo says that this is simply a way of examining Rosaline's beauty the more, implying that the others would merely suffer in comparison.

236–7 *These happy masks . . . hide the fair:* These fortunate masks that hide ladies' faces remind us of the beauty hidden below them. In Shakespeare's day ladies wore masks to many public functions. This habit was inspired by more than a sense of discretion. The ladies admired a pale or ivory complexion, and the masks, usually black, protected their faces from the sun.

242 *who passed that passing fair:* again a play on words. "Passed" means "surpassed." "Passing" means "exceedingly."

244 *I'll pay . . . in debt:* I'll teach you to forget or else die in the attempt.

ACT ONE, SCENE TWO

1 *bound:* obliged (to keep the peace).

4 *reckoning:* reputation.

8 *yet a stranger in the world:* still young. Capulet states this, but then goes right ahead and arranges the marriage. Perhaps he is merely going through the formality of being reluctant, or, perhaps, he talks himself into the whole thing in his next speech.

9 *fourteen years:* In Brooke's poem, Juliet is sixteen. In the earlier Italian sources, she is eighteen. Shakespeare may have been influenced by a contemporary play, Marlowe's *Jew of Malta,* in which the heroine is fourteen.

13 *marred:* An old proverb ran, "The maid that soon married is, soon marred is."

14 *Earth . . . but she:* His other children are dead and buried.

15 *hopeful lady:* the only woman who can carry on my posterity.

17 *My will to her consent is but a part:* I only agree if she does. This statement is either a mere formality or Capulet deceives himself. He later shows that he has no intention of giving Juliet a chance to say no.

19 *fair according voice:* happily agreeing voice.

30 *Inherit:* Possess.

32–3 *Which . . . none:* This is a difficult line, and scholars do not agree as to its meaning. Some maintain that Capulet is bragging about his daughter. A better reading seems to be, "Look all the ladies over. My daughter may be counted among them as one of them, but has no reputation for beauty." He is punning on the proverb, "One is no number." Capulet seems to be displaying a false modesty about Juliet's beauty.

34 *sirrah:* term of address to a servant or person of inferior rank.

37 *stay:* wait upon.

39–41 *shoemaker . . . nets:* The servant confuses four old proverbs; one, for example, is, "The shoemaker should stick to his last."

45 *in good time:* He sees Romeo and Benvolio approach.

48 *holp:* helped.

51 *rank:* corrupt.

52 *plantain leaf:* the leaf of a plant used for medicinal purposes. It was considered especially good for bruises or for stopping the flow of blood.

57 *God-den:* good evening.

65 *rest you merry:* may you remain happy, an expression similar to our "so long." Obviously the servant is confused by Romeo and thinks he cannot read.

85–6 *crush a cup of wine:* drink a cup of wine. This is a slang phrase akin to our "crack a bottle."

87 *ancient:* old, in the sense of long established.

90 *unattainted:* impartial.

95 *these:* these eyes.

96 *Transparent heretics:* Obvious disbelievers. Romeo holds Rosaline's beauty to be the religion of his eyes and that, if those eyes saw equal beauty, they would be heretics to their faith in Rosaline.

100 *poised:* weighed or balanced.
104 *scant:* scarcely.
106 *of mine own:* of my own love, i.e., Rosaline.

ACT ONE, SCENE THREE

2 *What:* An exclamation used in calling, such as "oh." *God forbid:* that anything is wrong, since she does not answer. Another possible explanation of the line is that a lady-bird, though a term of endearment, is also a term for a tart. Hence the Nurse, realizing the double meaning, says, "God forbid."

6 *give leave awhile:* leave us alone awhile.

9 *Thou's:* Thou shalt.

10 *a pretty age:* a fitting age to discuss marriage.

12 *lay:* bet. We still use the term in this sense today; *teen:* sorrow.

14 *Lammas-tide:* August 1, the feast of the first fruits and the hottest season of the year. In Brooke's poem, the incident took place on Easter Sunday.

22 *marry:* indeed. See Scene one, line 44.

29 *I do bear a brain:* I've got a head on my shoulders.

31 *fool:* affectionate term like "foolish darling."

32 *techy:* irritable or peevish.

33–4 *Shake . . . trudge:* When the quake hit, the dove-house began to shake and it was a sigh as though it had said to the Nurse "shake a leg" or "get moving." She says there was no need to tell her to get moving (*trudge*). *trow:* think, guess.

36 *high-lone:* all alone; *by th' rood:* by the cross, a mild oath.

38 *broke her brow:* cut her forehead.

40 *'A:* he.

43 *by my holidame:* originally a "halidom," a holy relic, on which an oath was taken. Afterward it became confused with the Virgin Mary, holy dame.

48 *stinted:* stopped.

53 *young cockerel's stone:* young rooster's testicle.

59 *mark thee to:* mark you out for or select you for.

72 *much upon these years:* at about the same age.

76 *why he's a man of wax:* a perfect specimen, as though an artist modeled him in wax.

83 *married lineament:* harmonizing feature.

84 *one another lends content:* each feature sets off the other.

85 *what obscured in that fair volume lies:* what is not seen in that beautiful face.

86 *margent:* margin. It was customary at that time for scholars to explain the meaning of a text in the margin of a book. This technique is still used on an informal basis today, but for formal comment we use footnotes. The figure of speech could be translated, "What you don't find in the volume of his face, look for in the footnotes of his eyes."

88 *cover:* the cover of the beautiful book that is Paris. As a wife Juliet would complete his beauty and enfold him in her caresses.

89–90 *The fish . . . to hide:* Here Lady Capulet continues the figure of speech of Paris as a book, but she also puns on the word "fish." There is a fish in the sea, Juliet, who will cover his handsome book with her beautiful appearance. Fishskins were used as book covers in those days.

97 *I'll look to like, if looking liking move:* I'll look at him and like him, if looking will make me like him.

101–2 *nurse cursed in the pantry:* they were angry with her in the kitchen because she was not there to help.

103 *straight:* immediately.

ACT ONE, SCENE FOUR

1 *What, shall . . . without apology?:* Romeo and his friends are in costume and masks in preparation for "crashing" the Capulet ball. It was customary for such groups of revelers to have someone make a speech of dedication as a reason or excuse for their appearance. Romeo asks if they should observe this custom or go on without a formal reason (*apology*).

3 *prolixity:* wordiness. "Such wordiness is old-fashioned."

4 *Cupid hoodwinked:* Cupid blindfolded. The speech might be given by someone so costumed.

5 *Tartar's painted bow of lath:* an imitation Tartar's bow.

6 *crow-keeper:* a young boy in the fields who acted as a scarecrow. He carried a bow and arrow.

7–8 *without-book . . . prompter:* an introductory speech that is not properly memorized from the book but is spoken by an actor, without confidence, as the prompter gives it to him.

9–10 *measure . . . measure:* another pun. The first means "judge." The last two mean "perform a dance."

11 *ambling:* mincing.

12 *heavy:* sad.

18 *bound:* a pun on "boundary" and "leap."

21 *pitch:* a height; therefore any distance above dull woe.

29 *case:* mask.

30 *visor for a visor:* literally "a mask for a mask." He asks for a grotesque mask to cover the grotesque mask of his face.

31 *quote:* note.

32 *beetle brows:* thick or overhanging brows of the mask.

35 *wantons:* light-hearted or playful ones.

36 *senseless rushes:* insensitive mats used to cover the floor.

37-9 *For I am . . . am done:* An old proverb warns me to keep out of the dancing. The proverb was, "Stop, while the game is fair." Romeo puns on *fair* ("at its height" and "light") and on *done* ("finished" and "drab").

40 *dun's the mouse:* Mercutio puns on Romeo's "done." The idiom means, "Be quiet."

41 *Dun:* a horse in a game called "Dun is in the mire." It was a Christmas game in which a heavy log representing Dun was placed in the center of the room and had to be lifted by the players.

42 *sir-reverence:* from the Latin salve-reverentia, save-reverence. The expression was used as a substitute for an improper or obscene word. Mercutio puns, "If you are Dun ['the horse' or 'finished'], we'll pull you from the mud of this obscene love."

43 *burn daylight:* waste time.

46 *good:* right.

47 *that:* refers to "right meaning"; *five wits:* five faculties or senses.

43-7 Mercutio says, "We delay [burn daylight]." Romeo says, "No, we don't," meaning "It's nighttime." Mercutio explains the figure of speech that he used and says it is better to understand his figurative meaning (good meaning) because it shows five times more good sense (judgment) than does understanding merely literal meaning.

49 *tonight:* last night.

53 *Queen Mab:* A fairy queen in Celtic literature.

55 *agate stone:* a gem stone in a ring. Tiny figures were often carved in the stone.

57 *atomies:* atom or mote; therefore, tiny.

59 *spinners':* spiders'.

61 *traces:* harness.

65 *worm:* An old superstition was that worms bred in the fingers of the idle.

68 *joiner:* cabinet maker.

70 *state:* pomp, as a queen travels in state.

78 *suit:* a pun on suit (clothes) and suit (plea). Courtiers often made good fees by carrying persons' pleas to court.

79 *tithe-pig's:* of the tenth pig born. Parsons were entitled to a tithe, or one-tenth, of all a parishioner's property as tax.

81 *benefice:* a good deed or a position with an assured income.

84 *ambuscadoes:* ambushes.

89 *plats:* plaits or tangles.

90 *elf-locks:* matted knots of hair in horses' manes or on human heads. The belief was that elfs caused these knots.

106 *misgives:* has misgivings, forbodes.

107 *consequences:* future events brought about by the stars. See note to line 6, Scene one.

108 *date:* time.

109 *expire:* end. Romeo speaks of ending the term of his life as though it were the end of his lease on life.

ACT ONE, SCENE FIVE

2 *trencher:* wooden platter.

7 *joint-stools:* stools made by a joiner, or cabinet maker.

7–8 *court-cupboard:* sideboard.

9 *marchpane:* almond and sugar candy molded into an ornamental shape; marzipan.

14 *great chamber:* a large common room in the homes of wealthy Elizabethans. The room could be used as a large dining room, and with the tables turned up (stood up against the walls) it could be used as a ball room.

16 *the longer liver take all:* the one who outlives or outlasts the others gets all that is left.

18 *walk a bout:* cut a caper, dance a figure.

21 *makes dainty:* makes a shy refusal.

22 *Am I come near ye now?:* Did I hit the mark? Am I close to home?

23 *Welcome gentlemen:* addressed to Romeo, Mercutio and their followers.

28 *A hall:* Make the room into a hall for dancing.

29 *turn the tables up:* See note to line 14 *supra.*

30 *quench the fire:* This fire is in conflict with the fact that it is August 1st (see note to line 14, Scene three). Perhaps Shakespeare was thinking of the Easter season of Brooke's poem or perhaps, when writing the scene, he simply envisioned the Elizabethan hall with its great fireplace. Such minor conflicts frequently occur in Shakespeare's plays. Perhaps he considered minute consistency of detail a trivial matter.

31 *unlooked for sport:* Perhaps Capulet is referring to the

appearance of the uninvited guests who relieved the monotony of the "ancient feast."

38 *Pentecost:* a church feast occurring in late spring.

40 *elder:* older than twenty-five years.

49 *dear:* a play on words: *Dear* means "precious" (as metal), "sweet," and "expensive."

56 *by his voice:* Tybalt apparently recognizes Romeo's voice.

58 *antic:* fantastic. He is masked.

59 *fleer:* mock or sneer; *solemnity:* festivity or celebration.

68 *portly:* dignified, carrying himself well.

75 *Show a fair presence:* show a happy face.

77 *It fits:* My frown is fitting.

79 *goodman boy:* a doubly insulting phrase. A *goodman* was a man who ranked below a gentleman. *go to:* an expression of impatience: "Be off with you."

81 *God shall mend my soul:* "God bless my soul," another expression of impatience.

83 *set cock-a-hoop:* start a riot. Originally the phrase meant to pull the cork out of a barrel and let the wine flow freely.

86 *trick:* trick or habit of starting quarrels; *scathe:* harm.

87 *contrary:* oppose or cross.

88 *my hearts:* my hearties. During his talk with Tybalt, Capulet is also conscious of his position as host. He addresses the dancers and gives orders to the servants. *princox:* impertinent youth.

91 *Patience perforce:* Enforced patience.

92 *different greeting:* opposition. In lines 91 and 92 Tybalt says that enforced patience in opposition with his anger (choler) makes his flesh tremble.

99 *pilgrim:* Romeo was probably costumed as a pilgrim. Thus his approach to Juliet is as a pilgrim to a shrine.

102 *palmers:* another term for a pilgrim. Actually, a palmer was a pilgrim who had been to the Holy Land. He carried a palm as a sign that he made such a pilgrimage.

107 *Saints . . . prayers' sake:* Saints do not take the initiative (move) in helping us, but will grant our requests if we pray to them.

111 *urged:* argued.

112 *You kiss by the book:* according to rules or with bookish phrases.

119 *chinks:* money.

120 *dear:* again in the double sense of "expensive" and "lovely"; *my life is my foe's debt:* my life is owed to my enemy. Juliet is now his life.

121 *the sport is at the best:* the fun has reached its high point. It is time to leave since what follows will be anti-climactic.

124 *trifling foolish banquet towards:* a little insignificant supper awaiting.

128 *fay:* faith.

130 *What:* Who.

141 *Too early seen unknown, and known too late:* I saw him too soon, before I knew who he was, and I knew who he was too late (to stop from falling in love with him).

142 *Prodigious:* Portentous, Unnatural.

ACT TWO, PROLOGUE

1 *old desire:* Romeo's love for Rosaline.

3 *fair:* fair one, namely, Rosaline.

4 *matched:* compared.

6 *alike:* equally.

10 *use to swear:* one in the habit of swearing.

13 *passion:* strong feeling.

14 *Temp'ring extremities:* modifying differences.

ACT TWO, SCENE ONE

2 *dull earth:* Romeo's body; *centre:* Juliet. In the figure of speech Romeo refers to his earth (body) finding the center of the universe (Juliet).

6 *conjure:* call up a spirit by magic.

11 *gossip:* intimate friend.

12 *purblind:* very blind.

13 *Abraham Cupid:* Eighteenth-century scholars seemed to think that Shakespeare meant Adam Cupid, after Adam Bell, a famous archer in an old ballad. Abraham, which is another form of "auburn," may refer to Cupid's hair.

14 *King Cophetua:* a character from an old ballad called "King Cophetua and the Beggar Maid." Cupid wounds the King with his arrow and causes the king to fall in love with a beggar maid at first sight.

16 *The ape is dead:* Romeo, as does a trained monkey, plays dead.

20 *demesnes:* regions.

25 *strange:* distant or belonging to another.

27 *spite:* outrage or annoyance.

28 *fair and honest:* proper and chaste, as opposed to the

obscene implications of the five previous lines of his speech.

34 *medlar:* the fruit of the *Mespilus germanica,* which can be eaten only when it is slightly rotten. A medlar is a play on "meddle," which meant "to have sexual intercourse." The fruit turns out to be a poperin pear. All of this is a part of Mercutio's obscene figure of speech.

38 *et cetera:* can be read "so and so."

38 *poperin pear:* a pear from the Flemish town of Poperinghe, but a slang term for the male genital organs.

39 *truckle bed:* a trundle bed. It was a bed on castors, which could be shoved under a larger bed. It was used by children or personal servants.

ACT TWO, SCENE TWO

4 *envious moon:* The moon is also Diana, goddess of chastity and virginity.

7 *Be not her maid:* Be not a follower of the virgin Diana.

8 *vestal:* virginal; *sick:* of a sick color, melancholy.

9 *fools do wear it:* court fools often wore green costumes.

17 *spheres:* heavenly bodies were thought to be contained in transparent concentric spheres that revolved around the earth.

33 *wherefore:* why, often misread as "where." This, of course, completely changes the meaning of the line. Juliet is saying, "Why are you Romeo?" It is his name that causes the problem.

39 *Thou . . . Montague:* You are yourself, even if you were not a Montague.

46 *owes:* owns.

47 *doff:* put off, discard.

53 *counsel:* intimate thoughts.

55 *dear saint:* as he addressed her in their previous meeting.

61 *if either thee dislike:* if either displease thee.

66 *o'er perch:* fly over and perch beyond.

73 *proof:* protected by armor; hence invulnerable.

76 *And but:* If only.

78 *prorogued:* postponed; *wanting of:* lacking.

88 *Fain:* Gladly; *dwell on form:* follow convention.

89 *compliment:* ceremony, polite behavior.

98 *fond:* foolish or doting.

99 *light:* unmaidenly.

101 *strange:* distant or reserved.

110 *orb:* sphere. See line 17 *supra.*

117 *contract:* betrothal.
118 *unadvised:* unthought-out, heedless.
131 *frank:* generous or liberal.
143 *thy bent of love:* the purpose of your love.
145 *procure:* cause.
152 *By and by:* Right away.
159 *falconer's:* of one who trains hawks to hunt birds.
160 *tassel-gentle:* the male hawk.
161 *Bondage . . . aloud:* Being confined, my voice is hoarse and I must speak softly.
173 *still:* always.
178 *wanton's:* spoiled child's.
180 *gyves:* fetter or shackles.
189 *ghostly:* spiritual.
190 *hap:* luck or fortune.

ACT TWO, SCENE THREE

3 *fleckeled:* spotted or streaked.
4 *Titan's:* Helios was the sun god. He was a son of Hyperion and one of the race of Titans, the early gods who inhabited Mount Olympus. Often Helios was simply referred to as Titan.
7 *osier-cage:* wicker basket.
14 *None but for some:* Even though all are not for some excellent virtue, all are for some purpose.
15 *mickle:* great; *grace:* source of divine help, power of goodness.
19 *strained:* pulled away from.
20 *Revolts from true birth:* Turns against its birthright.
25 *For this . . . each part:* the flower being smelled with the nose cheers each part of the body.
26 *with the heart:* by destroying the heart.
28 *rude will:* crude desire, lust.
30 *canker:* cankerworm, an insect that eats flowers.
31 *Benedicite:* Bless you.
33 *distempered:* disordered, diseased. The word refers to the upsetting of the humors in the body. See note to line 147, Act one, Scene one.
37 *unstuffed:* not overloaded, another reference to the humors.
50-1 *one hath . . . by me wounded:* Juliet has wounded him with Cupid's arrow as he has wounded her.
52 *physic:* remedy, healing powers.

54 *steads my foe:* aids my enemy. His plea will help Juliet (an enemy Capulet) as well as himself. Obviously, he wants the Friar to marry them.

55 *homely in thy drift:* simple in your meaning.

56 *shrift:* absolution. "Shrift" refers to both the act of confession and to the absolution, or forgiveness, obtained. Here it is obviously used in the latter sense.

60 *And all . . . must combine:* All is combined (agreed upon), except what you must combine (in marriage).

72 *To season . . . not taste:* Tears are shed for love (to salt it) but it has not the taste of the seasoning. In other words the tears do not help love.

79 *sentence:* maxim.

81 *chid'st:* scolded.

88 *by rote:* by mechanical memory. Friar Laurence says that Rosaline knew Romeo's love was mere formalized expression.

93 *stand on:* insist on.

ACT TWO, SCENE FOUR

11 *dared:* challenged.

15 *pin:* a peg at the center of a target.

16 *butt-shaft:* an unbarbed arrow with a blunt end. It was used for target practice. Mercutio says that Cupid needed only this target arrow to dispatch Romeo.

20 *Prince of Cats:* Tibert was a cat in the beast epic of *Reynard the Fox.* "Tybalt" is another form of the name.

21 *captain of compliments:* a master of polite behavior. There is also a pun here since a "compliment," in dueling, was a correct defense for a thrust.

21-2 *as you sing prick-song:* the melody that accompanied a song. It was pricked out, or written, on sheets. Tybalt's dueling was not improvised but followed a strict melody. *proportion:* rhythm.

23 *minim rests:* rests equal to half-notes.

24 *butcher of a silk button:* able to hit a button on his opponent's doublet.

25-6 *the very first house:* finest school of fencing. Mercutio is mocking Tybalt's skill with the newly popular rapier. See note to line 82, Act one Scene cne.

26 *first and second cause:* the causes for issuing a challenge according to the total code of honor. Tybalt was quick to take away cause.

27 *passado:* a forward thrust; *punto reverso:* a backhand

thrust; *the hay:* the home thrust. All three terms are from the Italian.

29 *pox:* plague; *fantasticoes:* dandies, affected persons.

30 *new turners of accent:* users of current jargon.

31 *tall:* brave.

33 *grandsire:* grandfather; addressed to Benvolio.

34 *flies:* water flies, used as a term for flatterers.

36 *form:* means "fashion" or "bench."

37 *bones:* play on English "bones" and French "bons."

39 *Without his roe, like a dried herring:* "Roe" is a short form of "Rosaline" (pronounced Rose-a-line). It is also the first sound of Romeo's name. Lastly it is used to indicate the sperm or testes (soft roe) of a male fish. Therefore, the pun runs thus: Without Rosaline he is nothing. Without his Ro, Meo (a sigh) is left. Without his roe, he is an emasculated fish.

41 *numbers:* verses; *Petrarch:* Italian sonnet writer. He dedicated his sonnets to his beloved Laura.

43 *Dido:* Queen of Carthage and beloved of Aeneas. When he abandoned her, she killed herself.

44 *Hero:* priestess of Aphrodite (Venus). Her lover Leander swam the Hellespont nightly to visit her. When he was drowned, she threw herself into the sea. *hildings:* good-for-nothings.

45 *Thisbe:* lover of Pyramus. They made love through a chink in the wall of her orchard. Their love, too, ended tragically. Shakespeare tells the story comically in a scene of *A Midsummer Night's Dream.*

47 *French slop:* baggy trousers.

51 *The slip:* A counterfeit coin was called a "slip" and getting away from someone was then called, as it is still today, "giving someone the slip."

57 *bow in the hams:* squat.

59 *kindly:* naturally.

61 *pink of courtesy:* perfection in manners.

64 *pump well flowered:* my shoe is pinked with a pattern of flowers. It is possible that Romeo here playfully kicked Mercutio. In other words if Mercutio is a flower, Romeo's shoe is flowered by kicking him.

67 *soley singular:* In two ways: (1) one sole left; (2) left markedly alone.

70 *O single . . . the singleness:* O, weak joke, outstanding for its feebleness.

73–4 *Switch and spurs . . . cry a match:* Go faster, go faster; or I'll claim a victory. A horseman would use his switch and spurs to urge on his mount. Romeo is in effect saying, "You'll have to be faster in your wit to keep up with me."

75 *wild-goose chase:* a race in which the leading horseman had to be followed in everything he did by the other horsemen in race.

76 *wild goose:* Here the phrase means "a silly person."

80 *Was I with you there for the goose?:* Did I prove you a goose?

84 *sweeting:* a kind of apple.

85 *sweet goose:* a popular dish of the time was goose and apple sauce.

86 *cheveril:* kid-leather; therefore, pliable.

87 *ell:* 45 inches.

89 *broad:* widely known, evident.

96 *natural:* a half-wit, a simpleminded person.

97 *bauble:* a fool's stick with a doll's head on the top of it. Mercutio is being obscene again.

99–100 *against the hair:* against the grain.

101 *Large:* licentious.

108 *goodly gear:* good stuff. He sees the nurse and Peter.

109 *a shirt and a smock:* a man and a woman.

116 *good den:* good evening.

119 *prick:* point. The obscenity of this pun even shocks the earthy nurse.

120 *Out upon you:* an expression of her indignation.

123 *By my troth:* In truth.

129 *fault:* want.

133 *I desire some confidence:* the nurse tries to be elegant in her language. She means conference.

135 *indite:* invite. Benvolio deliberately used the malapropism to mock the nurse.

136 *A bawd:* A procuress; *So ho:* the hunter's cry when he sights a hare.

139 *hare:* a slang term for a prostitute. *Lenten pie:* made during Lent, hence meatless.

140 *hoar:* "moldy," with a pun on "whore."

150–1 *Lady, lady, lady:* the refrain from the old ballad "Chaste Susanna."

153 *saucy merchant:* a rude fellow.

154 *ropery:* knavery.

160 *Jacks:* knaves.

161 *flirt-gills:* loose women; *skains-mates:* an unprincipled person.

181 *weak:* shifty.

183 *protest:* vow.

187 *mark:* pay attention.

201 *tackled stair:* rope ladder.

202 *top-gallant:* highest point. The top-gallant is the small mast on top of the main and fore masts of a sailing ship.

203 *convoy:* conveyance.

204 *quit thy pain:* reward your efforts.

208 *secret:* trustworthy.

209 *Two . . . away:* Two can keep a secret if only one of of them knows it.

212 *prating:* chattering.

213–4 *fain lay knife abroad:* steal something by force. This is merely her picturesque way of saying that Paris wants to marry Juliet.

214 *lief:* willingly.

216 *properer:* handsomer.

218 *clout:* dishrag; *versal:* universal.

220 *a letter:* the same letter.

223 *that's the dog's name:* The letter *R*, because it sounds like a growl, was called the "dog letter." Actually the nurse, who was undoubtedly illiterate, did not realize that the sound *rō* (Romeo and rosemary) was formed with an *r*.

225 *sententious:* the nurse's mistake for "sentences" or "maxims."

226 *rosemary:* a shrub that symbolized remembrance. The nurse is saying, "Juliet is writing the prettiest sentence about you and remembrance."

232 *Before, and apace:* Go before me and quickly.

ACT TWO, SCENE FIVE

6 *louring:* lowering and frowning.

7 *nimble-pinioned doves draw love:* light-winged doves were usually depicted pulling the chariot of Venus (love).

14 *bandy:* to hit back and forth as a tennis ball is hit; therefore to drive quickly.

16 *feign:* carry themselves.

21 *sad:* serious.

26 *jaunce:* jaunt, hard trip.

36 *stay the circumstance:* wait for the details. We still use a similar expression, "Under the circumstances," to mean conditions or details.

38 *simple:* simpleminded, silly.

52 *Beshrew:* curse.

64 *come up:* an expression of impatience like, "Come off it" or "Go to."

67 *coil:* fuss.

72 *Now . . . cheeks:* Now you begin to blush.

ACT TWO, SCENE SIX

4 *countervail:* counterbalance.

10 *like fire and powder:* Cannon were discharged by applying fire to loose powder.

12 *Is loathsome in his own deliciousness:* Becomes distasteful when overeaten.

15 *Too swift arrives as tardy as too slow:* Going too fast will make you just as late as going too slow.

17 *everlasting flint:* perhaps the stone floor of the Friar's cell.

18 *gossamers:* cobweb threads.

20 *vanity:* foolishness or dizziness, i.e., of love.

21 *ghostly:* spiritual.

23 *As much . . . too much:* The same greeting to him; i.e., good even, or else if it isn't, his thanks are too much

25 *that:* if that.

26 *blazon:* proclaim.

28 *Unfold:* Make known.

30 *Conceit:* Imagination, or Understanding.

32 *worth:* wealth.

ACT THREE, SCENE ONE

8 *by the operation of the second cup:* when the second drink begins to work on him.

9 *drawer:* the boy who brings the drinks in the tavern; a waiter.

13–4 *as soon moved to be moody, and as soon moody to be moved:* as inclined to get angry as he is angry when crossed.

33 *tutor me from quarrelling:* teach me how not to quarrel.

35 *fee-simple:* absolute ownership, a legal phrase; *an hour and a quarter:* a small fraction of the day, hence, cheaply.

48 *consortest:* keep company.

49 *consort:* Mercutio uses it here as combining to make musical harmony.

51 *fiddlestick:* rapier.

59 *my man:* the man I'm looking for. Mercutio deliberately twists it to meaning "my servant."

61 *field:* here used as a place for a duel.

66 *appertaining:* rightful or suitable.

68 *knowest me not:* He does not know that Romeo is now his kinsman by his marriage to Juliet.

69 *Boy:* a term of insult.

72 *devise:* think.

74 *tender:* regard or cherish.

77 *Alla stoccata carries it away:* A direct thrust wins the day. Mercutio means that Tybalt's bold insults have caused Romeo to back down.

78 *rat-catcher:* reference to his being King of Cats. See note to line 20, Act two, Scene four; *will you walk:* a phrase challenging him to fight; similar to the phrase in our Western movies, "I'm calling you out."

81 *make bold withal:* take liberties with.

82 *dry-beat:* beat without drawing blood. Mercutio says he will take one of his nine lives and, if his manners are not improved, he will beat to death the other eight lives.

84 *pilcher:* scabbard.

88 *passado:* a thrust. See note to line 27, Act two, Scene four.

90 *forbear:* stop.

92 *bandying:* fighting.

94 *sped:* finished.

101–2 *grave man:* Mercutio makes his last pun even though mortally wounded; *peppered:* finished.

106 *book of arithmetic:* by the rules set down in a book on fencing.

114 *ally:* kinsman.

122 *aspired:* risen to.

124 *on more days doth depend:* more days cast a shadow.

128 *respective lenity:* thoughtful gentleness.

129 *conduct:* guide or leader.

139 *amazed:* stunned; *doom:* condemn.

141 *fortune's fool:* the plaything of fortune.

147 *discover:* reveal.

148 *manage:* management or conduct.

158 *spoke him fair:* spoke to him civilly.

159 *nice:* trivial.

162 *take . . . spleen:* make peace with the wild anger.

163 *tilts:* strikes.

169 *Retorts:* Throws back.

173 *envious:* hateful.

174 *stout:* stout-hearted, brave.

175 *by and by:* at once.
176 *entertained:* considered.
182 *affection:* friendship.
194 *My blood:* Mercutio was the Prince's kinsman.
195 *amerce:* punish by a fine.
198 *purchase out abuses:* redeem or buy off misdeeds.
201 *attend our will:* wait on my judgment.

ACT THREE, SCENE TWO

2 *Phoebus:* Apollo, god of light, often confused with Helios, the sun god, who drew the fiery sun across the sky each day with his chariot.

3 *Phaethon:* son of the sun god, here Phoebus, who stole his father's chariot and attempted to drive the sun across the heaven. He could not hold the reins and the runaway team threatened to destroy the world. Zeus, to prevent this, killed Phaethon with a thunderbolt.

6 *runaway's eyes may wink:* a very controversial phrase. The "runaway" is probably Phaethon. Juliet asks that the eyes of day close (wink) so that it will be night.

10 *civil:* refined or courteous.

12 *learn:* teach.

14 *Hood:* Cover; a term from falconry. A hood was placed over the head of an excited falcon in order to calm him down. *unmanned:* untamed, again from falconry. *bating:* fluttering, again from falconry.

15 *strange:* reserved or shy.

46 *I:* ay. Even Juliet uses word play.

47 *cockatrice:* a mythological serpent that was supposed to be able to kill at a glance.

49 *those eyes:* Romeo's, and the conclusion of Juliet's pun on *ay, I,* and *eye.*

53 *God save the mark:* an oath to keep off bad luck.

54 *corse:* corpse.

56 *gore-blood:* clotted blood; *swounded:* swooned. The nurse again mixes up a word.

59 *Vile earth, to earth resign:* The vile earth is her body. She demands it to be committed to earth or buried.

67 *dreadful trumpet:* the trumpet that heralds the end of the world; *general doom:* day of judgment.

73–9 These lines are filled with oxymoron (see note on to

lines 177–82, Act one Scene one). The bittersweet images express Juliet's ambivalence toward Romeo.

81 *bower:* give lodging to.

87 *forsworn:* faithless. One who forswears is a breaker of vows.

88 *aqua-vitae:* spirits, liquor.

117 *needly:* necessarily.

120 *modern:* ordinary.

121 *rearward:* rear guard. She puns on "ward," which is pronounced as "word," and picks up "word" again in her next line.

139 *wot:* know.

ACT THREE, SCENE THREE

1 *fearful:* full of fear.

4 *doom:* judgment.

10 *vanished:* issued.

20 *world's exile:* exile from the world.

26 *rushed aside:* thrust violently aside.

28 *dear:* important, worthy, extraordinary.

33 *validity:* value.

34 *courtship:* a pun; he means both "courtliness" and "pursuit of love."

45 *mean of death:* means of death; *so mean:* so bare.

52 *fond:* foolish.

59 *Displant:* Remove.

63 *Let me dispute with thee of thy estate:* Let me discuss reasonably with you your circumstances.

77 *simpleness:* foolishness.

84 *even:* exactly.

85 *woeful sympathy:* Romeo and Juliet feel their sorrow together.

90 *O:* a sigh or exclamation of grief.

94 *old:* established, hardened.

98 *concealed:* The fact that she is married to Romeo is concealed to the world.

103 *level:* aim.

106 *anatomy:* body.

113 *Or ill-beseeming beast in seeming both:* Oh shameful beast in appearing to be both man and woman.

115 *tempered:* blended or mixed.

126 *form of wax:* a dummy. The nurse used "man of wax"

to describe Paris's beauty. (See note to line 76, Act one Scene three.) Friar Laurence is not impressed with external parts.

134 *And thou dismembered with thine own defence:* And you blown up with your own gun powder.

137 *There art thou happy:* In that you are lucky.

148 *watch:* guard.

151 *blaze:* proclaim; *your friends:* families.

157 *apt:* inclined.

166 *here stands all your state:* everything depends on what I'm going to tell you now.

174 *so brief:* so quickly.

ACT THREE, SCENE FOUR

1 *fall'n out:* happened or resulted.

2 *move:* make your proposal to.

11 *mewed up:* cooped up, a term from falconry.

12 *desperate tender:* bold offer.

16 *my son:* Paris, of course, will be his son-in-law.

24 *late:* lately.

25 *held him carelessly:* cared not enough for him.

32 *against:* in anticipation of.

34 *Afore me:* Most scholars think this phrase a mild oath like "before God." The phrase may, however, be a command by Capulet to Paris or to the torchbearers to precede him.

ACT THREE, SCENE FIVE

8 *lace:* ornament, stripe; *severing:* breaking up.

9 *Night's candles:* the stars.

13 *exhales:* Meteors were thought to be formed by fiery gases sucked up and "exhaled" by the sun.

20 *reflex of Cynthia's brow:* reflection of the moon. Cynthia, (a Renaissance name for Diana) was often depicted with a crescent moon on her forehead.

23 *care:* desire.

28 *sharps:* shrill notes.

29 *division:* musical variety.

31 *change eyes:* The toad has bright eyes and an ugly voice; the lark has ugly eyes and a lovely voice.

33 *affray:* frighten.

34 *hunt's-up:* an early-morning cry used to arouse huntsmen.

54 *ill divining:* evil-foreboding [in my].

59 *Dry sorrow drinks our blood:* A popular belief of the time was that sighing and sorrow caused the blood to descend to the bowels, where the heat sucked up the heart's blood, thus causing paleness.

67 *down:* abed.

68 *procures her:* causes her to come.

75 *feeling:* heartfelt.

84 *like he:* as much as he.

90 *runagate:* a renegade or vagabond.

91 *unaccustomed dram:* strange dose.

95 *dead:* Can be read with the line that precedes it or the line that follows it. Juliet is deliberately equivocating here.

98 *temper:* Again Juliet equivocates. She knows her mother will take the word to mean "mix" but she means "modify."

102 *wreak:* (1) to revenge; (2) to gratify.

110 *sorted out:* chosen.

112 *in happy time:* a vague phrase that can have several meanings. Here it seems to mean "indeed" or "by the way."

130 *conduit:* fountain or water pipe.

132 *Thou counterfeits a bark:* You imitate a boat.

140 *will none:* refuses.

142 *Soft, take me with you:* Wait a minute, let me understand you.

145 *wrought:* procured.

150 *chop-logic:* one who argues with oversubtle distinctions, a hairsplitter.

152 *minion:* a darling or pet child.

154 *fettle:* make ready.

156 *hurdle:* a wooden cart on which prisoners were carried to execution.

157 *green sickness carrion:* pale piece of flesh. Green-sickness was a kind of anemia that made young girls pale.

165 *My fingers itch:* He wants to strike her.

169 *hilding:* good for nothing, wretch.

170 *rate:* berate, scold.

172 *smatter:* chatter.

173 *O God ye god-den:* God give you good evening. He is dismissing her.

175 *Utter your gravity o'er a gossip's bowl:* Speak your wisdom over a punch bowl.

177 *God's bread:* an oath on the Blessed Sacrament.

182 *demesnes:* estates.

183 *parts:* qualities.

185 *puling:* whining.

186 *mammet:* doll, puppet; *in her fortunes tender:* in the offer of good fortune that she has received.

189 *I'll pardon you:* read sarcastically.

191 *I do not use to jest:* I am not used to making jokes.

192 *advise:* be advised.

197 *be forsworn:* break my oath.

207 *my faith in heaven:* my marriage vow is recorded in heaven.

211 *practise stratagems:* play violent tricks.

215 *all the world to nothing:* The nurse quotes odds. The phrase is like saying, "It's a million to one."

216 *challenge:* claim.

219 *county:* The count Paris.

222 *green:* Green eyes were much admired; *quick:* lively.

223 *Beshrew:* curse.

227 *here:* on this earth.

235 *Ancient damnation:* You damned old woman.

236 *forsworn:* breaking my vow to Romeo.

ACT FOUR, SCENE ONE

2 *father:* future father-in-law.

3 *nothing slow to slack his haste:* not so slow as to slow him down.

10 *That she do give her sorrow so much sway:* That she gives way to grief too much.

13 *minded by herself alone:* only in the case of herself; too much alone.

40 *entreat the time alone:* ask that you leave us alone.

41 *shield:* forbid.

47 *compass of my wits:* limits of my intelligence.

48 *prorogue:* postpone.

54 *presently:* at once.

57 *label:* a seal on a legal document; *deed:* a certificate of ownership. Juliet says that before she will put her hand to a false document (marriage to Paris) she will kill herself.

62 *extremes:* straits or difficulties.

63 *arbitrating:* judging or deciding.

64 *commission:* authority.

75 *cop'st:* contends or vies.

79 *thievish ways:* highways that robbers frequent.

81 *charnel house:* a human bone house. Graves were used over and over. Old bones were dug up and deposited in the charnel house.

83 *reeky:* reeking or stinking; *chapless:* jawless.
94 *distilling:* permeating.
97 *surcease:* shall stop.
100 *waned:* pale.
102 *supple government:* control of movement.
110 *uncovered:* with face exposed.
113 *against:* in anticipation of.
114 *drift:* purpose.
119 *toy:* whim or fancy.

ACT FOUR, SCENE TWO

6–7 *'tis an ill cook that cannot lick his own fingers:* Only a poor cook won't eat his own cooking.
10 *unfurnished:* unprepared.
14 *peevish:* silly; *harlotry:* hussy.
26 *becomed:* fitting, proper.
33 *closet:* private room.
34 *sort:* select.
35 *furnish:* fit out.
38 *provision:* supplies.
45 *prepare up:* prepare thoroughly.

ACT FOUR, SCENE THREE

3 *orisons:* prayers.
5 *cross:* perverse.
8 *behoveful:* needed; *state:* ceremony.
15 *faint:* causing faintness.
25 *ministered:* administered.
29 *tried:* proved, shown by trial.
36 *like:* likely.
37 *conceit:* idea or imagining.
42 *green in earth:* recently buried.
47 *mandrakes:* roots of a mandragora plant. The roots were used as a narcotic. The plant, shaped like a human, was supposed to shriek when pulled up and cause madness to the hearer.
53 *rage:* madness.
58 *stay:* stop. Juliet imagines that she sees Tybalt trying to kill Romeo.

ACT FOUR, SCENE FOUR

2 *pastry:* room where the pastry is made.

4 *curfew bell:* originally a name for the evening bell. Later it was applied to other ringings.

5 *baked meats:* pies and pastries including meat pies.

6 *cot-queen:* a man too concerned with household affairs. Notice the familiarity with which the Nurse addresses Capulet. She obviously had great freedom in the household.

8 *watching:* staying awake.

11 *mouse-hunt:* a slang phrase meaning "woman-hunter."

13 *Jealous-hood:* A woman's jealousy; perhaps, because she wore a hood.

19 *Mass:* by the Mass; *whoreson:* literally, "a bastard," but used in a good-natured sense to mean "fellow."

20 *logger-head:* blockhead.

ACT FOUR, SCENE FIVE

1 *Fast:* fast asleep.

2 *you slug-a-bed:* you sleepy-head.

4 *pennyworths:* little naps.

6 *set up his rest:* resolved. The phrase is from a card game called "primero."

26 *settled:* congealed.

40 *living:* livelihood and property.

43 *unhappy:* fatal.

60 *Uncomfortable:* Joyless.

61 *solemnity:* festive celebration.

65 *Confusion's:* Destruction's. The word is played off on the modern sense of the word in the next line.

72 *advanced:* exalted, played off against "advanced" in the next line.

83 *nature's tears are reason's merriment:* Our emotions make us feel sad about things that reason tells us are good. The Friar apparently speaks of the fact that Juliet's soul has gone to heaven. He really knows, of course, that she still lives.

87 *cheer:* feast.

99 *case:* The nurse means "situation." The musician means "cover" (for his instrument).

101 *heart's ease:* a popular tune of the day.

108 *dump:* sad tune.

115 *gleek:* jest, mocking.

116 *the minstrel:* apparently intended as some sort of insult, although the term is not known in this sense today.

120 *carry no crotchets:* put up with none of your fancy no-

tions. Crotchets were also musical quarter-notes.

122 *note:* a pun: (1) notice, (2) put me to music.

128–30 *When . . . sound:* from a song by Richard Edwards, published in the *Paradyse of Daynty Devises* (1576).

132 *Catling:* a small lute made of catgut. The surnames of musicians indicated their professions.

135 *Rebeck:* a fiddle with three strings.

137 *Soundpost:* a small peg that supports the body of a stringed instrument.

141 *cry you mercy:* beg your pardon.

144 *sounding:* playing.

147 *pestilent:* pesty, bothersome.

150 *stay:* remain for.

ACT FIVE, SCENE ONE

1–2 *If . . . hand:* If I can trust my dreams, I'm about to receive good news.

3 *bosom's lord:* heart.

7 *gives a dead man leave:* allows a dead man.

11 *shadows:* phantoms or images.

21 *took post:* hired a post horse.

23 *office:* duty.

24 *I defy you, stars:* another reference to fate. Here Romeo will decide his own fate.

39 *weeds:* clothing. We still use the term "widow's weeds." *overwhelming:* overhanging.

40 *Culling:* sorting; *simples:* medicinal herbs.

45 *beggarly account:* meager amount.

47 *packthread:* twine used for tying parcels; *cakes of roses:* small cakes of dried rose petals.

52 *caitiff:* miserable.

59 *ducats:* coins, usually gold, of various values.

60 *dram:* drink; *gear:* matter.

63 *trunk:* body.

66 *mortal:* deadly.

67 *any he:* any man; *utters:* circulates or sells.

85 *cordial:* a heart stimulant.

ACT FIVE, SCENE TWO

4 *mind:* thoughts.

6 *associate:* accompany.

8 *searchers:* officials who check on sanitary conditions and report of plague.

18 *nice:* trivial; *charge:* weight.

19 *dear import:* great importance.

21 *crow:* crowbar.

26 *accidents:* events.

ACT FIVE, SCENE THREE

3 *lay thee all along:* lie at full length.

14 *sweet water:* perfumed water.

16 *obsequies:* ceremonies performed in honor of the dead.

20 *cross:* thwart.

21 *Muffle:* Hide.

22 *mattock:* pickaxe.

33 *jealous:* suspicious.

39 *empty:* hungry.

41 *Take thou that:* Romeo gives him a purse of money.

45 *maw:* stomach.

48 *despite:* scorn.

56 *apprehend:* arrest, seize.

68 *conjurations:* entreaties.

77 *attend:* listen to.

83 *triumphant:* splendid.

84 *lantern:* a tower with many windows. Romeo says that Juliet's grave is such a tower.

86 *feasting presence:* festive chamber where a king appears on occasions of state.

89 *keepers:* nurses.

90 *lightning:* last surge of life.

96 *advanced:* raised.

105 *paramour:* lover.

110 *set up my everlasting rest:* remain forever.

115 *dateless bargain to engrossing death:* Eternal agreement with monopolizing death.

116 *conduct:* leader.

121 *speed:* bring me here on time.

122 *stumbled at graves:* a bad omen.

142 *masterless:* discarded by their owners.

148 *comfortable:* able to give comfort.

162 *timeless:* untimely.

163 *churl:* miser.

165 *Haply:* Perhaps.

166 *restorative:* Romeo's life.

169 *happy:* opportune.

173 *attach:* seize or arrest.

179 *woes:* sorrowful things.

181 *circumstance:* particulars; *descry:* discover.

203 *house:* scabbard.

207 *my old age:* Lady Capulet is not yet thirty years old. Shakespeare may have been careless here, but then again such an ordeal would make many women feel that youth is passed.

214 *manners:* The old should be allowed to pass first.

216 *Seal up the mouth of outrage:* Stop this outcry. Not only is the Prince asking them to stop the emotional outburst, but he is also directing the servants to close the tomb. On the Elizabethan stage, the bodies would be on an inner stage and with these words the curtains would be closed on them.

221 *be slave to patience:* give way to patience, i.e., bear your sorrow patiently.

222 *parties of suspicion:* the suspects, those under suspicion.

226 *impeach:* charge with crime; *purge:* clean.

229 *short date of breath:* short time to live.

238 *perforce:* by force, against his will.

247 *as this:* on this very.

253 *prefixed hour:* previously agreed upon time.

255 *closely:* secretly.

266 *privy:* aware of the secret.

270 *still:* always.

273 *post:* haste.

279 *raised:* aroused.

280 *made:* did.

293 *joys:* the two children.

295 *brace of kinsmen:* pair of relatives; i.e., Mercutio and Paris.

297 *jointure:* part of a dowry reserved for a widow.

301 *at such rate be set:* of such value.

305 *glooming:* gloomy.

ABOUT THE AUTHORS

William Shakespeare

William Shakespeare was born in April 1564 at Stratford-on-Avon, the son of John Shakespeare and Mary Arden. At age eighteen he married Anne Hathaway; she was eight years older than he and pregnant with their first child, Susanna. Later, they also had twins—Hamnet (who died at age eleven) and Judith. By 1592 Shakespeare had gone to London and become known as an actor and a playwright. In 1594 he became a member of the Lord Chamberlain's company of actors, and he went on with members of that group to found the famous Globe Theatre in 1599. By 1597 Shakespeare had written at least a dozen plays, including *Romeo and Juliet* in 1596. At the end of his lifetime Shakespeare had written 37 plays, 154 sonnets, and much poetry. Shakespeare died on April 23, 1616, and was buried in Holy Trinity Church, Stratford.

Baz Luhrmann

The director, co-writer, and producer of *William Shakespeare's Romeo & Juliet*, Baz Luhrmann collaborated with several members of the film's creative team on his previous film, *Strictly Ballroom*. This critically acclaimed film won the 1992 Cannes Film Festival's Prix de Jeunesse and a Special Mention for the Caméra d'Or, as well as eight Australian Film Institute Awards, three British Academy Awards, and a Golden Globe nomination. Luhrmann was born in Australia, where he attended the National Institute of Dramatic Arts in

Sydney. Luhrmann has also staged many award-winning operas and has directed music videos. He began his career as an actor, appearing opposite Judy Davis in the film *Winter of Our Dreams*.

Craig Pearce

Craig Pearce previously worked with Baz Luhrmann as the co-writer of the film *Strictly Ballroom*. The Australian native graduated from Sydney's National Institute of Drama and began his career as an actor. He has worked extensively in film, television, and theater. Pearce lives in Sydney, where he is currently developing a number of projects.